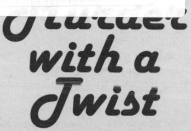

Murder
with a
Twist

Allyson K.
Abbott

KENSINGTON BOOKS
http://www.kensingtonbooks.com

KENSINGTON BOOKS are published by

Kensington Publishing Corp.
119 West 40th Street
New York, NY 10018

All Kensington titles, imprints and distributed lines are available at special quantity discounts for bulk purchases for sales promotion, premiums, fund-raising, educational or institutional use. Special book excerpts or customized printings can also be created to fit specific needs. For details, write or phone the office of the Kensington Special Sales Manager: Kensington Publishing Corp., 119 West 40th Street, New York, NY, 10018. Attn. Special Sales Department. Phone: 1-800-221-2647.

Kensington and the K logo Reg. U.S. Pat. & TM Off.

ISBN-13: 978-0-7582-8017-6
ISBN-10: 0-7582-8017-3
First Kensington Mass Market Edition: August 2014

eISBN-13: 978-0-7582-8018-3
eISBN-10: 0-7582-8018-1
First Kensington Electronic Edition: August 2014

10 9 8 7 6 5 4 3 2 1

Printed in the United States of America

"Have you ever been in Dan's apartment?"

"Sure," Theo said with yet another shrug. I was beginning to think it was a nervous tic. "We all hang out together a lot outside of work. We put in long hours most days and that doesn't leave much time or energy for a social life. Dan and I are both gamers. We get together a lot to play, sometimes at his place and sometimes at mine. Why? Does it matter?"

"It does," Duncan said, "because then we have a reasonable explanation for finding your fingerprints inside his apartment."

"Oh . . . right. Yeah, I've been there a lot." He was clearly nervous, but I wasn't sure if it was the situation in general or guilt that was causing it.

"Tell me what you do at Stratford and Weber."

As Theo began a lengthy, detailed explanation of his usual workday, the mundane nature of the topic allowed him to relax some. I wondered if Duncan had asked about work for just this reason. Theo's voice as I heard it through the wall speaker tasted like sweetened cream, but Duncan's next question made the taste change. "How long have you known that Dan Thornton was stealing his clients' money?"

Theo leaned back against his seat as if to distance himself from the question. "I . . . he . . . Dan . . ." Theo paused, sucked in a deep breath, and blew it out slowly before trying again. "I didn't know Dan was doing anything illegal," he said finally. "He always seemed like a straight-up guy to me. I can't believe he would do something like that."

Theo's taste had turned bad, like soured milk. "He's very unsettled right now," I said into the microphone Duncan had given me. "I can't tell if it's because he's lying, or if he's just extremely nervous."

Duncan gave a very slight nod of his head to let me know he'd heard me. But before he could ask another question, Theo moved himself up the suspect ladder with his next comment.

Books by Allyson K. Abbott

Murder on the Rocks

Murder with a Twist

Published by Kensington Publishing Corp.

This one is for Jen. Thanks for all you've done and all you do.

ACKNOWLEDGMENTS

There are so many people in my life who play a part in the creation of my books. There are my family members, who give me the time and space to write and who support my efforts with encouragement and love. There are my friends and coworkers, who contribute lines and ideas that I steal shamelessly. There is my genius editor, Peter Senftleben, with Kensington Books, whose wisdom and insight is always spot on, and my brilliant, hardworking agent, Adam Chromy, whose tireless efforts and constant cheerleading keep me going through the hard parts.

Last, but hardly least, there are all you wonderful readers out there who support my efforts by buying the books, e-mailing me your thoughts, and spreading the word. You keep me on my toes and give me the motivation to keep on keeping on. Thank you from the bottom of my heart, for I couldn't do any of it without you. Cheers!

Chapter 1

Something about the man in front of me bothered me, something more than the simple fact that he was dead. The death part was easy enough to discern based on the purple color of his face, the swollen protrusion of his tongue, the noose around his neck, and the way his feet hung just above the floor. Beneath his body, a little off to one side, was a turned-over wooden chair, the mates of which were gathered around the small oak dining table in another part of the room. The other end of the yellow vinyl rope around his neck was tied to the metal railing on a staircase that led up to a loft bedroom.

The sight made my stomach churn and I wasn't sure if this was a genuine visceral reaction to what I was seeing, or one of my unique responses. You see, I don't experience the world the way others do because sometimes my senses don't make any sense, or rather they make too much sense. Plus they have a tendency to go a little haywire when I feel stress or strong emotion of any kind, and looking at dead people tends to do that to me.

My name is Mackenzie Dalton, though most people

just call me Mack. I own and run a bar in downtown Milwaukee, a duty I shared with my father, Big Mack, until his death nearly a year ago. It was a bit of a leap to go from bartending to the scene before me, but oddly enough, I'd been preparing for this moment for several weeks with the help of a Milwaukee detective named Duncan Albright.

I was once told by a sociology professor who came into my bar that the biggest differences between human thought and that of animals are the ability to tell time and an understanding of the permanence of death. Certainly animals resist death when it comes on them, as do most of us humans. But the sociologist claimed that the animals have no understanding of the finality behind it. I understand it all too well because I've experienced it firsthand recently with the death of my father and his girlfriend, Ginny, both of whom were murdered. Given that, you might think I would want to avoid death as much as possible now. But I've decided this is my way to make a difference in this life because, on most days, I believe this is it. I've got one chance to make a mark. And if I'm wrong, I figure the karma can't hurt.

It all started six weeks ago in early October when I met Duncan Albright for the first time. He was there to investigate the death of a woman whose body I found next to a Dumpster in the alley behind my bar. That woman was Ginny Rifkin, a highly successful local Realtor and my father's girlfriend at the time of his death. I was the prime suspect in both murders at some point, and it was a combination of police instincts, luck, and my unique ability that kept me out of prison.

My so-called unique ability is actually a neurological disorder called synesthesia, which causes my senses to be cross-wired. As a result I tend to experience things in multiple ways . . . ways that others don't. For instance I not only smell odors, I may hear or feel them. And I not only hear sounds, I may taste or see them. All of my senses are like this, and Duncan Albright has taken to calling me his personal bloodhound. It does seem as if my senses are not only mixed but heightened, and Duncan, along with a group of my bar patrons, decided my quirk could be put to good use when it came to solving crimes. Over the past few weeks, Duncan focused his efforts on staged crime scenes where he'd set up a room and have me enter it, look around, and then leave. Then he would alter something in the room and have me come back to see if I could detect what the alteration was. At first it was simple things, like a missing item, or an added item, or an item that was moved to a different position. When I passed those tests with flying colors, he moved on to smells. He would spray a tiny amount of perfume somewhere and see if I could pick up on it. After the perfume, he ramped things up a little by simply rubbing an item with one of those scented dryer cloths. Or he would bring a scented candle—unlit—into the room and let it sit for a few minutes before he took it out again. Not only was I able to identify the smell and where it had been the most concentrated, I was able to tell that he had brought something into the room that he had then removed.

Duncan was fairly impressed with these little parlor tricks, but he was truly awed when we started playing around with sounds. He set up several scenarios where he would create some kind of noise in a room in a way that kept me from hearing it. Several times he had me wear headphones with music playing through them—something that triggered a fun display of shapes and colors—and another time he had me go outside while he made the noise in an enclosed restroom in my bar. Upon entering the room, I could typically tell from where the sound had emanated, how loud it had been, and, a few times, I was even able to identify the specific noise because I recognized the associated taste or visual manifestation it triggered as one I had experienced before.

We discovered timing played a role to some degree. The longer it had been since a sound occurred, or since something was moved or removed, the harder it was for me to identify. The time span was longer for smells, and in a way it all made sense when I considered the theory put forth by the neurologist who had finally diagnosed me in my teens, saving me from a cornucopia of psych drugs, or worse, shock treatments and a mini-vacation in a mental institution. His theory was that I was somehow able to detect minute particles of things. So if something is moved or removed, it creates a disturbance in the surrounding air and space that I am able to detect. If a sound is made, it disturbs the air around it and some part of my body is aware of this disruption. For smells, actual molecules of an item may often linger in a place where the smell occurred. That's why I seem to be able to pick up smells for a longer period of time after the causative item is gone. All humans can do this to some degree, like when people pick up the scent of cigarette smoke on a smoker, or even on someone who hung out with smokers. But my ability seems to be more sensitive than most.

The one I can't quite make sense of is my ability to detect emotional highs and lows in other people, even when I have never met them and they are no longer around. When I visit places where highly emotional events have occurred, I can sometimes tell. There is an odd visual sensation—like the heat waves one might see in the desert or above a hot tarmac—that clouds my vision. I can still see clearly, thank goodness, but the waves come on my visual field like they do in the ocean.

Some of my customers participated in a few of Duncan's tests, part of his reassurance that I wasn't cheating. While I excelled at the parlor trick aspect of things, I haven't done nearly as well with what Duncan and my customers call deductive reasoning. In an effort to help me in that regard, they started thinking up scenarios for me to analyze. These tests proved far more difficult for me because they were imagined only, hypothetical or historical cases that were relayed to me verbally. Because of this, none of my extra senses proved useful even though they were always active and giving me constant feedback on my current environment. In fact, they often proved to be something of a nuisance. And for some reason, my mind doesn't seem to want to work in a deductive way. Maybe it's because I've spent so many years trying to shut it, and all the extraneous senses that come with it, down.

Still, I do enjoy my new role despite the fact that it focuses more on death and bad things than on life and good things. I enjoy the challenge of puzzle solving and trying to think outside the box as I apply my unique talent to the art of crime solving. Enjoyment isn't skill, however, and while I haven't done well with the deductive reasoning tests, it doesn't stop me from trying. Plus, it just so happens to be good publicity for my business.

Six weeks ago, Mack's Bar was featured in the local paper and slapped with the title "the CSI Bar" because of the crimes we'd been able to solve—Ginny's murder and my father's—and because of all the cops who now frequent the place. At first it was only Duncan, who was filmed by a TV crew mixing drinks behind the bar, though he was actually working undercover at the time and only a few people knew he was a cop. But other cops who were involved with the investigation discovered that they liked my coffee while on the job, and the bar's ambience when off the job. Initially, my police clientele were limited to those who worked in Duncan's district, but the word spread and soon I was seeing off-duty cops from other districts in Milwaukee. It gives me a strong sense of security, because at any given moment, my bar is likely to have a cop in it somewhere.

Shortly after the CSI Bar article, it seemed as if a discussion of some crime or another was going on in the bar at any given time. Newspaper articles were being scoured, TV newscasts were getting dissected, and cops were getting grilled for the inside scoop on crimes of all kinds going on in the city and elsewhere. A core group of folks who participated in the crime discussions dubbed themselves the Capone Club after we learned of a connection between the notorious gangster Al Capone and some of the buildings in the area.

I figured it was a topical, trendy thing that would eventually die down. But when it didn't after several weeks, I decided to adopt an if–you–can't–beat–'em–join–'em attitude about the whole thing. I started by creating several new cocktails with catchy crime-solving names and featuring one each night of the week as a special with a discounted price. Mondays have become Fraud Day, so the crime or puzzle of the day has to be something related to fraud, and my cocktail special of the day is a Sneaky Pete, a drink made with an ounce each of a coffee-flavored liqueur and whisky or bourbon, topped off with four ounces of milk or cream and served over ice. Tuesday is Vandalism Day, and Wednesday is Larceny Day. Thursdays are Assault and Battery Day, and the drink du jour is a Sledgehammer, aptly named since it combines two ounces of vodka, two shots of rum, three ounces of Galliano, one ounce of apricot brandy, and two ounces of pineapple juice, served over ice. Fridays and Saturdays are dedicated to homicides or other death-related puzzles, and Sundays are a free-for-all.

Given my theme days, I suppose it's fitting that it was on a Saturday when Duncan brought me to my first real-life death scene . . . though I was puzzled by something at first. I remember someone saying that it's against the law to attempt suicide, but not to succeed at it. I suppose that makes sense in a way. I mean, who are you going to convict for a successful suicide? But that made me wonder why Duncan brought me to the hanging man. Because, at first blush it sure looked like a suicide to me, given that there was a tipped-over chair beneath him and a suicide note on the table. And it was also obvious that the victim was successful in his attempt, leaving no one to prosecute for a crime. I didn't need any special senses to know that he was dead.

But it turns out things aren't always what they seem and, in this case, the death turned out to be a convictable crime.

Chapter 2

There's another reason why it was ironic to find myself looking at a hanging victim: last night's test case at the bar had also involved a hanging.

It was a Friday night and I was doing a thriving business. Several of my regular customers were gathered near the bar; they often rearrange the tables and chairs to make one big table they can all sit around. The group included Cora, a forty-something, single, compulsive flirt and computer nerd. She has red hair like me, though hers comes from a bottle, and she owns her own computer troubleshooting company. She and one of her employees are working on a software program that will help analyze crime evidence and suspects—sort of a computerized version of the game Clue—and come up with the name of the most likely culprit. While the software still has a lot of bugs in it, so far it has done slightly better than I have when it comes to solving the proposed cases that come up at the bar, although it still falls far short of any acceptable grade.

Cora is also using her computer skills in another way. She is helping me build a database of my sensory reactions to things, so Duncan and I can consult it anytime I'm unable to recall the connection between one of my synesthetic reactions and a real sense.

Also part of the Friday night group were the Signoriello brothers, Frank and Joe, two seventy-something retired insurance salesmen who are like kindly old uncles to me. I've known the brothers my entire life, because my dad and I lived in an apartment above the bar and the brothers have been patronizing the place since before I was born. And, ever since my dad died, they've taken on a more active role in watching out for me.

Tad Amundsen, a very attractive man in his late thirties who works as a CPA and financial advisor in an office near my bar, was also part of the group. Tad, like the others, is a regular at my bar, primarily because he is very unhappily married to a wealthy woman he is unwilling to divorce. Consequently, he spends a lot of time in my bar under the guise of working late, often fending off women—and the occasional man—who flirt with him. Tad has movie star looks, and I'm pretty sure his wife, Suzanne Collier, who is eleven years his senior, married him so she could have some eye candy to sport on her arm and escort her to the many functions she attends. Since Suzanne and Tad live in an upscale condo that is within walking distance of my bar, Tad often drops by during nonworking hours, too.

While Cora, Joe, Frank, and Tad are longtime regular customers, I also have a new batch of regulars who have been coming on a steady basis for the past six weeks.

On this particular Friday night, the newer regulars in attendance at the CSI table included two women friends named Holly Martinson and Alicia Maldonado, and their male companions, Sam Warner and Carter

Fitzpatrick. Holly and Alicia both work at a nearby bank and have become frequent lunchtime and evening customers. They are good friends and an interesting duo in that they are like the yin and yang of women. Holly is tall, blond, blue eyed, and slender, whereas Alicia is short, heavy, dark skinned, and has brown eyes and hair. Carter, who is Holly's boyfriend, is also tall and slender, with strawberry blond hair and green eyes. He's a part-time waiter and wannabe writer who is always working on the next great novel or screenplay. Whenever he comes into the bar, he brings his laptop along, and his standard uniform every time I see him is jeans with a corduroy shirt. So far, he hasn't managed to sell any of his written works, but that doesn't keep him from trying, and the CSI angle of my bar intrigues him because he says it keeps his mind churning and thinking up new ideas. Sam Warner is Carter's friend— the two have known each other since grade school— and a grad student studying psychology with the hope of eventually becoming a practicing psychologist. He, too, is intrigued by the crime-solving aspects of the bar life at Mack's, and his insight into human nature gives him an edge from time to time.

I suspect Alicia's primary motivation for coming to the bar stems from the giant crush she has on my bartender, Billy Hughes, who is working to pay his way through law school. She finds endless excuses to talk to Billy, manages to sneak in plenty of supposedly casual touches to his arms and hands, and laces every conversation they share with sexual undertones and innuendo. Unfortunately for Alicia, Billy has a girlfriend named Whitney who he seems to be serious about, which is also unfortunate for him, in my opinion. I don't like Whitney much. She deems bartending to be a job far beneath Billy's talents and has made it clear she thinks being in my bar is akin to hanging in the slums. She's all about appearances, snobbish, and rude, and it's hard for me to see Billy with her since his personality is the exact opposite. At least he stands up to her and defends both his job and my bar, but I sense that if the relationship continues, Whitney will soon be the one in charge.

I keep hoping Billy will succumb to someone else's charms and dump Whitney. But aside from the gently flirtatious banter he uses on all the women who come into the bar, Billy, like Tad, never gives Alicia, or anyone else, any hope that her feelings are reciprocated, even though he has plenty of opportunities. With his tall, lanky build, emerald green eyes, and café au lait–colored skin, the man is a looker, and his charming, fun personality round out the package. Despite all the attention he gets, Billy manages to keep his admirers at a safe distance without pissing any of them off. And because he is a law student, he seems to enjoy the crime-solving games as much as anyone. Not only is he good at thinking outside the box, he's smart enough to figure things out a lot of the time. My goal is to train myself to think more like Billy.

On the flip side of the coin is my cocktail waitress, Missy, the female version of Billy—a lovely girl with silky blond hair, a curvaceous body, huge blue eyes, and milky smooth skin. Men flirt with her all the time, and I have several customers who I know come in to my bar solely to see her. Unfortunately, Missy doesn't have Billy's ability to keep her admirers at a safe distance. As a result, she is now a single mother of two and lives with her parents. Missy is very intrigued by the crime games despite her inability to understand the most basic connections and concepts, and on that Friday night before I came face to face with the real hanging man, she was hovering by the tables where the others were sitting, listening when she probably should have been making rounds and taking drink orders.

Unfortunately, Missy isn't my smartest employee. She's about as sharp as a bowl of oatmeal, at least when it comes to everyday knowledge and common sense, although she has a savantlike ability to match a face with a drink. If you are someone who orders the same drink most of the time, you'll only have to tell Missy once. She'll remember it forever after that. She might not remember your name or anything else about you, but she'll get that drink order right every time. While I know I should probably get on Missy more about hanging around the crime game folks—something she does every time she works—I often let her get away with it for one simple reason I'm not proud of: Missy's dim-witted attempts to solve the crimes make my comments and feeble guesses look almost brilliant by comparison.

Since it was a Friday night and therefore a homicide night, the drink special was an Alibi—a vodka-based drink flavored with ginger and lime—which was offered half price to all customers, and free, along with something to eat, to anyone who solved the "crime" for the night. Most of the folks at the CSI table had ordered one in preparation for the night's crime-solving puzzle.

I smiled when I saw that both of the Signoriello brothers had pens and little notepads just like the one Duncan uses, so they could take notes as Cora talked. The brothers love these little crime-solving sessions, and lately they spend as much time in my bar as they do at home. They are like eager children, which is funny given that they are both in their seventies with salt-and-pepper hair and a lot of well-earned wrinkles.

"To justice," Cora said, offering up a toast. Everyone clicked glasses and drank. When they were done, Cora kicked off the night's crime solver. "Here's our scenario. Listen carefully.

"A woman named Penelope comes home from an overnight visit to her daughter's and finds her husband, Harry, dead, hanging in the utility room in the basement from a pipe in the ceiling. Harry had been ill with cancer, but according to his wife, he was in full remission and on the mend. The open ceiling in the basement is ten feet high. There is no chair, stool, or anything else in the room that Harry could have stood on, and his feet are dangling a good foot above the floor.

"The noose is fashioned from a long utility-style extension cord, one end of which is around Harry's neck and tied in the back using a typical hangman's knot. The other end has been looped over two pipes in the ceiling and is then tied around a floor-to-ceiling beam several feet away. Harry's hands are secured in front of him with a zip tie and his wrists are slightly bloodied, presumably from his attempts to escape his restraints. The sink in the basement utility room is plugged and the hot water faucet is turned on, resulting in the sink overflowing. There is a drain in the utility room floor, but it has been blocked by an empty plastic kitchen-size trash bag, resulting in three to four inches of standing water in the basement. Some recyclable trash—an empty, half-gallon-size plastic milk carton, the soggy remnants of a large cardboard box, and three plastic containers from some microwaveable meals, all of which are presumed to have come from the trash bag—is floating on top of the water.

"The house has been ransacked and, according to Penelope, there are electronics and jewelry missing, along with some cash from a money jar the couple had. The police investigate and find that the couple is financially drained, as both were self-employed and much of Harry's cancer treatment was paid for out of pocket. Harry does have life insurance, and the payout doubles for an accidental death. However, a death from his cancer is excluded for a period of five years because he had it at the time he applied for the policy and there are still two years to go before this exclusion expires. Fortunately for the wife, the settlement from the insurance company will be enough to pay off all the debts the couple has incurred and still leave her with a tidy nest egg.

"At first the cops decide poor Harry was the unfortunate victim of a break-in and burglary gone wrong. They surmise that the water in the sink was left running and intentionally allowed to flood to eliminate or compromise any trace evidence. They later begin to wonder if Harry committed suicide, but they can't figure out how. Since Harry's hands were secured in front of him, and there was nothing found in the room that he could have stood on in order to hang himself, could Harry have committed suicide, or was he murdered? Go."

Cora then sat back and smiled at the group. Since the purpose behind these games was for me to try to learn to be more deductive in my reasoning and think like a detective, everyone turned and stared at me. Duncan had recently prepped me by suggesting that I analyze each crime scene with an eye toward motive, means, and opportunity. So I started there.

"Hanging seems like a rather extreme way to kill someone on the spur of the moment," I said. "So I can see why the cops might have been suspicious. Maybe the killers were sadistic. It does seem like they used stuff that was readily available, so maybe they were surprised by Harry's presence and had to think on the fly."

"However," Sam said, "the apparent randomness of the crime suggests a killer or killers who aren't very organized in their thinking. Could the wife have strung him up?"

Cora shook her head. "Penelope's alibi is verified. She was nowhere near the house at the time of the crime. And even though Harry was thin, he was still quite a bit heavier than Penelope."

"Did Harry have any drugs in his system?" I asked.

"Good question," Cora said. "As a matter of fact, he did. The coroner found morphine in his blood, but not enough to have killed him. A chat with Harry's doctor reveals that his cancer had recurred, something he had kept from Penelope, and he had a prescription for morphine that he was taking on a regular basis."

Carter jumped in then. "Is it possible he committed suicide and staged it to look like a murder?"

"Excellent!" Cora said. "While processing the house, one of the crime scene techs notices a very tiny drop of blood on the broken window of the door, which is assumed to be the mode of entry the burglars used. DNA typing shows that this tiny drop of blood belongs to the victim. No trace of anyone else is found in the house except for Penelope. After further investigation by the insurance company and the police, it is determined that Harry's death wasn't a murder at all, but rather a cleverly staged suicide meant to look like a murder. Eventually, they find all the missing jewelry and cash in a trash bin behind a convenience store. They also discover that the insurance policy excludes suicide as a payable death for five years, meaning that if Harry did himself in, Penelope gets nothing. But you still have to figure out how he did it."

I frowned, unable to come up with an answer. Apparently, I wasn't alone, because no one else offered up a solution, either. Someone suggested that Harry somehow jumped up and grabbed an overhead pipe and then managed to get his head in the noose and tighten it. Cora nixed that one pretty fast. I could see why. It would take a talented and very fit contortionist to manage all that with his hands zip tied together.

After several minutes of discussion, Carter suggested that the zip ties could have been applied by Harry himself easily enough and Cora said he was correct in that assumption. But no one had an idea about how Harry had managed to then hang himself a foot above the floor without anything to stand on.

Before long, the group was busy drawing pictures on napkins of elaborate setups that used physics to perform the feat, but one by one each idea was discarded. Even Duncan was stumped.

After another fifteen minutes of thinking about it and listening in on the ideas the others proposed, I announced that I gave up. "I'm just not built to think this way," I said.

"Give it time," Cora said. "Mull it over. Let your subconscious do the work."

I felt certain no amount of mulling was going to help, so I stepped away from the group and went back behind the bar to help wait on customers so Billy could participate in the game for a while. Duncan followed me and helped out as well. He has a knack for the job, and while doing his undercover stint several weeks back, he discovered he liked it.

Debra Landers—one of my other cocktail waitresses and the mother of two teenage boys—came up to the bar and ordered a round of beers. Duncan helped me pour them from the tap and, as we worked, our bodies came into incidental contact several times. Every touch was like an electric charge coursing through me and by the time we had the beers poured, I was a hormonal mess of synesthetic reactions.

Duncan must have felt something, too, because after Debra left to deliver her drinks, he leaned down close to my ear and whispered, "Any chance you'd let me spend the night here? I have to get up early in the morning and staying here would save me the drive time."

I knew his request to spend the night meant my apartment upstairs rather than the bar, and it both frightened and excited me. This was a step I'd been anticipating in our relationship for weeks since it was obvious we shared an attraction to one another. But, for whatever reason, Duncan had so far kept things on a platonic level.

"What about your clothes?" I whispered back to Duncan, feeling flustered. It was an inane question, but at the moment, it was all my addled brain could come up with. I looked around to see if anyone was close enough to overhear. Fortunately, no one was.

"I always keep a suitcase in the back of my car," he said. His breath was warm on my face and neck, and my mouth was bursting with the taste of sweet milk chocolate. Duncan's voice always tastes like chocolate.

I looked up at him, knowing I wanted him to stay. But then I had a second of doubt. Was I reading more into this than he meant? What if he was simply asking to sleep on my couch? I didn't want to jump to any conclusions, so I said, "You can stay if you want. I'll have to make up the spare bed, or if you prefer, the couch in my office is quite comfortable."

Duncan frowned at that, and then flashed me a crooked smile. "I was hoping for something a little more . . . cozy."

Based on that response, I decided to take the plunge. "Well, if your goal is to get some sleep, I don't think cozy is the answer. Neither of us will get any sleep."

"Trust me," Duncan said, "by the time I'm done with you, we'll both get the best sleep we've ever had."

I looked away from him then and swallowed hard, my thoughts whirling with the possibilities. "Do I have to cook breakfast?" I said. It was another utterly inane question, but my mind was spinning.

Fortunately, Duncan didn't answer because Billy chose that moment to approach us. "Cora came up with a tough one tonight," he said. "I gave up, too."

Missy came up to the bar and ordered another round of Alibis for the crime-solving group and I used it as an excuse to move away from Duncan, hoping I could rein in my thoughts. I stayed focused on the task at hand, mentally ticking off each step even though I could make the drink blindfolded. It was as I was scooping the crushed ice into the shakers that I had my epiphany. I stopped what I was doing and froze for a few seconds, the shakers in hand.

"Mack, are you okay?" Billy asked, staring at me.

I looked over at him and smiled. "I'm fine," I told him. "But I think I just figured out how Harry did it." I handed the shakers off to him and made my way around the bar and back to the group table. Billy took over making the drinks, but I could tell he was intrigued, because he moved to the end of the bar to finish mixing them so he could be closer to the group and hear what I was about to say. Duncan followed me, a curious grin on his face.

"Cora, how big was the box they found in Harry's basement when it was in its original shape?"

I could tell from the smile on her face that I was moving along the right track. "It was a good-size carton, about two feet high and two feet wide."

"We already went there, Mack," Carter said. "Cora said Harry weighed around one-eighty, and there is no way an empty cardboard box like that would hold up that kind of weight."

"You're right, an empty box wouldn't," I said. "Did Harry make any purchases right before he died?" I asked, turning my attention back to Cora.

"In fact, he did," she said, her smile widening. "After checking out stores in the area, the cops discovered that Harry made a purchase at one that was only two minutes away. It was a convenience store and the receipt wasn't itemized, but the cops knew that he spent just over thirty bucks."

I did a quick calculation in my head. "Enough for about ten twenty-pound bags of ice?"

"Yes!" Cora said, now gleaming.

"That's how he did it, then," I said. I saw a glimmer in the eyes of several of the others and a few nods of grudging admiration.

"Of course!" Carter said. "He filled the box with crushed ice and stood on that. That's why he had the hot water tap running, so it would melt the ice and disintegrate the cardboard box."

"But what about the bags the ice came in?" Joe asked.

"He was close enough to the convenience store to pour the ice into the box and then run the empty bags back to the store and dump them in the trash there," I said. "The ice wouldn't melt that much in the four or five minutes it took him to do that."

"Well done, Mack," Frank Signoriello said. Then, with a wink he added, "Only you thought more inside the box than outside it."

I received kudos from around the table, and for the

next two hours until the bar closed, I was on a high. I felt good, better than I had in a long, long time.

Though once the bar was closed, the cleanup was done, and everyone else had gone home for the night, Duncan proved that I could feel much, much better.

Chapter 3

And that brings me back to the real hanging man.
The call came a little after eight the next morning
while Duncan and I were still in bed, and despite Duncan's
promises, neither of us had had much sleep, not that I was
going to complain. He carried his phone into the bathroom and shut the door, eliminating any chance I had of
overhearing. When he came back out, he told me he had
a crime scene to go to, and based on my success with the
crime-solving task the night before, he declared me offi-
cially ready for the real thing and invited me to come
along. I agreed, but not without trepidation.

I had thought our little crime games, along with all
the preparations I'd been making with Duncan over the
past six weeks, would make a real crime scene easier to
take. But that wasn't the case. Our little "test runs" had
been clean, sanitary, pretend situations where we
laughed and had fun. The crimes were all make-believe,
or ones we only heard or read about, and the stakes
were small. But the hanging man before me that morning was real, frightening, and all too dead. I don't like

death, and staring it in the face that way was very unnerving.

A few minutes after we entered the apartment of the dead man, I turned to Duncan, who was standing next to me, and said, "I don't know if I can do this."

"Would it help if you stepped outside for a few minutes?"

I shook my head and squeezed my eyes closed. "No. When I come back inside, everything will still be the same." I sighed heavily. "How do you do this?" I asked him. "How can you face this sort of misery, cruelty, and sadness day in and day out?"

He shrugged. "I hesitate to say that you get used to it, but the fact is you do. I think after a while you start putting up mental fences, little guards around your inner emotional self. You only let your objective self out; you need to keep your inner self, the emotional self, protected and secluded."

I had opened my eyes while he talked, but I was staring at my feet, which were covered with blue paper booties. In my mind, I was doing a little trick I've learned over the years, something that helps me clear away the noise and make my world more manageable. It worked; the majority of the noises, smells, and sounds that were assaulting me moments ago dissipated. Slowly I raised my eyes to look at the hanging man again. Some of the noise returned, and I sucked in a deep breath and blew it out very slowly, trying to focus on each reaction individually. But the sight of that bloated, purple face kept triggering a veritable locust plague of reactions. I shook my head, sighed, and looked back down at the floor.

"Maybe it would be easier if we started with the room," Duncan said, handing me a pair of latex gloves.

"Look around and see if there's anything that leaps out at you."

I nodded, pulled on the gloves, and then shifted my gaze to the area behind Duncan. His partner, Jimmy, was standing there looking at me with an expression of impatience and disapproval. I knew Jimmy was skeptical about my ability to help out with this sort of thing, and I also knew that Duncan had convinced him to give me a chance. I didn't want to let Duncan down, but to be honest, I, like Jimmy, was feeling pretty doubtful about my abilities at the moment, even on the heels of last night's game success.

I turned my back on the hanging corpse and went back to the door we had come through moments before. I'd had an experience as we entered the place and I'd meant to comment on it right away, but then the sight of the man hanging from the stairway balustrade wiped the thought from my mind. Recalling it now, I decided to test the experience to see if I could replicate it. Turned out, I could.

"When we first came in here," I said over my shoulder to Duncan, "I heard this sound. It was a swishing, watery sound, like clothes getting agitated in a washing machine, or dishes getting cleaned in the dishwasher." I had reached the door and I turned back and looked at Duncan, making an effort not to let my gaze go toward the hanging corpse. "Can you hear it?" I asked him.

Duncan cocked his head to one side, closed his eyes, and listened for a few seconds. Then he shook his head. "I don't hear anything like that," he said.

"Okay, good. I thought at first that it was a real sound, something coming from a neighboring apartment. But I can tell now that it's not." I walked away from the door and headed right, toward the kitchen area. The sound grew in intensity. Then I turned left and walked toward the hanging man, keeping my eyes averted. The sound rapidly diminished, only to crescendo again when I approached the small bathroom that was off to one side of the entry door.

"I often hear smells," I said. "I think that's the case here, because I can smell something by the entry door, and in the kitchen and bathroom, that fades as I get closer to the victim. And the sound I hear does the same thing."

Jimmy frowned and asked, "Meaning what, exactly?"

"I'm not sure," I said, feeling as frustrated as he looked. "I just know that it seems out of place, that there is something wrong about it. I'm still feeling my way through this stuff."

Jimmy rolled his eyes and let out an exasperated sigh. "Duncan, you can't seriously believe this is going to be useful."

Before Duncan could answer, I spoke. "If I'm interpreting the sensation correctly, it suggests to me that someone else was here in this apartment very recently. The smell and the sound that I think goes with it is strongest in the kitchen, bathroom, and by the door, and it all but disappears when I move closer to the victim. That implies to me that whoever was here with that particular smell on them didn't go near where the man is now."

Apparently, this interpretation made Duncan happy, because he looked over at Jimmy with a smug expression. "There you go, Jimmy," he said. "If there was someone here in this apartment around the time this man hung himself, we need to find out who it was and talk to them."

I went over to the bathroom by the entrance and

stopped after stepping over the threshold. It was small, and most likely meant to be a guest bath since it only contained a toilet and a vanity sink and cupboard. As I stood there, I felt an annoying itch on the back of my neck, as if I had a tag on my shirt that was irritating my skin. I reached back but there was no tag, making me think it was a synesthetic reaction. Had something in here been moved, added, or removed recently? Or was the itch a reaction to some lingering odor? It nagged at me because I was certain I'd felt this same experience before, plenty of times, but I've spent so much of my life trying to ignore and suppress my reactions that trying to identify the cause now was hard to do. I tucked it away for the time being and stepped out of the bathroom.

I meandered my way toward the small dining-room table just off the kitchen. On top of the table was a drinking glass with a smidge of whisky at the bottom and a nearly empty bottle of Johnnie Walker Black. The glass rested on one corner of the victim's suicide note, a single sheet of paper typed out and presumably printed from a laptop computer and printer, which were also on the table. I read the note.

If I could return the money I would, but it is gone, lost to a series of bad bets I made with a bookie. I thought I could borrow it, make myself a little profit, and return it before anyone knew. But it didn't work out the way I planned and I can't bear the thought of spending the rest of my life in some jail. I'd rather be dead. I didn't mean to hurt anyone. I know it's not nearly enough, but maybe the proceeds from my life insurance policy can provide some restitution to those I stole from.

I'm truly sorry,

The name *Dan Thornton* was typed at the bottom of the page.

During the time it took me to read the note, I heard an odd twangy sound like the strum of an out-of-tune guitar. This was a sound I'd heard before and this time I knew what it meant. Just to be sure, I bent down closer to the paper and inhaled deeply. Then I did the same thing on the keyboard of the laptop computer next to it. As I expected, the twangy sound increased as I got closer to the paper or the keyboard, and then decreased as I straightened and backed away from them. Puzzled, I looked around the rest of the small studio-like apartment in search of an explanation.

"Is there any indication our victim smokes?" I asked no one in particular.

The two men both looked around the room. "No," Duncan said. "At least nothing obvious. Why?"

"Because the person who typed this note and handled the paper it's written on is someone who smokes."

"Are you sure?" Duncan asked.

At the same time, Jimmy said, "How can you possibly know that?"

"When I get close to the paper or the keyboard on the laptop, I hear the same twangy guitar sound I hear when I smell cigarette smoke." I looked over at Duncan. "Remember? It's one of the reactions we logged from before."

"I do," Duncan said. "And if you're right, it suggests that someone other than the victim wrote that suicide note."

"Wait a minute," Jimmy said, looking suspicious. "Did you hear this sound over by the door?"

I shook my head.

"Why wouldn't you hear it by the door? If someone smells like cigarette smoke, I would imagine you would be able to hear that sound anywhere they were in the apartment."

"Not necessarily," I told him. "Some smells come and go quickly. They are easily dispersed by breezes, showers, whatever. Other smells are more ingrained, or perhaps their molecules are just heavier and as a result they tend to linger on surfaces. For instance, no matter how hard I try, I can't eliminate the smell of lemons and limes from my hands because I cut them up every day, often several times a day. And even though I wash my hands dozens of times a day, the smell never completely goes away. It's the same for someone who has smoked for a long time. Even if they haven't had a cigarette in several hours, or even several days, the smell from holding so many cigarettes over the years lingers on their hands and fingers. I suspect that's the case with this smell. It's coming only from his—or her—hands. It's on the things that he or she touched."

"And this other sound you heard . . . ," Jimmy said, still looking skeptical.

I didn't know what point he was trying to make, so I gave him a questioning look.

"You don't hear this other sound, the washing machine thing, near the suicide note and the computer?"

"I do, but it's very faint. I don't think the person who had that smell spent much time by the note, or touched it."

Duncan said, "So you're suggesting there were not one, but at least two other people here in this apartment along with the victim?"

"I'm not telling you anything except what I'm experiencing. How you choose to interpret that is up to you."

Duncan could tell I had my dander up, and he placed a reassuring hand on my shoulder. "Look, I know this is difficult for you," he said. "But I truly believe that your experiences can help us interpret these crime scenes, maybe even help us catch a few culprits. It might take some trial and error to figure it all out, but that's okay. The more we practice, the better we will get at this."

I looked back up at the hanging man and grimaced. "I'm not sure this is something I want to get better at."

"Understandable," Duncan said. "I'm sorry, Mack. I suspect I may have pushed you too fast with this and, let's face it, this particular scene is a grim one to start with. So let's call it a day. I'll get one of the uniforms downstairs to drive you back to the bar."

"No!" I was a little startled by my outburst, and judging from the expressions on both Duncan's and Jimmy's faces, so were they. "I told you I would help with this," I said. "I promised I would try and I will."

I felt I owed Duncan my efforts in exchange for what he did to solve both Ginny's murder and my father's. I know he was just doing his job, but the way he did it had made it more personal, more meaningful. And then there was the little fact of my own apparent guilt in both cases, which at one point seemed like a given. Even I had to admit that the evidence against me had been quite damning, but Duncan had kept an open mind throughout it all, working as much on instinct as he did on facts. There are some who might say that's not the best way to function in a job like his, but I disagree.

Granted, some of Duncan's skepticism about my guilt stemmed from his attraction to me, a fact he admitted to during the investigation into Ginny's murder. At one point, I thought his flirtatious manner was simply a ploy he used on women to get them to relax and open up to him, but over time I came to believe that his attraction to me was genuine. Lest I had any lingering doubts, last night had eliminated them, though I still wondered why it had taken Duncan so long to make that move. I also wondered if Duncan feared a personal relationship might cloud my decision making and the professional relationship he was trying to foster.

In addition to repaying Duncan for the extra business he brings me amongst the cop crowd, and the free labor he provides behind the bar on a regular basis, I have another motivation for wanting to do this crime stuff: my synesthesia, which has been a curse to me for most of my life. I'm far from being the only person who has it, but apparently my case is a unique and severe form of the disorder, something the doctors think might have been triggered by my traumatic beginnings. My mother was seriously injured in a car accident while pregnant with me and she was kept alive on machines while she lay in a brain-dead coma. As soon as the doctors thought she was far enough along in her pregnancy, they induced her. That's how I was born, and a short while later, the machines were turned off and my mother was allowed to die.

It took me awhile to realize that my view of the world differed vastly from that of my playmates. When my father realized I was seeing things other people didn't, hearing things other people didn't, and experiencing odd tastes, smells, and sensations that others were not aware of, he became intrigued. He discovered my ability to tell when small things in a room had changed, to detect odors most people couldn't, and to generally sense things on a level most people couldn't understand. We played games for a while—the same sort of games Duncan had been organizing for me over the past few weeks—little mini-tests where my father would show me a room, make me leave, make some small change, and then bring me back to see if I could tell what was different. I was able to do it every time and, when I saw how it pleased him, I embraced both the games and my disorder.

Then puberty came and my hormones kicked in. This had an odd effect on me, ramping up my synesthetic reactions so that they were stronger and more frequent. As a result, my father's intrigue turned to concern. A parade of doctors and tests followed, and the mental illness labels started getting slapped on me. I was saved by a wise and kind neurologist who recognized my disorder for what it was, albeit my own unique variety of the species. He said he'd never seen a case quite as severe as mine, and when my father told him about the little tricks I was able to perform, the doctor theorized that my senses were not only cross-wired but extremely sensitive.

In addition to the normal five senses, I also have a very keen sense of thermoception, making me able to feel subtle changes in temperature. If I walk through a space where someone has recently been standing, I can feel a change in the air temperature. The same thing happens if I walk past a refrigerator whose door has recently been opened, or by a door that someone has recently exited or entered. Most people have experienced something similar at some point in their lives, such as when they sit in a chair someone else just vacated and the body warmth of the first sitter is still palpable.

What I took away from my experiences as a teenager was the knowledge that my disorder was something to be ashamed of, something to hide, something to suppress. And that's what I've done for the past twenty years: suppress, ignore, and hide. My father was aware of it, of course, and while the two of us still occasionally played a game of "What's Different?" up until his death, for the most part, he respected my desire to keep my disorder secret.

That all changed when Duncan Albright came into my life. The discovery of Ginny Rifkin's body had triggered all kinds of confusing reactions . . . reactions that I was then forced to explain to Duncan. But, in a way, those reactions also helped us figure out who killed her. That, and the fact that Duncan didn't automatically assume I was weird or crazy, has made me more open about my disorder. And when Duncan proposed this collaboration, it gave me the chance to turn my synesthesia into something useful as opposed to something shameful that I needed to hide.

Not that I'm ready to go public with my ability. Duncan knows, his partner Jimmy knows, and several of my employees and patrons at the bar know. I swore all of them to secrecy, but it was like shutting the proverbial barn door after the horses have escaped. Word had already spread. Most of the folks in the crime games group know, but there are some who don't. They think I'm playing simply for the fun of it and I'd like to keep it that way for now. For one thing, those adolescent nightmares are never far from my mind and I'm scared that someone, somewhere, will again try to declare me insane. For another, I'm not sure yet if my unique ability will actually prove helpful. Duncan seems to think so and that's why he and I, with the help of Cora, spent the past month or so cataloging the meanings behind as many of my experiences as we could.

All of that was in preparation for my first visit to a real crime scene, which is how I came face to face with a real hanging man. And thanks to last night's game—or perhaps because of it, since it taught me not to jump to conclusions—it's also how I became certain that Dan Thornton was a victim of homicide rather than suicide.

Chapter 4

The representative from the medical examiner's office arrived and, with the help of Duncan, Jimmy, and two police officers who were there, the body of Dan Thornton was taken down and laid out atop a white sheet on a stretcher that had been wheeled into the room. While this was going on, I spent my time surveying the rest of the apartment, sorting through all the sensations I was getting.

"The chair is wrong," I said to no one in particular. The others in the room ignored me, but Duncan heard what I said and walked over to me.

"How so?" he asked.

"I don't think the chair was ever upright anywhere near Mr. Thornton's body. Someone carried it over there and laid it down on its side to make it look like Thornton stood on it and then kicked it over. This carpet is new. If Thornton had ever stood on the chair, there should be deep imprints in the carpet from its legs. I can sense other irregularities in the pile but I don't feel any from the chair legs anywhere beneath where the body was."

"Interesting," Duncan said, staring at the carpet with a curious expression.

"I don't think he hanged himself."

"Because of the smell on the laptop and the note?"

"And the chair thing."

"What else are you picking up?"

I kept hearing the sound of high-pitched flute music, louder in some areas than others. It was something I'd experienced before but once again I didn't know what was triggering it. Like the annoying tag sensation, I kept this one to myself for now, and instead shared the things I could interpret.

"Well, when I look at the carpet I also feel pressure spots along my arms. Most of them feel the same, but in some areas, the pressure is lighter or heavier. I'm not sure what it means, but I think it might be footprints I'm picking up on. For instance, over there by the end of the couch you can see a depression left by someone's foot. I think that's the victim's footprint, because the pressure I feel when I look at the majority of the rest of the room is the same. But over by the dining table, and here by the stairs, I feel lighter and heavier pressures when I look at the carpet. It's as if other people were walking in here—someone with a bigger, heavier footprint and someone with a lighter one."

Duncan cast a smug look toward Jimmy before telling me, "The person who called nine-one-one was the victim's girlfriend, and she found him pretty much the way you see him now. She told us she didn't go near him, and that the only places she went in the apartment once she let herself inside were the bathroom and the kitchen. Apparently the sight of her boyfriend hanging there made her ill and she ran into the bathroom because she thought she might vomit. She didn't, and she then went into the kitchen and poured herself a glass of water. Then she went out into the hallway and used her cell phone to call nine-one-one."

"That probably explains the sound I picked up on in those areas," I said, "though I can't tell if the smell that caused it was something on her body like a perfume, lotion, or shampoo, or if it was her laundry detergent."

I looked away from the carpet and toward Duncan to assess his reaction. He cocked his head to one side and smiled at me.

"What?"

"I knew your little talent would come in handy."

"I'm not sure how handy it is telling you stuff you already know," I said.

"We knew about the girlfriend being in here, but not anyone else."

"Those other footprints could well be yours, or Jimmy's, or the other cops who've been here."

Duncan nodded and gave me a grudging look. "You may be right, but it's still useful information. You have to understand, it's rarely just one thing that helps us solve these cases. More often it's a combination of things. We have to take bits of evidence and lay them out so we can see a pattern, and most of the time it's the pattern that provides the solution, not the individual bits."

"You didn't seem surprised when I mentioned the chair or the smoke smell on the note and laptop. You knew this wasn't a suicide when you brought me here, didn't you?"

Duncan's smile turned apologetic. "Busted! But without you we might not have known that the position of the chair was staged, or that the person who typed the fake suicide note is a smoker."

"Is his girlfriend a smoker?"

"I don't know," Duncan said. "We'll ask her, but she may lie. We can search her credit card records, and check at stores near here and ask if she buys cigarettes. But that all takes time and it isn't necessarily proof, because she could say she bought the cigarettes for someone else. We could also search her apartment to see if there are ashtrays filled with butts. However, that requires a warrant if she doesn't give us permission. Or I can simply introduce you to her and you can tell me if the same smell exists on her hands."

"You want me to sniff her hands?"

"Based on what I've seen so far, I don't think you'll have to do that. I think just standing next to her will suffice. Wouldn't you agree?"

"Probably," I said grudgingly. "If you didn't know about the chair or the note before I got here, how did you know this wasn't a suicide?"

"Walter Finch, who was the first police officer on the scene, figured it out. Jimmy clued me in during his call. Walter's a sharp cookie and he was able to tell it wasn't a suicide by the marks on the victim's neck. That was lucky for us, because it kept more of the scene preserved. Walter has seen several hanging victims and he knew this one was beyond any medical help, so we were also able to avoid having EMS tromp all over our scene. Thus far we've allowed only two officers to enter the apartment, so up until the arrival of the medical examiner, the only people who have been in here are Walter Finch, his partner, me, and Jimmy . . . and now you, of course. Jimmy got the initial call, and when he told me what we had, I decided to bring you along to see what you could figure out."

I glanced over at the body, curious about what Duncan had just said.

Duncan called over to the man from the Medical Examiner's Office. "Hey, Martin, can you show Ms. Dalton here the marks on our victim's neck?"

Martin, who was standing alongside the stretcher on the opposite side of the body from us, grabbed a hold of Thornton's shoulder and hip, and rolled him up onto his side, exposing his back to us. The rope, which was still around Thornton's neck, was slack now.

"You can see where the rope came in contact with the victim's neck," Martin said. "Everywhere it touched the skin is blanched white."

Even though I could see what he was referring to easily enough, he traced the path of the rope on Thornton's skin with his gloved finger. The white stripe ran along the front and sides of the man's neck, under his jawline, and up behind his ears, where it then disappeared. Martin then took hold of the rope above the knot and pulled it up behind the back of Thornton's head, mimicking the position it had been in when he was still hanging.

"You see how the rope forms an upside-down *V* when the knot is located at the back of the head, as it was in this case?" Martin said. "It doesn't touch the back of the neck, so the blanched area stops just behind the ear. It's a typical finding in a hanging of this nature."

I must have looked confused because Duncan leaned into me and whispered, "Wait for it."

"What isn't a typical finding for a hanging like this is the bruising we see here," Martin said, returning Thornton to his back and tracing a finger along a dark, somewhat linear mark at the base of the man's neck near his collarbone. The bruise appeared to crisscross just under Thornton's chin. "This bruising, along with the color of the man's face, tells me he was strangled and then hanged."

"How can you tell the difference?" I asked.

"Frontal strangulation will typically cut off the flow of the jugular vein before it cuts off the flow from the carotid arteries, thereby blocking the return of blood flow from the head to the heart, but not the flow from the heart to the head," Martin said, continuing my education. "Hence the congestion and the purple coloring that we see here. He also has what we call petechiae—tiny burst capillaries—on his face and in his eyes. These are also classic signs of strangulation that typically aren't seen in a hanging. In general, hanging causes a much quicker loss of consciousness because the flow from the carotid arteries is interrupted. A lot of people think the cause of death in hanging is suffocation, assuming the neck isn't broken, but it's actually the obstruction of the carotid arteries and a lack of oxygen to the brain that causes death most of the time. The trachea is a fairly rigid structure and it's more difficult than most people realize to compress it hard enough or long enough to cause death."

Martin picked up the hand closest to him. "Also, his fingernails are too clean," he said. "If someone was on top of him, or in front of him strangling him, I would expect him to have clawed at his attacker. Even if this was a suicide, I would expect to see something under the nails or, at the very least, some broken nails. It's common to see scratch marks at the neck and fragments of the rope or whatever else was used under the victim's nails. It's an instinctive reaction to the hanging process if there isn't a broken neck. This guy's neck doesn't appear to be broken and yet he has nothing under his nails and none of them are broken."

Duncan said, "He didn't struggle?"

"It doesn't appear so," Martin said.

"Can you give me an approximate time of death?" Duncan asked.

Martin probed the man's face, arms, and torso with his fingers. "There are some indications of rigor mortis in his upper body. Based on that and room temperature, I would say he died around six hours ago, give or take an hour."

Duncan glanced at his watch and said, "So between two and four this morning."

I approached the man's body, trying to inure myself to the sight and smell of it. As I drew closer, I heard a rhythmic grating sound, as if a stick was being scraped over a cheese grater. It was a sound I knew well, one I heard all the time, except this time it was off. In addition to the grating sound, I heard a high-pitched whine.

When I reached Thornton's body, I bent down close over his face and sniffed, making Martin back up a step and mutter, "What the hell?"

I turned around and looked at Duncan. "You're right; he didn't struggle. I suspect he was sedated with something and I think it was probably in his drink," I said.

"Why do you think that?" Duncan asked.

"I know the smell of Johnnie Walker Black. I know the smell of all the liquors and the sounds that go with them. This Thornton guy drank Johnnie Walker Black, all right, but it had something else mixed in it. The sound of it over there by the table where the glass and the bottle are sitting is the way it should be, but the sound of it over here by his mouth is off. The smell is off."

"Could it be off because he imbibed it, and he's dead?" Duncan asked.

It was a good question, and I wasn't sure of the answer.

"And if the glass on the table didn't seem off to you,

how could it be the source of whatever was given to him?" Duncan added.

It was another good question and another answer I wasn't sure of. As I thought about it, I walked past Duncan and went back into the kitchen. On the counter beside the sink was a small dish rack with a bowl, a spoon, a coffee mug, and a drinking glass in it. I bent down close to the drinking glass and took a big sniff. Then I whirled back toward Duncan.

"This is the glass he drank the bad whisky out of," I said, pointing to the culprit. "It may have been rinsed, but I can still smell it or, rather, I can still hear it. It makes a rhythmic grating sound. I know this glass had the Johnnie Walker in it, but it also had something else mixed in, something one wouldn't normally expect to find, something that makes me hear an odd undulating high-pitched whine that I've never heard before." I felt pretty confident of this last claim. After working in a bar virtually my entire life, I know the smells and attached sounds associated with every possible mix of drink.

"That glass is the one his girlfriend said she used," Jimmy said. "Maybe that's the reason it seems off to you."

Despite his questioning of my claim, this comment from Jimmy was definite progress. Normally he would have dismissed my take outright with a sneer of skepticism.

"Not unless she rinsed her mouth out with the Johnnie Walker," I countered. "There was whisky in this glass."

"She said she used water," Jimmy said.

At this point, Martin was staring at me like I was someone who had just escaped from the insane asylum.

Duncan jumped in to shift the focus onto something else. "The crime scene techs should be here anytime. Make sure they bag all those dishes in the rack," he said to Karl Jensen, a uniformed officer who was guarding the doorway. "And ask them to limit their efforts to the kitchen area until I get back here." Then he turned to Martin and said, "Let me know what you find when you finish his autopsy. Call me on my cell."

Martin, who had been staring at me agape for the past minute or so, managed to shake off the trance he appeared to be in and refocused his efforts on securing Thornton's body to the stretcher.

"You, come with me," Duncan said, and he cupped my elbow and steered me out of the apartment and into the hallway. "I've got a special project for you."

Chapter 5

Duncan said, "Walter Finch and his partner, Adam, have the girlfriend in her apartment, which is in this building, one floor up. I need to go talk to her and, if you don't mind, I'd like you to come along. You don't need to talk, but I'd like you to observe her and see what type of reactions you have, if any. I'm particularly interested in the cigarette thing, but I haven't been in her apartment myself yet to see if there's any obvious evidence that she's a smoker. If there is, you won't need to sniff her hands."

He winked at me to let me know he was joking, at least a little bit, although his next words sort of belied that. "If there is no obvious odor in the apartment, or any ashtrays or packs of cigarettes lying around, then I'd be curious to see if you can detect anything on her. How close do you think you need to be to her if that becomes necessary?"

"I don't need to snuggle with her, if that's what you're asking," I said. "If we are sitting relatively close, like at the same table, I should be able to pick it up."

A few minutes later, I met Shelly Dominsky, a tall,

slender woman who looked to be in her midthirties. She had short, curly brown hair with bangs, thin lips, and blue eyes that at the moment were puffy and rimmed in red from crying. Glasses with a modern rectangular frame sat atop her head, their proximity making me suspect she needed them for vision and wasn't just wearing them as a fashion statement.

Duncan introduced me as a consultant, a title that made Adam shoot me a curious look. Both Walter and Adam were regulars at my bar, frequently stopping in at the end of their shift for a nightcap or two, but as far as I knew, only Walter was in on my little secret. Though, to be honest, what I knew about cop partners led me to believe they shared pretty much everything. So I figured there was one more person who would know my secret if he didn't already, which didn't bode well for my goal of keeping it under wraps.

There was no odor of cigarette smoke in Shelly's apartment, nor was there any visible evidence of smoking, such as an ashtray. Even before Duncan began his questioning of the woman, I knew she wasn't the person who had typed the suicide note. The sound I typically heard whenever I smelled cigarette smoke was absent. I did, however, hear the faint washing machine sound I'd heard in Dan's apartment and knew that it must be a manifestation of some odor on Shelly's body, hair, or clothing.

Shelly's apartment was nearly identical to Thornton's. We sat at a small table similar to the one that had held the suicide note, and I listened as Duncan questioned Shelly about her relationship with Dan Thornton. Shelly told him that they had originally met at work, but had known each other for more than a year before they started dating.

"Dan was the one who helped me get this apartment," Shelly said. "I was in a bad situation with a roommate I couldn't stand and I wanted to move. Finding something I could afford seemed impossible until Dan told me that a couple living in the apartment above him bought a house and they were moving out at the end of the month. He put in a good word for me with the landlord, and I was able to move in right away. I've been here three months now."

"How long had you and Dan been dating?" Duncan asked.

"Our six-month anniversary is . . ." She stopped herself and hiccuped a sob. "It would have been next week," she concluded, tears welling in her eyes. "We were happy . . . or at least I thought we were. I spent some time with him last evening and he seemed fine."

"What time did you leave?" Duncan asked.

"Around ten. We were in bed and he wanted me to spend the night, but I wasn't feeling so hot all of a sudden. I think the fish I ate for dinner might have been bad because I spent most of the night running to the bathroom. Dan was fine when I left, I swear." Tears were flowing freely now, and she swiped at them irritably as they tracked down her cheeks. "I tried to call him this morning to let him know I was okay, but he didn't answer. After several tries, I went down and let myself in. We swapped keys a while back."

"Did Dan ever say anything to you about playing fast with the company money?" Duncan asked.

Shelly shook her head vehemently. "I read that note, but I don't believe it," she said. "Dan's the most honest and moral person I know. I just can't see him stealing money from people. And as far as I know, he doesn't make bets or gamble." She swiped at her tears, sighed, and then combed a hand through her hair, pushing the fringe of bangs off her forehead. "It just doesn't make any sense," she said, shaking her head.

"Did you touch the note at all?" Duncan asked.

Shelly shook her head again. "I read it from a few feet away. I didn't want to get anywhere near it."

"You two worked together, is that right?"

Shelly nodded. "Yeah, Dan's been with Stratford and Weber for two years now. I was there for several years before he came on board. He joined us straight out of college, but he has a master's degree and I only have a bachelor's. I'm going back, though, just as soon as I get my feet on the ground financially."

"How has Dan done at Stratford and Weber?"

"Really well," Shelly said. "In fact, he passed over several people when he got a promotion six months ago. It opened up a position in his group and I took it. That's when he and I got close. But we keep things strictly professional at work because we're not supposed to date people from our own investment group."

"Did Dan's promotion create some bad feelings?"

Shelly shrugged and blew her nose. "There was some grumbling from some of the others, but it was hard to argue with Dan's success. He works . . . *worked* hard and earned that promotion."

Duncan spent a little more time with her, verifying the calls she said she made this morning by checking her cell phone, and getting the names and numbers of the people she and Dan worked and socialized with. Shelly responded in a sad, bereaved monotone interspersed with sniffles. I felt sorry for her, and what's more, I believed her. Her words, her tone of voice, her expressions . . . they all felt—and tasted—right to me.

When we left her apartment, I told Duncan this and explained that I meant it in the most literal sense. At the risk of branding myself as some sort of freakish human lie detector, most of the time I can tell when someone is lying. I don't know if it's a quality in their voice that I pick up on, or if it's some subtle body language or facial tic, but most of the time I can tell. Unfortunately, most of the time isn't all of the time, and I've been fooled before. I think the cause on those occasions was the extraordinary ability of the other person to lie without guilt, remorse, or compunction. I'm not a shrink—though bartenders seem to come close at times—but I do know that there are certain types of personality disorders that make some people professionals when it comes to deception.

The crime scene techs were onsite in Thornton's apartment, and all the dishes had been bagged and tagged. The body had been removed, and the technicians—a group of three women and one man, all of them dressed in gray jumpsuits, gloves, and paper bonnets and booties—were standing in the foyer along with Karl Jensen awaiting Duncan's return and instructions.

"I'm sorry to keep you all waiting," Duncan said to the techs. "But I want to take a look around the rest of the apartment with my consultant before you guys go anywhere else in here."

"If there's something in particular you're looking for, all you have to do is tell us," one of the women techs said, looking annoyed.

"I don't think that will work in this situation," Duncan said cryptically, winking at me. "Have you guys had lunch yet?"

There was a mumbled chorus of nos from the evidence techs, and a "Hell, no!" from Karl Jensen. Duncan took out his cell phone, punched in a number, and ordered two pizzas to be delivered to the apartment. He paid for them by giving his credit card number and when he was done, he said to the group, "You can eat out in the hallway. Hopefully by the time you're done, we will be, too."

He then turned and grabbed some booties and gloves from the technicians' supply, and handed me a pair of each. "I want to walk you through the entire place once before we leave," he said as I put the booties on. "Try not to bump into or touch anything. We can go as slow or as fast as you like. Just walk around and absorb. Do that thing that you do. Okay?"

I shrugged and nodded. The techs all exchanged looks that told me what they thought of the idea, but no one said anything. I suspected they didn't want to bite the hand that was literally feeding them.

The techs headed out to the hallway, and over the next forty minutes, Duncan and I walked around the small apartment. He handed me a notebook and a pencil at the start, and I jotted down some notes as we went along. I experienced several episodes of strong reactions to things, some of which I understood, and some of which I didn't.

When we were done, he said, "When we get back to the bar, I want to sort through any experiences you've had here and try to figure out what they might mean while they're still fresh in your mind. We can search Cora's database to see if we can figure out any of the ones you don't understand."

We headed back out into the hallway. It smelled wonderful, a rich aroma of tomatoes and Italian spices that made my stomach rumble and triggered a sound like the hum of a well-tuned engine. The food had done much to ameliorate the frustration of the evidence techs and the on-duty officer. They all looked sated, happy, and like they would be content to sit in the hallway for another hour or so.

Jimmy arrived—I hadn't realized he was gone until he came back—and took Duncan off into a far corner where they shared a whispered conversation. I could tell from the looks I was getting that it somehow involved me. After five minutes or so of this heated but whispered give-and-take, Jimmy left looking frustrated. Duncan came back over to me and said, "Jimmy is going to round up some of the people Dan Thornton worked and socialized with and bring them down to the station for questioning. Would you be willing to come along and observe?"

"Just observe?" I asked, suspicious that he wanted more.

"Busted," Duncan said with a guilty grin. "I want to see what kind of sensations you get from them."

"I want to help, but I need to get back to the bar," I said, glancing at my watch.

"Billy, Debra, and that new cook, Jon, you hired can handle it. Plus I happen to know that you gave keys to Billy, Debra, and your day bartender, Pete, even though I advised you not to. They not only manage fine when things are open, they come in early to do prep work. Nice try, but face it, you've set things up so that the bar functions just fine without you. You aren't going to wiggle out of this that easily."

He had me there. With a reluctant smile, I said, "Fine."

"I am willing to compromise, however. Since I have to wait for Jimmy to track down the people we need to talk to, we have a little time to kill. Are you hungry?"

"Sure. I haven't eaten anything since the coffee and muffin I grabbed just before we left this morning."

"Why don't we head back to your bar for lunch and fix a couple of those outstanding BLTs of yours."

I do make a mean BLT with sourdough bread,

Nueske's bacon, heirloom tomatoes, and herbed mayonnaise with a pinch of basil and garlic in it. They are the most popular item on my bar menu.

As we drove back to the bar, Duncan took several calls, leaving us little time to talk about anything else. Jimmy was one of those callers, and he let Duncan know that he had arranged for three of Dan Thornton's coworkers to come down to the station an hour from now. Apparently his job was made easy because all three of them were having lunch at a competing bar in town, and they agreed to come down to the station as a group.

When we got to the bar, I did a quick check-in with my staff and then headed toward the kitchen to make the sandwiches. But Duncan steered me down the back hallway instead, grabbed my arm, and pulled me up against his chest, making my body explode with both real and synesthetic reactions.

"I need to make our sandwiches," I said, breathless. I have a talent for uttering inane things at the most inopportune moments.

"I think we need an appetizer first," he said, his voice hoarse and bittersweet. Then he took me by the hand and led me upstairs to my apartment.

Chapter 6

When we arrived at the police station just under an hour later, still as hungry as we were before—for food, anyway—Duncan led me through a maze of doors and hallways until we ended up in a small room with windows on three sides, each one looking into another room. These rooms, which Duncan informed me were used for interrogations, were simple and small, each one fitted with a table, a couple of chairs, and blank walls.

"You can observe directly from in here," Duncan told me, indicating a chair I could sit on that was as high as one of my bar stools. "Each room is equipped with a video camera and everything that takes place is recorded. You're welcome to look at the recordings if you like, but you've told me it's easier for you when things are live, so to speak." He made little finger air quotes when he said the word *live*.

"It is," I agreed. "I don't get the same sensations when I'm looking at a picture of something that I get when I'm looking at the real thing. I'm not sure how a video recording will affect me, but I do find that some of my reactions are either missing or minimized when I'm watching TV or a movie. So I'm assuming it would be the same here."

"Make yourself comfortable," Duncan said, gesturing toward the chair. He then handed me a tablet and a pencil. "Here's something to write with so you can record your reactions. I'd also like to fix you with a small microphone that will be connected to an earpiece I'll be wearing. That way you can provide me with direct feedback while I'm talking to these people."

I nodded and climbed onto the chair, which Duncan had turned so that it was facing the room straight ahead, opposite the door we had come in. Then he handed me a headset with an attached mouthpiece.

"I'm not sure if you should just hold onto this and use it as a microphone only, or wear the headpiece with the earphones," Duncan said. "There are two ways for you to listen in on my interrogations. You can either use the switch on the wall here," he said, pointing to a speaker box with a knob below it that could be turned to point to a number one, two, or three. Duncan turned the knob so that it was pointing to the two. "Or you can listen through the headphones. We typically use the headphones when there's more than one interrogation going on because having more than one speaker on in here gets confusing. At the moment, there are no plans to use the other rooms, so I doubt that will be an issue for you, but I'm not sure which method will work best for you with regard to your synesthesia."

"I'm not sure, either," I said. "In fact, just being behind this window may interfere. So many of my reactions are dependent upon my immediacy to the person or object in question—to things like air currents, and subtle temperature changes, and small molecules of smell. If I'm not in the room with the person you're talking to, I'm not sure how much I'll be able to pick up."

"I'd rather not have you in the room with these people if we can avoid it," Duncan said. "It might be too much of a distraction and I don't want to jeopardize the interviews in any way by having a third party in there who's not part of the legal system. I know this is hard enough for you as it is and I want to minimize your exposure as much as I can. However, if it turns out that being in the room is the only way you can do what you need to do, I'll figure something out."

"Who are you going to be talking to?"

"Jimmy had a chat with Dan Thornton's boss. The firm operates under a peer group structure so that each of the investment counselors, like Dan, is part of a group. All of their investment decisions are discussed and decided upon by that group, and each group has at least one junior partner, plus a senior partner who oversees things. The individuals in the group are still allowed to make some independent decisions as to what they do with their money, and apparently that's where Dan Thornton excelled. This peer group structure seems to have worked well for the company, and their returns on investment are a tad bit higher than the industry average. Anyway, we figured it made sense to talk with the members of Dan's group first. We have all three of the people Shelly mentioned sitting out front waiting. That's all I'm going to tell you about them for now. I'll let you draw your own conclusions from what you hear. You okay with that?"

"That will be fine."

"If you have anything you want to tell me while I'm in there, speak into the headset, okay?"

I nodded, and Duncan left the room. I settled back on the chair to wait, and a minute or so later, Duncan

entered the interrogation room with a man who looked
to be in his late twenties. He was short, maybe five-six,
with blond, nappy hair cut close to his head, a broad
face with very pale blue eyes that looked huge behind
thick-lensed glasses, and milky white skin. He had a
pudgy build and a soft look about him that made me
think exercise was relatively low on his priority list. I
knew the names of the group of people Dan worked
with from our talk with Shelly, and I tried to guess
which one of them this might be. Based on his coloring
and his Slavic looks, I guessed right.

Duncan directed him to the chair farthest from the
door and then took the one across from him, offering
me a profile view of the two of them.

"Everything we say in this room is being recorded
with both video and audio," Duncan began. Then he
stated his own name, the date and time, and that this in-
terview was with Theodore Petrovski as part of an investigation into the death—I noticed he didn't mention
what type of death—of Dan Thornton. When he was
done with these preliminaries, he looked at Theodore
and said, "For the record, can you please state your full
name."

"Theodore Petrovski." It was obvious he was nervous.
His left leg was bouncing up and down at a rapid pace,
he had both hands shoved down between his legs, and
his voice had a hesitant, high-pitched tone to it. "People
call me Theo."

"Where do you work, Theo?"

"At Stratford and Weber."

"That's an investment firm, correct?"

Theo nodded and then Duncan reminded him of
the recording. "I need you to verbalize your answers if
you would, please."

"Oh . . . sorry. Yes, Stratford and Weber is an investment firm."

"You worked there with Dan Thornton?"

Theo nodded again and then caught himself. "Yes." There were a few seconds of silence and then he added, "I can't believe Dan is dead. I was just talking to him yesterday. We went out to a bar and had a beer together."

I wondered how Theo had heard the news, and exactly what news it had been. I suspected Dan's girlfriend had called or texted someone in the group, and that started the grapevine working. Hot news like that typically spreads very quickly, and in this day and age, with instant messaging, Facebook, Twitter, and the like, news travels lightning fast.

"Where was this bar?" Duncan asked.

Theo provided the name of a local downtown bar, one of my competitors. I wondered if it was the same one he and the others had patronized earlier today.

"What time were you there?"

"We went straight from work. I think that was around six. We had a couple of beers and then left. I got home around eight-thirty."

"Did you and Dan work closely together?"

"I guess so," Theo said with a shrug. "My cubicle was right behind his. We're part of the same peer group, and we hang out together a lot."

"How long have you worked at Stratford and Weber?"

"A little over three years."

"And did you work with Dan Thornton the entire time he worked there?"

"I did. Dan was added to our peer group right out of school. I was responsible for most of his training and orientation. We hit it off pretty well from the start, both at work and outside of it."

"How many people are in your peer group?"

"Six. Each peer group has one senior partner, a junior partner, and four associates. Dan was promoted to junior partner six months ago. That's when Shelly joined our group."

Duncan raised his eyebrows, as if this was news to him. "How did you and the others feel about that? I mean, didn't you have seniority over Dan?"

Theo shrugged. "Yeah, but Dan earned it. He's a hard worker. He came from a poor family and had to work two jobs to put himself through school. The guy was pretty driven."

"What about the others in your group? How did they feel about Dan's promotion?"

Theo shrugged again. "As far as I know, there were no hard feelings, but I guess you'd have to ask them."

"Does everyone in your group get along?"

"Well, our senior partner, George, is a lot older than the rest of us. He's a bit of a fuddy-duddy and he can be abrupt at times, but I don't think anyone in our group hates him or anything like that."

"What is George's last name?"

"Weber," Theo said. "He's one of the founding partners."

"Have you ever been in Dan's apartment?"

"Sure," Theo said with yet another shrug. I was beginning to think it was a nervous tic. "We all hang out together a lot outside of work. We put in long hours most days and that doesn't leave much time or energy for a social life. Dan and I are both gamers. We get together a lot to play, sometimes at his place and sometimes at mine. Why? Does it matter?"

"It does," Duncan said, "because then we have a reasonable explanation for finding your fingerprints inside his apartment."

"Oh . . . right. Yeah, I've been there a lot." He was clearly nervous, but I wasn't sure if it was the situation in general or guilt that was causing it.

"Tell me what you do at Stratford and Weber."

As Theo began a lengthy, detailed explanation of his usual workday, the mundane nature of the topic allowed him to relax some. I wondered if Duncan had asked about work for just this reason. Theo's voice as I heard it through the wall speaker tasted like sweetened cream, but Duncan's next question made the taste change. "How long have you known that Dan Thornton was stealing his clients' money?"

Theo leaned back against his seat as if to distance himself from the question. "I . . . he . . . Dan . . ." Theo paused, sucked in a deep breath, and blew it out slowly before trying again. "I didn't know Dan was doing anything illegal," he said finally. "He always seemed like a straight-up guy to me. I can't believe he would do something like that."

Theo's taste had turned bad, like soured milk. "He's very unsettled right now," I said into the microphone Duncan had given me. "I can't tell if it's because he's lying, or if he's just extremely nervous."

Duncan gave a very slight nod of his head to let me know he'd heard me. But before he could ask another question, Theo moved himself up the suspect ladder with his next comment.

"Am I allowed to smoke in here?"

I saw Duncan's mouth twitch, a funny little half smile. "Sorry, no," he told Theo. "No one is allowed to smoke in any public buildings anymore. But we're almost done. I'm sure you can hold out a little longer."

Theo flashed him a smile that was half relief, half

nervous energy. "That's okay. I don't have any cigarettes on me anyway. I don't smoke all the time. If I want one, like when we're out drinking or something, I usually bum one off of Will or Cindy. I'm one of those annoying people who only smokes OPs."

"OPs?" Duncan echoed.

"Other people's," I said into the microphone, having heard the term in the bar many times before.

A second later Theo said the same thing. His voice still tasted sour, his leg was still bouncing, and one hand, which was no longer between his knees, was busy picking at one of his fingernails.

"Ask him to lie to you," I said into the microphone.

Duncan didn't take his eyes off Theo, but he cocked his head to one side with a curious expression.

"I need him to say something that's a known lie so I can see how it affects the taste I have with his voice," I explained further.

Still keeping his eyes focused on Theo, who was growing more agitated with each passing second of silence, Duncan gave a slight nod of his head to indicate he understood. "Have you ever stolen anything?" he asked Theo.

"No," Theo answered quickly . . . too quickly.

The taste of his voice became not just sour, but rancid.

"I mean, not at my job," Theo added. "I stole stuff when I was a kid; all kids do. But I've never stolen anything at work."

With this last sentence, the rancid taste disappeared, morphing back into a sweeter taste with just a hint of sourness.

"I think he's telling you the truth," I said into the microphone. "He hasn't stolen from his job, but I can't tell for sure if he knew anything about the missing money. That topic definitely rattled him, but it may have been nerves rather than lying that triggered it."

"All right, Mr. Petrovski," Duncan said, "I think I have what I need for now. If I have any other questions I'll give you a call. Thank you for your cooperation."

"You mean I can go?" Theo said, looking hopeful but suspicious.

"Yes, you can go," Duncan told him. "But don't leave town without telling me."

Theo got up from the table and headed for the door. "Yes, sir—I mean, no, sir—I mean, I understand. Thank you." With that he scurried out the door like the devil himself was on his tail.

Duncan looked over at the window and even though I knew his side of it was mirrored, I swore he could see me. He smiled, winked, and said, "Are you ready for the next one?"

"I am," I said into the microphone. "Bring it on. This part is kind of fun."

Chapter 7

"I'm going to talk to Will Dorner next, the other guy from Dan's group," Duncan said, "and after that the girl, whose name is Cindy Whitaker. I want you to come out when Cindy is done and find a way to get close to all of them."

"Why?"

"I'd rather not say."

"Fair enough." I knew he wanted to see what kind of reactions I had when I was near them. What I didn't know was why, or what he was looking for. And, I realized, that was probably for the best. At least that way I couldn't be accused of being swayed by the power of suggestion, though as I stared at Duncan's smiling face and warm brown eyes through the glass, I definitely felt swayed. Except, the types of suggestions that were running through my mind had nothing to do with the crime we were investigating.

Duncan left the interrogation room and returned a few minutes later with a tall, attractive fellow who had a thick head of brown hair with a shock that liked to fall down over one of his hazel eyes, and a typically masculine build: broad shoulders, narrow hips, and muscular arms. In response to Duncan's questions, he stated that his name was Will Dorner, and that he had worked for Stratford and Weber for a little over four years. He spoke easily and freely, and there was a relaxed confidence in his body language that told me he was comfortable around other people. He had a strong Boston accent, and when he spoke it triggered a sweet vanilla taste that bordered on being overpowering, kind of like eating a too-rich dessert. The flavor sensations I get are typically bursts of taste that hit hard and fade fast, but occasionally they linger. That was the case with Will and it created an interesting medley of flavors in my mouth when his voice's lingering flavor mixed with the various chocolate tastes that Duncan's voice always triggered for me.

Duncan ran Will through the same basic litany of questions he'd used on Theo, questions about the firm, the peer groups, how well he knew his coworkers, and whether he'd ever been inside Dan Thornton's apartment. Will answered each question without hesitation, providing basic minimal information, but never once providing more information than was asked for. He sat slightly slumped in the chair, one arm casually tossed over the back of it, his legs extended out to the side, his ankles crossed. The fingers on the hand of the arm that hung over the back of the chair were beating a gentle rhythm on the frame. The other hand was also in constant motion as Will played with a fifty-cent piece, flipping it back and forth between his fingers and occasionally rubbing his thumb along its edge. Aside from these nervous activities, he appeared to be someone who didn't have a care in the world. At one point, he looked over at the window and I could have sworn he was looking right at me. He flashed a little know-it-all grin, gave a slight nod of his head, and then turned his attention back to Duncan. Even though Duncan had told me the glass was a mirror on the other side, I reared back, unsettled by Will's glance.

His voice maintained its overly sweet flavor until Duncan asked him if he'd ever stolen anything. Unlike Theo, Will didn't answer right away. His hands stopped moving and he narrowed his eyes at Duncan before saying, "Are you asking me if I've ever stolen anything in my entire life?"

"Have you?" Duncan asked.

"Sure," Will said with a shrug. "When I was a kid, I used to take money from my father's dresser drawer and use it to buy candy. And I remember getting into trouble for stealing a kid's watch once when I was in grade school."

"How about on the job?" Duncan asked. "Have you ever stolen from an employer?"

"Hell no," Will said, looking indignant. His voice took on a salty, almost bitter, taste. He straightened up in the chair and leaned forward, resting his elbows on his knees. "And, frankly, I resent you asking that question. I thought you wanted to talk to me about Dan. From what I heard, he's the one who stole the money. Don't try to drag me into it."

"So it's common knowledge at Stratford and Weber that money is missing?" Duncan asked.

"Yeah, there was an internal audit at the end of last month and rumors have been circulating ever since. Everyone has been on pins and needles. And then we heard about Dan."

"So you think Dan took the money?"

"That's what I heard." It was a cagey answer, one that didn't require an out-and-out lie on his part if he was involved, but that also didn't implicate anyone else. The flavor of his voice when he said it was an odd mix of sweet vanilla and salt, like the taste of a salted pecan eaten in a spoonful of ice cream sundae.

I had the distinct impression that Will Dorner was a smooth operator, someone who was used to being able to sway people to his opinions and confident in his ability to do so. Given more time, I feared he would become one of those people who could lie easily and without guilt. But he hadn't made it to that stage yet. He was good, but I thought there was still enough self-awareness when he lied for me to be able to pick up on it. I spoke into the mike and gave Duncan some directions. He acknowledged that he'd heard me with a slight nod.

"Tell me exactly what it is you heard about Dan Thornton," Duncan said.

"Shelly told Cindy that he hanged himself and left a note that said he was sorry for taking people's money. Supposedly the note said something about borrowing the money and thinking he could make it back."

Once again I had to admire Will's ability to avoid an actual lie.

"Do you think Dan Thornton hanged himself?" Duncan asked.

Will hesitated before answering this time, chewing his lower lip and frowning as he thought about what to say. "Are you suggesting he didn't?" he said finally.

Damn! The kid was smarter than I'd given him credit for.

"I'm not suggesting anything," Duncan said, keeping his own voice even. "I'm simply asking you if you think Dan Thornton was the type of person who would hang himself."

"I'd say yes, given that, from what I heard, he did exactly that."

"And do you also think he stole money from the firm? Yes or no, please."

"Yes," Will said after a moment of hesitation. He was still leaning forward, elbows on his knees, but his feet tapped nervously, making it clear that he didn't like what Duncan was doing.

I said something into the mike and Duncan responded accordingly.

"Did you have anything to do with Dan Thornton's death or the money he stole?" he asked. Will opened his mouth to answer but before he could, Duncan added, "Yes or no, please."

"No." His answer, short as it was, tasted bitter and briny, like a mouthful of seaweed soaked in salt water.

"He didn't like that last question," I said through the mike. "His voice is different all of a sudden, but I can't be sure if he's actually involved or just angry that he's a suspect."

Duncan switched gears then, asking Will about his social life and the time he spent with his coworkers outside of the firm. Will talked about the group's outings, naming a couple of places they liked to go, and verified Dan and Theo's gaming sessions.

Whenever Will mentioned Cindy's name during this discussion, I detected a change in his voice that made me suspect something. I was about to share my suspicions with Duncan, but before I could, Duncan showed me that we were both thinking along the same lines.

That's when Dan Thornton's case got really interesting.

Chapter 8

"Are you dating Cindy Whitaker?" Duncan asked Will.

"No," Will said, and his voice turned bitter-tasting again, though without the brine this time. "It's against work rules to date someone in your group," he added.

"Ah, so you two are keeping it under wraps then," Duncan said. "We have no interest in sharing this information with your bosses, but I need you to be honest with me. If we find out you are lying about one thing, no matter how trivial, it makes everything you say suspect. So tell the truth . . . your relationship with Cindy is more than one of simple coworkers or friends, isn't it?"

Will tensed up in his chair; his cheek muscles twitched and his fingers fidgeted. After a few seconds, his facial muscles relaxed and he slumped down in his seat. "Yeah, okay," he said with a smarmy smile. "I'm doing Cindy Whitaker. But I mean, have you seen her?" he asked, his eyes growing big. "That's one hot package."

When Duncan asked Will where he was this morning

between the hours of two and four he said, "I was home . . . alone."

"You mean, Cindy wasn't *doing* you this morning?"

Will had the good grace to look uncomfortable when Duncan threw his own crass word back at him, but all he said was, "No."

Duncan dismissed Will with the same warning he had given to Theo, then he left the room and returned a short time later with Cindy Whitaker. She was a very attractive brunette with dark blue eyes rimmed with thick black lashes and a killer body that, based on the way she was currently dressed, I guessed she liked to show off. Can't say I blame her. If I had her long legs, tiny waist, perky breasts, and slender hips, I'd probably dress a lot more risqué than I do. As it is, I favor jeans and blouses most of the time, and if I'm feeling a need to get dressed up, I might trade the jeans for a skirt. Since I like green and it's a color that goes well with my red hair, my wardrobe is heavily weighted toward the green end of the color spectrum. Cindy Whitaker, however, had no such restrictions and today she was wearing tight-fitting, black skinny jeans with bright red heels, and a body-hugging top cut low in front that was a kaleidoscope of colors on some sort of shiny fabric. The bright, shiny hues in the blouse were dampened some by the red bolero-style jacket she wore over it, but the overall effect was a definite eye-catcher.

In fact, it caught Duncan's eye more than I liked. And when the chocolate taste of his voice became sweeter and smoother as he started chatting with Cindy, it didn't sit well with me.

Cindy's voice had no flavor. Men's voices almost always have a flavor, but women's sometimes do and sometimes don't. Those who don't typically have an image that goes with their voices, typically undulating lines of color that sometimes appear to breathe right along with the person who is speaking. Cindy was one of those, except I'd never encountered anyone with such a specific image before. Her voice appeared in my mind as a single flame, like one might see from a steadily held cigarette lighter, blue at the bottom, yellow at the top, flickering ever so slightly with her breaths. But as soon as she finished answering the basic questions, such as who she was and where she worked, that flame grew into a roaring fire. Cindy Whitaker was hiding something; I had no doubt. And I suspected that several of the answers she gave were lies. Her interrogation went about the same as the other two with one exception. Not only was she not intimidated by anything Duncan said or asked, she appeared relaxed, composed, and amused, and she flirted with Duncan the entire time.

She answered her questions with more composure than Will had shown and she readily admitted to suspecting that Dan was the one who was stealing money. "I mean, come on," she said. "The guy was right out of school when he was hired and the rest of us have been at this awhile. For him to earn such remarkable returns so early in his career didn't make sense. I knew something was up."

Cindy, who had joined the firm around the same time as Will, was the only one of the three to admit that Dan's being promoted ahead of her had pissed her off. "Yeah, the guy worked hard and often put in hours way later than the rest of us, but I think that was so he could manipulate funds without being under the watchful eye of the senior partners."

As soon as her interrogation came to a close, I hopped off my chair and made my way out to the main portion of the station. Cindy Whitaker was taking her time leaving, continuing her flirtation with Duncan. Across the room, in some scarred-up, molded plastic chairs that were lined against the wall, sat Will and Theo. The two of them watched Cindy with lovelorn, infatuated expressions that made me realize they *both* had the hots for her. Whether Cindy was interested in reciprocating either boy's interest, I couldn't tell. She was too busy focusing on Duncan at the moment.

I walked over to her and Duncan, and knew immediately that Cindy was a heavy smoker. The loud, twangy guitar sound I heard left no doubt. Perhaps even more significantly, I caught a whiff of her perfume, and in the same instant, I heard high-pitched flute music. Duncan introduced me as a consultant, giving Cindy my first name only. I appreciated his efforts to maintain some level of anonymity for me, particularly since what I was doing had the potential to be dangerous for me. To help me figure out my reaction and to keep things on a friendly note, I commented on Cindy's perfume.

"I love that fragrance you're wearing."

"Thanks," she said, with a fake-looking smile.

"What is it?"

"Chanel No. 5."

We accompanied Cindy over to the chairs where Theo and Will were waiting. Though I had seen and heard both of them before, this was my first opportunity to experience what I thought of as "their space." I typically have to have a certain level of proximity to someone in order to experience some of my synesthetic reactions, and while I believe the space I deal with has a larger perimeter than what most people think of as personal space, the basic concepts are the same. Within moments of arriving at the spot where the boys were, I knew that what Theo had said earlier about not being a regular smoker was likely true, and that Will was as heavy a smoker as Cindy.

Duncan told all three of them that he might want to talk with them again, and reminded them that they had to let him know if they needed to leave town for any reason. They then walked away—Theo trailing behind the other two—looking conspiratorial, their heads bowed together as they whispered something to one another. As they rounded a corner at the end of the hall, we heard the echo of their laughter. Though I couldn't see them, I knew the laughter came from Cindy and Will because I could see Cindy's flame and taste Will's salty sweetness. Clearly they weren't intimidated by Duncan's interrogation. Was that because they were innocent, or because they were so sure of themselves that they felt they had nothing to worry about?

Duncan looked at me and said, "Interesting group, eh?"

"That they are."

"What's your take on them?"

"I'm pretty sure Cindy and Will are a couple, though they're trying hard to hide that fact. I think both of them are comfortably smug about things and don't rattle easily. With a little more practice, they'll both become accomplished liars. Theo is a bit starry eyed around them, in part because he has a crush on Cindy, and in part because Will is everything he isn't. All three of them are smart; in fact, I'd wager they are all smarter than most people their age. And I suspect all three of them know something about Dan Thornton and that missing money that they aren't telling."

"Do you think they were involved with his death?"

"I'm not sure I'm ready to make that leap yet. You're asking me to condemn people based on something that may well be pseudoscience. I don't think they can be trusted, and I don't think they are necessarily nice people, but I'm not convinced they're killers. I need more time to think about it."

"Time, we have," Duncan said. "Jimmy has been talking to the folks in management at Stratford and Weber, and we have a forensic accountant looking through their files. It's pretty clear that there's money missing, and from what we've been told, it appears that Dan Thornton is the one who took it. But it will probably take a couple of days to sort through all the files, and to talk to the necessary people at the firm. Plus, we haven't been able to find any irregularities in Thornton's finances, so if he took the money, we don't know what he did with it. The good news is, the missing money hasn't been communicated to or noticed by any of their clients yet, so we don't need to worry that any of them might be a suspect."

"It might be helpful to revisit Thornton's apartment with each of those three," I said. "I'd be interested in seeing what reactions, if any, I get from them there."

"Good idea. I'll call Jimmy and have him set it up for later today. In the meantime, my stomach is growling and I think we really do need to get a bite to eat."

"I agree. Our last attempt didn't work out so well."

He shot me a sidelong glance, looking worried.

"I mean, it went very well for what we did," I said, feeling my face flush hot. I imagined it was probably the same color as my hair by now. "But we never did get to eat."

Duncan smiled and looked relieved.

"If you're not up for a BLT, Jon was going to make a batch of his famous five-alarm chili today," I said, mentioning my new cook.

"That sounds good, but I was hoping we might be

able to go somewhere else, somewhere a little more private."

My heartbeat sped up a notch at his suggestion. "Did you have somewhere in mind?"

"Yeah . . . my place. I make a mean takeout."

This was a big step. I hadn't yet been to Duncan's place and, in fact, had no idea where he lived other than a vague "in the neighborhood" comment he'd made once. "I could go for that," I said, letting all the implications ride with the words. We shared a moment of staring at one another, our eyes smoldering, our hearts pounding, our breaths quickened. I could hear, see, smell, and taste Duncan's desire mixing with my own bodily sensations and it was the most exhilarating, exciting, mind-numbingly *awesome* thing I had ever felt before in my life. I felt pretty certain food would once again be low on the list of priorities.

I wasn't sure my stomach—or my heart—would survive it.

And I didn't much care.

Chapter 9

As it turned out, we did get to eat, but only because Duncan ordered the food with his cell phone and we picked it up along the way, right after he called Jimmy to have him invite Will, Theo, Cindy, and Shelly to meet us at Dan's apartment in two hours. He instructed Jimmy to tell the group that we thought some items might have been taken from Dan's apartment, and that since all four of them admitted to being in the place from time to time, we needed their help in determining what, if anything, might be missing. Along the way, I asked Duncan about George Weber, the senior partner, and why we weren't talking to him, too.

"Several reasons," Duncan said. "First, he's stinking rich already and doesn't need to steal funds from the business. Second, he's in Europe right now, so we know he couldn't have killed Thornton. Jimmy Skyped with Weber earlier today and saw the Eiffel Tower out his hotel-room window, so unless he set up a very elaborate scam, there's no way he could have killed Thornton in the wee hours this morning and made it to Paris a few

hours later. Eventually, we'll check his tickets and pass-
port to verify everything, but it's not a high priority."

Duncan's house was a surprise. For some reason, I
had pictured him in one of the many apartment buildings or condos in the area, but he lived in a turn-of-the-
century bungalow in an older residential section of
town. The place was small and the inside was tidy and
definitely lacking any female touch. The curtains were
bedsheets strung on rods, the furniture was well used
and mismatched—most likely yard sale stuff or rentals—
and the kitchen was so bare it looked like whoever lived
there had been on vacation for weeks. While Duncan
might not have been big on décor, he was, thankfully,
clean. The place was neat, the surfaces all shined, and
there were no stray whiskers, spilled toothpaste, or
funky specks on the mirror in the bathroom. I haven't
been in many bachelor-pad bathrooms in my life, but
those I have seen were always a mess. Duncan's was both
a relief and a delight by comparison . . . a pleasant surprise.

We ate our takeout Chinese on the coffee table in
the small living room using mismatched plates. The
food was delicious and a welcome change for me. I almost always eat my own bar food and don't get out as
often as I should. Hopefully that will change soon, because I've been able to hire on some extra help.

"Do you own this house?" I asked Duncan.

"Sort of," he said cryptically. "My grandparents bought
it years ago when they first migrated here from Scotland.
When they died, my parents lived in it for a short time,
but then they moved to Chicago. They kept the house
and used it as a rental until last year. When I got a job
offer here with the Milwaukee PD, my parents said I
could live in it rent free in exchange for fixing up what

the renters destroyed. I did most of the major fixes in the month before I started working and I've been doing bits and pieces ever since." He looked around the room as if seeing the place for the first time. "It looks pretty bare, doesn't it?"

"Not bare, so much," I said. "More like early college student, first apartment, bachelor pad."

Duncan sighed. "I suppose it could use a bit of a female touch."

"Not female, necessarily, but maybe a little something to warm it up, make it cozier. At the very least, you might want to hire someone to give you suggestions on décor, paint colors, that sort of thing." I glanced at my watch and said, "You know, you haven't seen the new section of the bar for several weeks now and it's almost done. All the walls are painted, the woodwork is finished, and other than a few pieces of furniture, everything is ready to go. I'm planning on opening it next weekend if the last stuff arrives like it's supposed to next week. Why don't we go look at it? It might give you some ideas."

"Okay. We have the time and I have to admit I've been curious about what's going on back there."

Just under twenty minutes later, we arrived at the bar and headed inside. The place was crowded—a good thing for my bottom line, though it made me feel guilty that I hadn't been there to help. Fortunately, my staff had everything under control and the members of the Capone Club were in their usual spot, with several tables pushed together near one end of the bar. If business stayed at this level through the winter, I'd be looking good.

When I'd discovered that Ginny Rifkin—my father's murdered girlfriend—had listed me as the beneficiary on her life insurance policy, it had come as a total surprise. It also nearly landed me in jail since it gave me a stellar motive for her murder. Lucky for me, that didn't happen. What's more, the money couldn't have come at a better time. I'd been living week to week with my cash flows after some costly problems that had come up, and Ginny's money not only allowed me to get caught up on the bills so I had some breathing room, it was enough for me to expand the bar by buying the recently vacated space next door, something I considered a risky but necessary decision. If I was going to continue to make a living off my profits in the years to come, I needed to invest some money in the place.

I'd had some misgivings about the whole Capone Club, crime-solving thing in the beginning, but it had attracted a lot of new business—customers who came from a variety of knowledgeable backgrounds. While we seemed to have developed a core group of regulars for the Capone Club, other customers in the bar would often join in on the discussions, too. The cops who frequent my bar like the Capone Club because it provides them with a variety of expert consultants for free. On any given night, I might have customers with finance experience, science experience, computer experience, medical experience, psychology experience, and plenty of folks with passels of simple human nature experience.

I led Duncan through an opening along the side where there used to be a shared wall with the neighboring building I bought. Now it was scaffolding with plastic sheeting that hid a metal gate that kept people from entering the new area without permission. I unlocked the gate and led Duncan into the next room, relocking it behind us. It was one big open area with a platform stage at the back.

"I'm thinking I'm going to start bringing in live

music on Thursday, Friday, and Saturday nights," I told Duncan. "There's a local band I like that does Irish music. And maybe down the road, I'll look at bringing in a DJ on some of the other nights."

"That ought to liven up the place."

"That's what I'm hoping."

"Just tell me you aren't going to do a polka night. I hate the polka and it seems like I hear it everywhere I go up here."

"Sorry to tell you, but here in Milwaukee it's practically a tradition, particularly given the large German and Polish populations we have. And you might be surprised to learn that Ireland was introduced to the polka in the late 1800s and it's the base for some of the most popular Irish folk dances."

Duncan looked skeptical but he apparently decided to let the matter drop. "You've done a nice job of blending the new area into the old," he said. "You've matched up the wood and the general décor really well."

"Thanks. It cost me a little extra to do it that way, but I wanted the addition to look as seamless as possible, like it had always been there."

"You have good taste. Maybe I should hire *you* to recommend a décor and paint colors for my house."

I didn't respond right away because I couldn't think of anything to say. On the one hand, I was flattered that he thought I had good taste. I was also excited about the long-term relationship it hinted at. But a split second later, I was second-guessing myself, wondering if I was reading too much into it. Was he even serious? Or was he just spouting out random thoughts that he would later regret or forget? Finally I said, "I'd be happy to give you some ideas, or help you pick stuff out. That sort of thing is fun. But I think doing one extra job for you is enough for right now."

Instead of responding to what I said, Duncan came back with a non sequitur. "It's going to get loud down here if you have live music. That will make it harder for your Capone Club members to do their thing."

"I already thought of that. I've made accommodations for them in the upstairs area. Come and see."

I led him up to the second floor where I had structured the expanded area by creating smaller rooms, each one with limited seating, a cozy feel, and something of a theme. One of the rooms was set up as a library with wood-paneled walls, bookshelves filled with both novels and nonfiction books that could be swapped out using an honor system, and large, cozy chairs that could be set up in small conversation circles or left alone in a corner. I'd splurged on recessed lighting and lots of lamps to create a cozy feel as well as the ability to see well enough to read, and a gas fireplace for both heat and ambience. While several people told me I was crazy for doing the fireplace, now that the weather was turning colder and winter was just around the corner, those same people were asking me how soon it would be functional. It was this room that I had in mind for the Capone Club.

I also had a room set up to be a sports and gaming spot—my regular customers had already nicknamed it the Man Cave—replete with large-screen TVs, a pool table, a foosball table, a dart board, a putting green, and computers with game systems. I had some large, comfy reclining chairs on order that were supposed to come in next week.

The third room was more ordinary, a smaller version of the bar area downstairs, with several small tables that could be pushed together to form larger ones. This room could be rented out to local companies for meetings or small parties. To service the rooms, I had set aside a spot in the common area for a second bar, which was contained in its own room. It had a garage-style door that could be opened or closed, depending on whether or not it was being used and staffed.

"This all looks very nice," Duncan said. "Just be careful that you don't overdo it."

"I will," I said, hoping this was true. "It just feels like the right thing to do."

Despite my optimistic posturing, Duncan's words echoed my own fears. I now had enough money to survive even if the business went belly-up, but my entire life was the bar. If it closed, I'd be heartbroken. I'd hoped the expansion would prevent that and provide me with a future nest egg of sorts, but I was leery for a couple of reasons. One was the investment I was making and the gamble it carried with it. Though my business was definitely on the rise at the moment, I worried that the publicity surrounding the recent murders and the whole CSI Bar thing might yet prove to be transitory.

The second reason I was leery was because I wanted to keep a neighborhood feel to the bar. Wisconsin is third in the country in the number of taverns and bars it has per capita, falling behind only Montana and North Dakota. And Iron County, Wisconsin, has the highest per capita bar rate of anywhere, with one bar for every 240 people. Small watering holes are a way of life for Wisconsinites, and people in many places treat them like a home away from home. That's fine if you live in a small town, but here in Milwaukee, where more than a million other people share your air, achieving that small, cozy neighborhood feel can be a bit of a challenge. Plus, my location means that I frequently pull in tourists or visitors to the downtown area who are here on business, or I might pull in some distant locals, folks who come into town for the night to see a show or a game at the Bradley Center, which is walking distance away.

My hope was to find a happy medium between expanding the business enough to keep my revenues flowing while still keeping that home-away-from-home feel. That was easy enough for me since it really was my home. And now, with both of my parents dead and no other relatives I knew of, many of my regular customers were my family.

We finished the tour and after checking in with my staff, Duncan and I headed back to Thornton's place to meet up with Dan's coworkers.

"Will it be okay for them to go into the apartment?" I asked.

"Sure, as long as we're with them and control where they go, what they do, and what they touch. The techs are done processing the place."

"I had some reactions earlier that I couldn't identify, one of which was Cindy Whitaker's perfume. So I'm curious to see what the apartment is like for me without them in there first."

"We can do that. You and I will go in first and once you've absorbed it all, we'll bring the others in."

I was skeptical of this idea but also curious. Knowing the dead body was no longer there made it easier for me to face the idea of going back. And what Duncan was suggesting was more along the lines of the sort of games he—and my father—would play with me from time to time.

"Okay," I said. "Let the games begin."

Chapter 10

We beat Jimmy and the others to Dan Thornton's apartment. There was a uniformed police officer sitting in a chair in the hallway and the door was now sealed with crime scene tape. Duncan greeted the officer and then sliced through the tape so we could go inside.

I felt a definite difference when we entered that I suspect was because of the time that had elapsed between my first visit and now. Many, if not most, of the smells and sounds that I experienced before were either diminished or absent, but I also experienced some new reactions to things like the fingerprint dust. I recognized this one because the cops had dusted my bar with the stuff when both my father and Ginny were murdered, and I knew from my previous exposure that it triggered a chalky, slightly bitter taste if I came into contact with it. And the sight of it—at least the black powder kind, though I learned that it comes in a multitude of colors—made me taste dirt. I think it was the color that triggered this last reaction because black in general always triggers a dirt taste to some degree, often overlaid with other tastes. And I also noticed some lighter-colored fingerprint dust—white and pink—on the dark wood credenza and the tabletop, and those spots didn't trigger the dirt taste.

I realized right away that things were missing. I could sense some of the voids and figured out what some of them were—the chair Dan Thornton had supposedly stood on, the laptop, the suicide note, the glasses and other dishes that had been in the dish rack—by using a combination of my memory and my synesthesia. I wandered into the half bathroom and could tell things were missing here, too: the trash, the hand soap, the towel. Every surface appeared to have been dusted for prints: the countertop, the light switch, the sink surfaces, the mirror, the toilet handle . . . even the underside of the toilet seat, which was now in the up position. That struck me as clever, as I might never have thought to look there for prints, given that we women typically only lift the seat if we are cleaning the bowl. I logged this fact away, thinking that it might help in my deductive training.

The techs had left behind the toilet paper, however, which looked to be a nearly full roll. At first I thought this was so the crew could use the bathroom if they needed to. Then I realized that would most likely be considered scene contamination and would therefore be forbidden. Yet something about that toilet paper bothered me. I thought back to earlier in the day and recalled the irregular sensation I had felt on the back of my neck when looking at the bathroom. Such sensations are typically a response to something that has been moved or removed. Occasionally smells will register as a physical reaction, but most of the time they come across as sounds. That irritating tag feeling on my neck was gone now, though other sensations had occurred as the result of the stuff that was missing. As I stared at the toilet paper and thought about that nagging tag reaction, I finally realized what it related to.

I called Duncan over to the bathroom doorway. "Why didn't the techs collect the toilet paper in here along with everything else?"

He looked over at the roll. "It's that quilted stuff with the patterns in it. It's pretty much useless for getting any usable prints. We would have to spray it with ninhydrin and the tissue is so absorbent and textured that the end result would be an unusable mess. I suppose there is a faint possibility of DNA being on it, but most of what gets touched gets used and flushed. So there isn't much evidentiary value to it."

"What about the cardboard tube inside the roll, or the little roller thingy that goes through that cardboard tube? How would they be for prints?"

Duncan smiled at that. "Little roller thingy?" he teased. Then his smile froze and his eyes narrowed, I suspect because he saw where I was headed. "I imagine either one of those would be a good surface for prints," he said slowly.

"Well, that's a brand-new roll, or close to it," I said. "And if my hunch is right about my earlier reaction to looking at it and the lack of any similar reaction now, I'd venture to guess that it was changed pretty close to the time that we were all here earlier. Maybe the victim changed it before he was killed, but given how much time I imagine it must have taken to stage his supposed suicide, and how long we know my reactions typically last for something like this, I doubt it."

Duncan gaped at me like I'd just said the most inane thing he'd ever heard. For a moment, I thought I'd made a fool of myself somehow, but then he grabbed me by the shoulders and said, "Mack, you're a bloody genius!"

We heard voices then, and Duncan went over to the door to meet with Jimmy, who had arrived with Theo, Will, and Cindy. I stayed inside the apartment while they talked outside in the hallway and, after a few minutes, Duncan came back inside with the threesome in tow.

"Where is Shelly?" I asked Duncan.

"She said she couldn't do it. She didn't want to come back here. She's gone to stay at her mother's place in Wauwatosa."

Theo looked scared; his eyes darted back and forth nervously. Will and Cindy, on the other hand, appeared cool, calm, and indifferent.

Duncan turned to Cindy first. "When was the last time you were here?"

Cindy scrunched her face in thought for a few seconds and then said, "I don't know . . . a week or two, maybe." She turned and looked at Will. "When did Dan invite us over for that pizza thing?"

"Two weeks ago Friday," Will said.

Cindy turned to Duncan with a smug smile and said, "There you go, detective."

I couldn't tell if she was lying. Her flame flared for a few seconds before settling back down. The only thing I was sure of was that she was a smooth operator who didn't rattle easily.

Duncan turned to Will. "How about you, Will, when were you last here?"

Will thought a moment and said, "Monday, I think. Yeah, Monday. I gave Dan a ride home because his car was in the shop. He invited me in for a beer. I didn't stay long . . . maybe an hour or so."

I had a strong sense that Will was telling the truth. The taste of his voice stayed consistently sweet, no more bitterness.

"How about you, Theo?" Duncan asked. "When were you here last?"

His facial muscles started to twitch and he hesitated for a second or two. "Um . . . I think . . . it was last week some time." The sweet cream taste of his voice, and consequently his credibility, became spoiled.

"Have you ever used this bathroom?" Duncan asked, pointing toward the room.

Theo's eyes shifted even faster and I could tell he was trying to analyze his answer before he gave it. Was that because he was afraid? Guilty? Both? I'd been feeling a bubbly, watery sensation on my arms and legs, as if they were immersed in carbonated water. At first it was very faint, but it had gotten progressively stronger as the amount of sweat dripping off Theo's face increased. At the moment it felt like a spa tub jet.

"Yeah, I've used it," Theo said, trying unsuccessfully to not look rattled by the question. "What's that got to do with anything?"

"We just want to know where we might expect to find your fingerprints," Duncan explained in a calm, relaxed voice. The bubbly sensation eased as I saw Theo sigh with relief, but it was a short-lived reprieve. "Ever take a dump in there?" Duncan asked. He was still using his buddy tone and he smiled and tried to look abashed, I assumed to put Theo at ease. But it had the exact opposite effect.

"That's very personal," Theo said.

Will scoffed a laugh, but Cindy was staring at Theo with a laser-sharp focus and a very intense expression.

"Sometimes we have to get personal," Duncan said. "So, I'm sorry for the intrusion, but have you?"

Sweat was running down the sides of Theo's face now and he was shifting nervously from one foot to the other. "No, I haven't," he said, and I knew instantly he was lying because his taste grew rancid. "I don't like to do that anywhere but my own place, you know?"

Cindy let out a snort of derision that made Theo blush.

"I do know," Duncan said, smiling at Theo and ignoring Cindy. "In fact, I'm the same way. I'll do anything to be on my own pot. There has been a time or two when I had an emergency and had to do it somewhere else and, let me tell you, I hate that! Did that ever happen to you?"

Duncan's voice was relaxed and jovial, and for a split second it worked; Theo looked relaxed and the glimmer of a smile started to form. He gave a half nod and started to say something, but stopped himself. The frightened look returned and the bubbles were coming fast and furious.

"Did that ever happen to you here?" Duncan asked. Cindy's expression morphed into something scary as she stared at Theo. "Because if that's never happened to you here," Duncan pressed on, "we wouldn't find your fingerprints inside that roll of toilet paper in the bathroom, or on the spindle it's sitting on, right?"

It was intriguing to watch the emotions play over Theo's face and experience the kaleidoscope of sensations it triggered in me. Cindy was glaring at Theo; Will kept shifting his gaze from one person to another, looking utterly confused.

Theo, whose eyes were bugging, looked like he was about to drown in his own sweat. Suddenly he blurted out, "I didn't take the money and I didn't kill him, either! It was Cindy."

"Shut up, you lying little—" Cindy spat out, her voice a veritable conflagration of anger.

"I'm going to stop you both right there," Duncan said. He then recited the Miranda Warning and when he was done, he focused on Theo. "What do you want to tell me?"

"Shut the hell up, Theo," Cindy warned. Her fists were opening and closing, as if she wanted nothing more than to cold cock Theo. Despite the disparity in their sizes, I had a feeling she could do it with ease.

"She made me help her," Theo said, casting a nervous eye at Cindy, who was standing with both hands clenched, giving Theo a death stare. "But I didn't steal the money and I didn't kill him. Cindy did. I just helped her cover it up by faking the hanging thing."

"You lying bastard!" Cindy seethed. "I'm not going to stand here and listen to this." She shifted her angry gaze at Duncan. "I don't know what Theo is trying to do, but he's obviously not right in the head."

"She told me that if I helped her, she'd be my girlfriend," Theo said.

Will, whose look of confusion had only grown, gaped at Cindy. "Cindy, is he telling the truth?"

"Of course not!" Cindy insisted irritably. "He's obviously deluded. He must have a crush on me or something and he thinks we stand a chance as a couple." She shot a glance at Theo and sneered. "As if I'd sleep with someone like him."

"But she did," Theo said. "She did sleep with me, and I can prove it."

"This is ridiculous. *You* are ridiculous," Cindy said, and she turned as if to leave.

"I videotaped the whole thing," Theo said.

Cindy stopped dead in her tracks.

Duncan said, "You're not going anywhere, Cindy.

There is another detective and a uniformed officer outside that door who will see to it."

Cindy turned around and glared at him, her lips pursed, her face pinched.

Will said, "Jesus, Cindy . . . you slept with him?" The look of horror and disgust on his face left no doubt as to his feelings on the matter.

"Get over yourself," Cindy snapped at Will. Then she shifted her glare back to Theo. "I should have known you couldn't be trusted."

Duncan walked over, opened the apartment door, and ushered the uniformed cop and Jimmy inside. "Place all three of them under arrest," he said.

"I want a lawyer," Cindy said. Now her flame guttered, like a lit candle caught in a crosswind.

"Fine," Duncan said. "Take them down to the station and book them. If they don't want to talk, they can sit in jail and stew for a while."

Theo, who looked utterly petrified, said, "I'll tell you anything you want. I didn't kill Dan and I didn't take the money. Cindy did it. She told me she went over to Dan's late last night, doped up his drinks with some Xanax she had, and when he passed out, she sat on his chest and held that rope that was around his neck until he quit breathing. She's the one who killed him. She's the one who typed up that suicide note. And she's the one who's been stealing the money. She called me around four this morning after it was all done to come over to Dan's place and help her string him up because she wasn't strong enough to do it herself. She said she'd share the money with me if I helped her." Theo's voice was sweet, cool cream again and I believed every word he said.

"You're still an accessory," Duncan said. "However, if you're willing to talk, maybe you can work out a deal."

Cindy, who was being cuffed by the officer, shot a look of pure venom at Theo. "Shut your damned mouth, you cretin," she hissed. "If you don't, I swear I'll make you pay." She then looked at Duncan before fixing her glare on me. "I'll make you all pay. Every one of you . . . you bastards!" Her flame was at a roar again, and fire-licked bits, like drops of lit gasoline, fell to the ground.

The look on her face made me step back, away from her. I believed her threat of revenge and, knowing what I did about her now, it scared me. The fact that she was handcuffed and being hauled away to jail did little to lessen my fear.

Jimmy and Duncan helped cuff the boys and then escorted them down to the cars. Theo and Will were placed together in Jimmy's car and I could only imagine what their conversation would be on the way to the police station. I knew it would be interesting and almost wished I could ride along and listen in.

Despite my lingering fears regarding Cindy's threat, I felt good that the case had been solved so quickly, and that I'd had some small part in it. As I watched the cop cars drive away, I thought that, all in all, it had been a very satisfying day.

Unfortunately, it didn't last.

Chapter 11

The bar was still crowded when we got back—a good thing for my bottom line, though it again made me feel guilty that I hadn't been there to help. As usual, my very capable staff had things well under control, and the crime group was in their regular spot with several tables pushed together.

One of the things I had done with my inheritance was expand my staffing to handle the booming business so I'd have the option of not working all the time. At first, I'd thought it was a dumb move, one that didn't make a lot of fiscal sense. But I discovered that using that time to schmooze with my customers and to oversee the operations to make sure things ran smoothly was much smarter than being a part of the everyday workforce. I still tended bar quite often; it was something I loved to do. And occasionally I'd take a turn in the kitchen and experiment with some new food items that I would then try out on some of my customers. So far, things had gone as well as could be expected.

Duncan and I headed over to the Capone table where Carter, Sam, Alicia, Holly, Tad, and Cora were seated.

Cora was showing Sam something on her laptop, but she quickly closed it as we approached. I suspected that whatever she was showing him wasn't fit for public consumption, because Cora dallies in some rather questionable websites whose ratings look like a tic-tac-toe win.

After greeting everyone and making sure they had plenty of food and drinks, I leaned over and whispered in Cora's ear. "Join us in my office?"

Duncan and I headed that way and Cora followed as directed, bringing her laptop along.

"What's up?" Cora asked once we were behind closed doors.

"I did my first real crime scene today," I told her, settling onto the couch I had along one wall.

Cora took the chair behind my desk where I usually sit, and opened her laptop. "How did it go?" she asked. "Was it hard for you?"

I nodded. "It was definitely unpleasant. But I got through it."

"She did well," Duncan said. "She was able to pick up on some valuable clues."

"Clues you didn't really need. You already knew it was a staged suicide," I said.

"That's true," Duncan said. "But you definitely added insight into the process, particularly with the toilet paper thing."

"Toilet paper?" Cora said, looking back and forth between the two of us. "Should I ask?"

"It's not as bad as it sounds," I said. "I happened to sense that something was moved or different in the victim's bathroom when we were there the first time, but when we went back I didn't get the same feeling. And the toilet paper roll was obviously a new one. I mentally walked through what you do when you change a toilet paper roll and suggested there might be fingerprints inside the tube, or on the spindle the paper rolls on. Fortunately, one of the culprits involved was the one who had put that roll on. Revealing the fact that we knew that, or at least suspected it, and might be able to get prints from inside the roll was enough to elicit a confession."

"Impressive," Cora said. Duncan's cell phone rang and he put himself in the corner to talk. "And I'm guessing you have some new impressions for me to record as a result," Cora said to me.

"I do, if you don't mind."

"You know I'm happy to do it."

Cora and I spent the next few minutes recording some of my reactions until Duncan finished his call. "You were spot on, Mack," he said. "The techs found prints on the inside of the toilet paper roll and on the spindle. And Theo is singing like the proverbial bird. Apparently the whole thing with stringing up Dan's body made him so nervous, his bowels got in an uproar and he had to use the bathroom. He admits to putting a new roll of toilet paper on the spindle, so I'm pretty sure the prints will be his. And he said that Cindy was the mastermind behind the whole thing. She flirted with Theo and apparently slept with him, knowing he had a crush on her. She convinced him to help her by getting Dan's passwords, which she then used to move some money around and place it in her own offshore accounts. She knew that if anyone discovered the missing money, it would look like Dan was the one who had taken it. Once she heard that the theft had been discovered, she decided to kill Dan and make it look like a suicide so that the blame would stay with him. She planned it well until the end, but she couldn't stage the hanging by herself. Since she had to ensure Theo's silence, she got him to help her with the suicide staging, thinking that his involvement would keep him quiet."

"Well done, Mack," Cora said. "I knew you could do it."

I wasn't as convinced as Cora was. Cindy's final threat was still uppermost in my mind. It reminded me that my involvement was more than a simple game. The stakes were life and death, and that included my own.

I turned to Duncan and said, "If you already knew that Thornton didn't hang himself, why did you take me there? Was it some kind of test?"

"In a way, yes. But simply knowing it wasn't a suicide didn't solve the crime. I truly wanted your help. I thought it might help us figure things out quicker, and I was right."

"Still, it was rather harsh. You could have picked something a little less graphic for my first real case," I said, recalling Dan's purple, bloated face. "Especially since I'm not convinced you needed my input at all. You would've solved it on your own eventually. I'm pretty sure Theo would've caved at some point, even without the toilet paper thing."

"He probably would have," Duncan admitted. "But whether you admit it to yourself or not, you were a big help. I'm sorry if it was hard for you, but it wasn't a wasted effort. You provided us with insights we might not have otherwise had."

"But I could just as easily have led you down the wrong path. You admitted you already knew Thornton didn't hang himself, and that would have led you to suspect that the note wasn't legitimate, and that other people had to have been in the apartment at the time of his death."

"But we might not have known there were two people in there close to when he died. Or that one of them was a woman."

"I didn't say it was a woman, just that it was someone who was smaller, lighter."

"Hold up, guys," Cora said, looking at the two of us with a confused expression. "You're going too fast for me. What impression was this? I need to get it down."

"Sometimes it's not about what you know, but rather what the suspects think you know," Duncan said, ignoring Cora's protest. He narrowed his eyes at me. "And you knew there had been more than one person in that apartment close to the time of death."

He had me there. "I did," I admitted. "There were two distinct fragrances in there. And while it's true that smells can drift, they don't do so inside of a closed environment as much as people think. Molecules of smell tend to settle on things and linger there."

"I need to know more about these smells," Cora insisted.

"See, there you go," Duncan said with a smile. "If we hadn't already solved this case, your knowledge that there were two people inside that apartment around the time of death would have given us a better focus in our investigation."

Cora sighed with frustration and leaned back in her chair, arms folded over her chest. "If you want me to accurately record this stuff, you guys are going to have to explain yourselves better," she said.

"Sorry, Cora," I said, finally giving her the attention she wanted. "We knew that Dan's girlfriend, Shelly, was there in the apartment pretty close to the time of death because she was the one who found him. She swore she didn't go anywhere except the foyer, the kitchen, and the bathroom. And that was consistent with the smells I got from her when we talked to her and the smells I picked up elsewhere in the apartment. It made me hear something like a washing machine running . . . wet and mechanical."

"That doesn't sound particularly appealing," Cora said, making a face.

"I guess not, but it is what it is. I heard that washing machine sound elsewhere in the apartment, but only by the door, the kitchen, and the guest bathroom. Later, when we explored the rest of the apartment, the sound disappeared until we got into the bedroom. Then it surged when we were near Thornton's bed. I'm guessing her smell was stronger in the sheets for reasons we can all guess."

Duncan smiled and arched an eyebrow.

"The girlfriend told us she spent some time in Thornton's place last evening," I went on. "And I'll bet the majority of the time was spent in the bedroom. She wasn't feeling good so she probably left without dawdling, which is why her smell wasn't detectable elsewhere in the apartment except for the spots she was in when she came back later and found him. I'm guessing the victim must have showered after his girlfriend left, and that's why her smell wasn't on him. Plus, I knew there was someone in the apartment who smoked, and neither the girlfriend nor the victim did."

"The smoke smell could have come from Theo," Duncan said.

"True," I agreed, "but the Chanel No. 5 smell didn't. Cindy's perfume is what did her in."

"Chanel No. 5," Cora said, typing away. "What did that smell trigger for you?"

"High-pitched flute music."

We went on discussing the various impressions I'd had and what we thought had triggered them, while Cora typed it all in to her database. After an hour or so, we were finally done and I sent Cora out front to get a meal and a glass of wine on the house, my payment for her services.

As Cora packed up her laptop and left the room, Duncan got another call on his cell. When he was done, he turned to me and said, "That was Jimmy. He said they have no evidence that Will was involved so they let him go. They found Theo's sex tape, and both he and Cindy are locked up. I imagine if she had the chance, Cindy would probably kill Theo right now. She isn't talking, but Theo is telling everything he knows. He said Cindy told him she showed up at Dan's last night around eleven and told him she was locked out of her apartment and her roommate wasn't answering her cell phone and likely wouldn't be home until after two, so she needed a place to hang out for a while. Dan let her in and after they chatted and watched some TV for a while, she drugged Dan's drink with Xanax. Since she knew we wouldn't be able to find any unexplained funds in Thornton's accounts, she wrote the suicide note to explain why the missing money couldn't be found. I'm sure she was hoping that would keep us from looking for the money."

"The Xanax explains that high-pitched whine I heard mixed in with the rhythmic grating sound of the Johnnie Walker Black. Remind me to have Cora add that one to the database."

"See, you're better than you realize."

"But Will wasn't lying and I interpreted the changes in his voice that way. So you see, I'm not as good as you think."

"Just because we don't have evidence pointing to Will doesn't mean he's innocent. Maybe he *was* lying."

"Or maybe he was just very angry that we suspected him. That's why I'm not one hundred percent comfortable with this. What if you'd arrested him because of what I said? He could have ended up in jail simply because he was pissed off."

"I'm not going to arrest anyone based solely on your reactions, Mack. It's just one part of the puzzle. Without any concrete evidence, I can't arrest anyone or prove anything legally. I think that's why Jimmy is worried. He's afraid I'll rely too heavily on your input, but I promise you, I won't."

"He thinks I'm crazy, doesn't he?"

"Who, Jimmy?"

I nodded.

Duncan scrunched his face up into something that looked like a cross between a smile and a grimace. "To be honest, I think he's on the fence, but you're slowly winning him over. I think he believes you have a unique talent. He's just not convinced that using it is wise. He focuses on every miss you've had during our test runs and he's afraid that if I rely too much on what you say, it will lead us down some wrong paths and waste valuable time and resources. But he also can't deny that you've produced some accurate results, too, sometimes amazingly so. However, he tends to attribute those incidences to luck, or simply good powers of observation combined with a strong understanding of human nature."

"He's right that I seem to be hit and miss with this thing. So maybe he's also right in thinking this isn't such a good idea."

Duncan frowned. "There are bound to be a few mistakes until you get more experience. But I think they will lessen over time. You'll get more familiar with how to interpret your reactions, and what they mean. There's a learning curve and I think we just need to be patient."

"I'm not sure I agree. And I'm not sure that I want to

get involved with this death and misery on a regular basis."

I could tell Duncan was disappointed by my comments. I wanted to help him, but I just wasn't sure if I was cut out for this sort of thing.

"I can't force you to do it," Duncan said. "But I hope you'll stick with it."

With that, he got up, kissed me on the cheek, and left. I stayed in my office for a while to have some alone time and sort through the jumble of thoughts running through my mind. The only thing I knew for sure was that Duncan Albright had definitely complicated my life.

Chapter 12

When I finally left my office and went out to the main bar area, I looked around for Duncan, but he was nowhere in sight. I poured myself a glass of wine and carried it over to where Cora was sitting. Before I had a chance to say anything, she offered up the very information I wanted.

"If you're looking for the hunky detective, he left," she said. "And he looked really sad when he did. What did you do, Mack, break his heart?"

I didn't know about *his* heart, but mine was definitely aching. "It's complicated, Cora."

"How so? The two of you make a great team. And it's obvious that you both like each other. In fact, I'd say it's a little more than *like*." She punctuated this last statement with a salacious wiggle of her eyebrows.

She was right about one thing; I definitely felt something for Duncan Albright. That was part of my problem. I wasn't sure if I was helping him with this crime stuff because I truly wanted to be involved with doing something good that would better the community, or if I was doing it simply because I was attracted to him and wanted to please him and spend time with him. I suspected it was a combination of the two.

Plus I had some lingering doubts about his attraction to me. There were times when I felt confident Cora was right, but there were other, more cynical times when my inner voice suggested that his interest in me might be a fleeting infatuation, or be solely because of how my little talent could be of use to him. Was I just fooling myself? Was I behaving like some besotted teenager with a schoolgirl crush? I found it ironic that I possessed this so-called talent that made me more sensitive to the world around me, and yet I didn't seem to be able to sense anything with regard to my own love life.

I looked around the bar at my customers, many of whom, along with my employees, were like family to me. Were they all looking at me now with pity, seeing me as the poor lonely girl who would do anything for a little attention?

"Sit down," Cora said, gesturing toward the seat across from her. "I want to try something."

Curious, I did as she instructed. She tapped some keys on her laptop and after a moment she said, "What sort of sensations did you get when you were with your father?"

I gave her a confused look, unsure what she was going for.

"I mean, when the two of you shared a special moment," Cora explained. "When you were a child and you curled up in his lap, or hugged him, or had one of those special father–daughter moments, what sensations did you have?"

I saw where she was going then and thought I knew what she was aiming for. "Most of the time I felt a warm, secure pressure over my shoulders and back, as if I had a cozy blanket wrapped around me. I also remember times as a child when he would poke his head in on me at night after he'd closed down the bar and come up to the apartment. He always checked on me, and there were times when he would come and sit beside me on my bed and it would awaken me. When that happened, he would try to talk me back to sleep by telling me stories about things that happened in the bar, or sometimes things about my mother—how they met, the early days of their marriage, how excited she was about being pregnant, that sort of thing. Sometimes he would make up stories about fantasy lands populated with anthropomorphic creatures, most of whom were thinly disguised versions of some of our regular customers. For instance, the Signoriello brothers would appear as Neapolitan Mastiffs, an Italian breed of dog known for protecting home and family. It made sense because both the dogs and the brothers were big, and the brothers were insurance salesmen so, like the dogs, they were in the business of protecting home and family. And when I looked up the dogs in a book at the school library, they had these funny, sweet, kind of saggy faces like the Signoriello brothers have."

Frank and Joe Signoriello have a strong sense of family, though their own families have spread out like the tufts of a dandelion gone to seed. As a consequence, they have adopted me as their family, an arrangement that suits me just fine.

"Another character Dad often used was a chatty parrot named Lilly that was very vain and constantly preening," I went on. "The parrot talked with a heavy New York accent that my father pulled off surprisingly well. It was obvious to me that the parrot was based on a woman named Molly who used to come into the bar all the time hunting for men to date. She dressed in bright jewel colors, she had the New York accent, and she was forever taking a compact out of her purse and primping."

"How fun," Cora said.

"It was, and I loved it when my father would tell those stories. He only did it on Friday and Saturday nights during the school year because I would get so interested in the stories and the characters that I couldn't go back to sleep." I paused and smiled. "I always told Dad he should write those stories down and try to sell them as children's books."

"I take it he never did," Cora said.

I shook my head. "He kept saying he would, one of these days. Maybe once he retired he would have done it, but he never got the chance."

"I doubt your dad would've ever retired," Cora said.

"Yeah, you're probably right."

"But your memories of those times are exactly what I'm after," Cora went on. "Can you remember what other synesthetic reactions you had during those special moments you and your dad shared?"

"A taste," I said. "Warm and chocolaty, like hot cocoa."

Cora typed and said, "A taste for you is usually associated with a sound, something you see, or a tactile sensation. Which do you think this was?"

"Sound," I said without hesitation. "It was the sound of his voice when he talked to me in a certain way."

Cora shot me a curious look. "You seem pretty certain of that. Have you had the same experience with others?"

I nodded and felt myself start to blush. "Yes, with Duncan. His voice also makes me taste chocolate."

"Interesting," Cora said, tapping away on her keys. "Do you taste chocolate when you hear any other people's voices?"

I thought about it a moment and realized I didn't. "Not that I can recall. I do experience tastes when I hear other people's voices, particularly men's voices, but not chocolate. Most women's voices have a taste, too, but some manifest as a visual."

Cora looked up from her computer for a moment and narrowed her eyes at me. "Do you taste something when you hear my voice?"

I laughed. "It depends on your tone," I said. "You always taste like barbeque sauce, but sometimes it's a sweeter taste than other times. At the moment, you sound rather tangy."

She considered this a moment. "I'll take tangy," she said. "What about Zach?" she asked then, referring to my recent ex-boyfriend. "What did his voice taste like?"

"Fresh baked bread. Nice . . . comforting . . . ordinary," I concluded with a shrug.

"Interesting," Cora said, once again tapping away at her keys. "Let's get back to your dad. What other experiences did you have with him? What about when he touched you or hugged you? What did that trigger?"

"An undulating image of color—sort of a blue-green shade—like soothing waves on the ocean."

"I think that was your interpretation of the love you felt emanating from your father when he hugged you."

"Perhaps," I said, unsure.

"And when you touch Duncan, what happens then?" Cora asked. I blushed—a curse of us pale-skinned redheads—and Cora read me like a book. "I gather the two of you have touched a lot lately. Did you finally take your relationship to the next level?"

"We did," I admitted in a low voice after looking around to see who might be within hearing distance. "When he touches me, I get a zing of a shock, like an electric current, and I tend to see hot red-and-yellow jagged lines."

Cora cocked her head to one side and considered this. "What do you suppose that means?" she asked me.

I smiled. "Near as I can tell, it's the fires of hell."

Cora let out a hearty laugh. "Why would you think that?"

"I don't know. For me, the act of feeling includes both tactile senses and emotional ones. I can't always tell which is which if I'm touching someone I have strong feelings for, or who may have strong feelings for me. For instance, there were times when Zach and I were alone and I would catch him looking at me a certain way. I could tell just from his expression that he was having fond thoughts about me, and that would trigger a visual manifestation. The same thing happened at times with my father."

"What sorts of visual manifestations?" Cora asked, once again typing away.

"Typically swirls of colors—soothing, comforting, relaxing colors."

"So these visual things made you feel comforted and loved?" Cora suggested.

"Yes, I suppose they did."

"What do the visual manifestations you get with Duncan make you feel?"

"Fireworks," I said with a fond smile. Then the smile faded. "But at times I also feel unrest and discomfort. Maybe it's the things he sees in his work that cause it. I'm not sure if the manifestations are triggered by what I feel when he touches me, or by the emotion I sense coming from him."

"Maybe they're triggered by the emotion you sense coming from *you*," Cora suggested.

It was an unsettling thought, yet it made sense. Maybe my body and my skewed senses were trying to tell me something. It was then that I made the decision not to work with Duncan anymore. If there were shared feelings between us that might lead to something permanent, it would have to happen without our working relationship. The decision felt right to me, and I thanked Cora for her help and insight.

Unfortunately, my newfound resolve dissolved an hour later when Duncan called and told me about Davey Cooper.

Chapter 13

Duncan quickly filled me in on the basics: Davey Cooper was two years old and missing. His mother, Belinda, was found dead—murdered—in their house.

"Look, Mack," Duncan said, "I know you have some hesitations about working with me, but I could really use your help on this one. Time is of the essence. Every minute that goes by without us finding this little boy increases the likelihood that he'll end up dead if he's not already."

Just in case I had any remaining reservations after learning the victim's age and hearing Duncan's plea, he sent a picture of Davey Cooper to my cell phone to help seal the deal. I looked down at an adorable little boy with light brown hair, huge brown eyes, thick dark lashes, and a disarming, cherubic smile.

I was being manipulated and I knew it. Unfortunately, it worked. "What can I do to help?" I asked with a sigh, putting the phone back to my ear after looking at the picture.

"I want you to come here to the house, to the scene of the murder. I know this death stuff is hard for you, and I'm not going to lie, this one is particularly grue-some. Belinda Cooper didn't die a pleasant death."

The thought of having to look at another dead body made my spine prickle, but after looking at the little boy's picture, I knew I had no choice. My mind shifted into business mode and I glanced around the bar. We were doing a hopping business, but I knew the staff I had on duty could handle the place just fine for a few hours without me.

Duncan must have interpreted my silence as hesita-tion because he urged me along. "I have a car waiting out front to bring you here."

"Fine, I'll be there as soon as I can."

I disconnected the call and glanced over at my head bartender, Billy Hughes. He was eyeing me curiously and I could tell he sensed something was up.

"I need to leave again," I told him.

"You look like you just saw a ghost," Billy said. "Is everything okay?"

"I don't know. Duncan has another case he wants me to help him with. He warned me that it wasn't going to be pleasant."

"Are you sure you want to do this?" Billy asked, and I could tell he sensed my lingering reluctance. Billy's keen ability to read people will serve him well when he launches his new career.

"A little boy is missing," I told him. "I don't know if I'll be able to help, but if I can, I have to try. Do you mind taking over here while I'm gone?"

"Of course not," Billy said.

It was just past eight in the evening and in case I didn't get back in time to close, I asked Billy and Debra if they would mind doing it for me.

"We're happy to help out any time," Debra said.

"Plus, we have fun when you're gone," Billy added with a wink. "When the cat's away . . ."

"You little mice have a good time," I said. I then stepped from behind the bar and headed over to Cora's table.

"Heading out to help Duncan?" she asked. I'm not sure how she knew, though I suspect my face must have shown the angst I felt.

"I am. Can you do me a favor?"

"Name it," Cora said.

"Use your computer superpowers and dig up anything you can find on Belinda Cooper and her two-year-old son, Davey."

Cora looked troubled. "Don't tell me someone killed a child."

"I don't know. He's missing. Keep it to yourself for now and if you can stay by your cell phone while I'm out, I'd appreciate it. I might need your help in interpreting my reactions."

"No problem," Cora said. "You know you can always call me anytime, night or day, for any reason."

"Thanks, Cora." My mind conjured up some faint swirls of soothing colors like the ones we had discussed earlier and I had an overwhelming urge to reach down and hug her, but I didn't. Instead, I grabbed my coat from my office and headed out the front door. It was dark, the air felt heavy and damp, and I felt a chill that seeped through my skin all the way to my bones. I sensed there would be snow coming soon, though probably not tonight. I buttoned my coat clear to the top, unsure if the chill I felt in my bones was due to the weather or my thoughts about the situation I was heading into.

As Duncan had promised, there was a squad car waiting for me with two uniformed officers in the front seat. I knew them both by name because they had been frequenting my bar a lot in the past few weeks, both while on and off duty. On-duty cops come in for my coffee; the off-duty ones typically come in at the end of their shifts to enjoy a libation and some camaraderie. I was even considering expanding my hours of operation once I opened the new section to accommodate the night shifters. State law requires that bars be closed between the hours of two a.m. and six a.m. Monday through Friday, and two-thirty a.m. and six a.m. on Saturday and Sunday. The one exception allowed is on New Year's Eve, when no closing is required. But first I had to find staff willing to work those early morning hours, staff I could trust enough to open the place on their own.

The two cops waiting in the squad car for me were Nick, whose Polish parents had saddled him with the name Nicodemus, and Tyrese, an African American who, unlike his partner, insisted on being called by his full first name whenever anyone tried to shorten it to Ty. They greeted me with somber nods of their heads, which I took to be an indication of just how grim the scene I was about to visit would be. I climbed into the back, which promised an uncomfortable ride given the hard plastic of the seat and the confined space. The feel of cramped quarters made me see a red number zero floating around my field of vision.

Fortunately, because of the discomfort I was experiencing, and unfortunately, because of the crime scene's proximity to my bar, the ride was a short one. It was a little over ten minutes, despite a fair amount of traffic, before we pulled up in front of a house in the Halyard Park neighborhood. We were only a few blocks away from Duncan's house.

While the majority of the housing directly around my bar is condos, if you go a few blocks to the north, west, or east, you'll find yourself in one of several eclectic residential neighborhoods that contained a mix of condos and older single-family homes, as well as a mix of ethnic types. It wasn't hard to identify the particular residence we were headed for based on all the flashing lights and police tape strung up out front. It was a smaller bungalow-style house with a one-car attached garage, similar in style to Duncan's and, also like Duncan's, the place was in need of some repair. The pale blue wood siding was faded to near white on the south and east sides of the house, and the paint was peeling badly. A cracked concrete sidewalk led up to a small porch with a wood-post railing, a bead-board ceiling, and a heavy, arched wooden door with a small window at the top.

Nick let me out of the car—the back doors couldn't be opened from the inside—and he and Tyrese escorted me past the police tape to the front door. The number zero disappeared from my field of vision. As I approached the house I hesitated, and the two men seemed to sense my reluctance.

"Are you okay, Mack?" Tyrese asked, looking concerned. "I know Albright thinks you have some unique insights to offer, but maybe going in there is more than you can handle."

"You know about my . . . how I . . ." I didn't go on, unsure how to put my ability into words.

"Word has spread down at the precinct. Cops talk," Nick said with a shrug.

I frowned at this. Up until now, I'd thought that only a handful of cops knew, though I suppose it was naïve of me to think that something like this would be kept secret for long. You can't drag a lay person along to crime scenes and not raise some questions.

"Don't worry," Nick added. "Everyone understands that you don't want it known publicly and we're keeping it amongst ourselves."

"Do cops outside this district know, too?" I asked.

"I don't know," Tyrese said. "There's bound to be some talk sooner or later if word gets out that you're accompanying cops to crime scenes. But the official word from our station is simply that you're a consultant, though most of us are calling you Albright's secret weapon."

I didn't like the sound of that, or the pressure I felt it put on me. Plus, I knew there were skeptics and naysayers who disapproved of what Duncan was doing—people like Jimmy.

As if he were reading my mind, Nick said, "I don't know exactly what it is you do, but Albright definitely believes in you, and the guy knows his stuff. If he has faith in you, so do I."

"You're a psychic or something like that, right?" Tyrese asked.

"Not exactly," I told him. "Think of me more as a bloodhound, like a K-9 partner who can detect things normal humans can't."

"You sure as hell ain't no dog, Mack," Nick said. "In fact, I was wondering . . . do you and Albright have a thing between you? You know . . . a romantic thing? Are you two dating?"

Tyrese gave his partner an admonishing punch in the shoulder. "Sheesh, so not the time or the place, bro," he chastised.

"Yeah, I suppose you're right," Nick said. "Sorry, Mack."

"No harm done," I said, grateful I didn't have to answer his question about Duncan and me, since I had no idea if the two of us had a "thing," whatever the heck that was. And I wasn't about to admit to these two that Duncan and I had slept together. "In fact, I'm flattered. But Tyrese is right. We have more important things to focus on for the moment. So, as much as I'd rather be behind my bar right now whipping up some scrumptious hot toddy, I think we need to head inside."

Chapter 14

Tyrese led the way with Nick bringing up the rear. I stepped to one side just inside the threshold so I could take a moment to deal with the onslaught of visual images, the cacophony of sounds, and the host of bodily sensations that were triggered by what lay beyond. I closed my eyes and tried to sort through them, singling each one out and mentally filing it into one of several boxes I created in my mind. One of the boxes was for sounds, one was for smells, one was for visuals, and one was for touch. Hopefully I wouldn't need one for taste, but I did set aside a fifth box for the miscellany that I sometimes experience: manifestations triggered by emotional residue and by what I thought of as my sixth sense, for lack of a better description.

The first thing I filed was the most overwhelming one: the smell of blood. I knew that smell and its associated sound from my childhood, and I was reminded of it when both my father and Ginny were killed. My brain translated the sharp, acrid scent of blood into a sound I can only compare to shrill, high-pitched notes played on a trumpet. I forced my mind to push the sound aside, a trick I learned when I was very young. If not for my ability to filter through the many sensory experiences I have, I probably would've ended up in a nuthouse somewhere. The neurologist who diagnosed me said the sensory input I experience is akin to the voices a schizophrenic hears. He warned me that it might sometimes be difficult to distinguish my manifested experiences from the real ones, and if I didn't learn to ignore my synesthetic responses, it might make me as crazy as all the doctors I'd seen before him thought I was.

After pushing aside the smell of blood and its associated sound, the next thing I focused on was a terrible taste. It was as if I had bitten into something rotten, like a bad peanut, or meat that had begun to spoil. The experience was both unpleasant and new to me. I pushed it aside but didn't file it away in one of my mental boxes, knowing I would want to explore it more later on. Along with the taste, I felt cold, as if I were standing in a draft, and I wasn't sure if that sensation was real, an emotional reaction, or a synesthetic response.

I was standing in a small foyer and the entrance to the kitchen was straight ahead. I took a few more steps and looked at the room to my left. It was a small but tidy living room furnished with a mismatched chair and couch, and a yard sale coffee table. Off in the far corner of the room was a door that I assumed led to the garage. On the wall in front of me was a fireplace with a brick surround and the cold, ashy remnants of a fire beyond the hearth. Hanging above that was a flat-screen TV and on either side of it were built-in bookcases. While the bookcase on the left was filled with paperback novels and a few hardcovers, the bookcase on the right held a DVD player, a Wii console, several games, and an assortment of G-rated movies. There were several framed photos of Davey at various ages, one of which I recognized as the photo Duncan had sent to my phone. Most of the pictures were of Davey alone, from infancy on up, but two of them also featured a pretty, smiling blond woman. Based on her age and the adoration I could see in her eyes—even in a picture—I assumed this woman was Belinda.

The floors were hardwood and there was an inexpensive beige-colored area rug on the living-room floor that had the faint remnants of a pink stain by one corner of the coffee table. I imagined a little boy sitting on the floor watching a movie, or playing a game, taking the occasional drink from one of those little juice boxes that he then somehow managed to spill.

As I entered the living room, the nasty taste in my mouth lessened a little and the air felt warmer. I stood next to the stain in the rug, closed my eyes, and let my other senses absorb for a minute. Nothing seemed particularly dominant and, as I turned back toward the foyer, I saw Nick, Tyrese, and Duncan—who was holding a camera—all standing there watching me. The sight of Duncan made my heart skip a beat, but I wasn't sure if it was real or synesthetic.

"Thank you for coming," he said. As usual, the sound of Duncan's voice triggered the taste of chocolate in my mouth; it'd been that way since the first day I met him. Depending on his mood or the tone in his voice, the chocolate taste might be sweet or bitter, but it was always there. Duncan turned to my chauffeurs and said, "Thanks for bringing her."

Nick and Tyrese took this as their cue to leave and they exited via the front door.

"What do you want me to do first?" I asked Duncan once the others were gone.

"Let's go through the house a room at a time," he

said, handing me a pair of gloves that I dutifully donned. "Does anything leap out at you here in the living room?"

"I don't think so. There may be something about the bookcase over there on the right side of the fireplace, like something has been moved or removed, but I'm not sure."

Duncan said nothing, but he took a few moments to snap some pictures, including several of the bookcase I had mentioned. Then he turned to me and said, "Let's move on." He placed his hand at the small of my back and gently steered me into the kitchen.

I could tell from the strength of the blood smell and the lessening of the sound that went with it that little Davey's mom wasn't in the kitchen. But I didn't want to be surprised by the sight of her body, so I hesitated and turned back to Duncan. "Where is she?"

"In her bedroom, at the end of the hall on the left. We'll go there last and I'll warn you before we get there. For now, I'd like you to walk through the rest of the house and tell me what sort of reactions you get."

I told him about the acrid blood smell and the shrill trumpet sound it triggered, and then I told him about the taste and the chill I felt. "I've never experienced that particular taste before so I can't tell you what it means, and I'm not sure if the chilled feeling is real or not. But I can tell you that it was stronger in the foyer than it was in the living room, or than it is in here, for that matter."

Thus far, I had kept my eyes either on Duncan or the floor, purposely avoiding anything else in the kitchen. While this didn't block out any of the sound or smell triggers I was experiencing, it did minimize the visual ones. Most of the sound and smell manifestations were minor ones that I knew to be part and parcel of the more ordinary aspects of my surroundings. To prepare for a more involved experience with the kitchen, I closed my eyes for a few seconds to brace myself. Then I opened them and focused hard on the room.

One of the first things I noticed was a calendar hanging on a small section of wall beside the refrigerator. The top half had a picture of a lake with cloud-studded skies above and snow-capped mountains in the distance. The bottom half was the calendar itself, accurately flipped to the current month of November. Though some part of my mind registered the fact that the numbers for each day were printed in black, another part of my mind saw them in an array of colors. Numbers often appear to me as colors, with each of the digits from zero to nine having its own unique color. The number five, for whatever reason, is always yellow and two is always blue. Oddly enough, this unique way of envisioning the numbers makes me very good at math.

The other odd experience I have with calendars is that each month has a personality. November is kindly and comforting, a bit drowsy at times, and it always feels a little nostalgic. I ignored these sensations and focused instead on the handwritten items filled in on some of the days: *school closed* was written in on the day after Thanksgiving; *Dr. Fillmore, 10:00* was scribbled in two days ago on the twelfth; and *6:30 hair appt* was written in on the twentieth. I recognized the name of the doctor since it was the same OB-GYN doctor I use, and therefore guessed that the appointment was for Belinda rather than for her son. I mentioned this to Duncan before turning my attention to the rest of the room.

Most of the houses in this neighborhood date back to the 1920s and 1930s, and this kitchen looked like it had last been overhauled in the 1980s. The cabinets were faux wood with a white stripe of plastic trim, the floor was linoleum worn nearly through to the subfloor in front of the sink, and there was a built-in banquette in one corner of the room with a rectangular table sporting the same pink and black Formica that topped all the counters. I wondered if Belinda Cooper owned the house or was renting it and asked Duncan, who informed me the place was a rental.

As I approached the refrigerator, the nasty taste in my mouth grew and I started to wonder if it was somehow related to a bad smell emanating from inside it. But smells don't typically manifest themselves as tastes for me. I usually hear or feel smells. My neurologist suggested that I'm able to detect small molecules of odor that linger in the air and that these molecules trigger a wave pattern of sound, or a tactile sensation, or on rare occasions both, that I can discern from the rest of the air around me. My suspicion that in this case it wasn't a smell triggering the odd taste was supported when I opened the refrigerator door and looked inside. The interior sparkled with cleanliness and the contents were all carefully placed with their labels facing out. Duplicate items were lined up in neat little rows and, as I looked over it all, I sensed that something had been moved recently from a shelf on the left. There was a front-to-back row of yogurts and three front-to-back rows of single-serve juice boxes. As I stared at the juice boxes, the skin on my back registered an irregularity, as if someone was tracing a finger down my spine and skipped a spot.

"I think something was either moved or taken from this spot here," I said to Duncan, pointing to the juice boxes. After thinking on it for another second, I added, "Taken, I think, because I sense a void."

Duncan opened the refrigerator door wider and started snapping pictures of the contents. "I imagine the missing item is probably a drink that Belinda or Davey had," he said.

"Maybe," I said, not convinced. "How long ago did all this happen?"

"The first officer got here about five minutes after the elderly woman next door called because she thought she heard a child screaming," Duncan said, still snapping away. "She said she looked out her window but she couldn't see anything because it was dark and all the shades in the house were drawn. The woman said she tried several times over a period of ten minutes or so to call Belinda, but no one answered, so she called nine-one-one." He stopped what he was doing and glanced at his watch. "We've been here for just under half an hour and we got here minutes after the first officer called it in."

"I know from the games I used to play with my father that my sensations regarding missing or moved objects fade and disappear after about an hour or so, depending on how enclosed or exposed an area is, so whatever is missing here was likely removed within that time frame."

"Meaning we were very close to catching whoever did this. If the neighbor woman had called when she first heard the screams . . ." He didn't finish this thought, but the sad shake of his head said it all. "Anyway," he went on after a few seconds, "it's possible that whatever was removed was done so by the victim."

"Maybe. Have you seen any yogurt containers or juice boxes on top of the trash or lying around?"

"None so far," Duncan said, glancing around the kitchen. He walked over to a lidded trash can by the sink and opened it with a gloved hand. "Nothing here," he said, snapping a picture of the garbage. "We'll keep an eye out as we go through the rest of the house."

Both sides of the double kitchen sink were sparkling clean, and an empty dish rack sat on one side. A quick perusal of the cabinets and drawers showed neat rows of items, with food labels facing outward, dishes organized by size and color, pots and pans all polished to a gleam. It seemed Belinda Cooper was all about neatness and organization.

We left the kitchen and went down the hall to the first room on the right. It was small and likely meant to be a bedroom, but was being used as an office instead. There was a small wooden desk with a computer on top, a dented two-drawer metal filing cabinet, a standing lamp with a plastic shade, and a desk chair with a wheeled base and worn fabric on the seat. Everything looked old and used, but also clean and well cared for. The office offered me nothing in the way of interesting reactions and I told Duncan so. With that, we left the room and went across the hall to a bathroom.

Like the room we had just been in, the bathroom was also small though functional. Immediately inside the door and to the left was a small vanity, beside it was the toilet, and beside that was the combination shower and bathtub. While the vanity, toilet, and fiberglass bath and shower structure appeared to be newer, the tile on the floor reflected the age of the house. It was a basic black-and-white hexagon design, and in a few spots the tiles were cracked or missing.

Built into the wall across from the sink was a decent-size wooden cabinet, and tucked into the larger bottom section was an empty laundry bag. The cabinet shelves were as organized and neat as those in the kitchen had been and they were filled with typical bathroom items: towels, washcloths, cosmetics, soaps, shampoo, and other hair products. In the cabinet below the sink, we found tampons, toilet paper, and cleaning supplies. There was also a medicine cabinet above the sink, which contained deodorant, toothpaste, and some basic over-the-counter medications, both for adults and for children. In a cup sitting atop the faux marble vanity topper were two toothbrushes, one large and one small. Though the sight of the tiny toothbrush made my throat tighten, I thought this was nothing more than an emotional reaction since I already knew the child was missing. On one side of the sink was a hairbrush that looked as if it was brand new; there was a single short, brown hair in it that I guessed must have been Davey's since Belinda was blond.

We left the bathroom and went to the end of the hall, where there were two more bedrooms. Even if Duncan hadn't already told me, I would have been able to tell from the smell that Belinda Cooper was in the bedroom on the left, so it didn't surprise me when he steered me into the bedroom on the right.

It was obvious this was little Davey's room. A colorful area rug done up to look like a collection of children's wooden alphabet blocks covered most of the floor. In the far corner was a bunk bed, the top level covered with stuffed animals, the bottom one made up with a Thomas the Tank Engine comforter set. Even though the lower bunk was neatly made, I sensed a void there because I felt a hollow sensation on my back between my shoulder blades. I also heard a faint sound, the distant tinkle of music from a child's toy, something like a jack-in-the-box. I mentioned it to Duncan, even though I didn't understand what it meant.

A long, wooden dresser with two columns of drawers stood to the left just inside the door. It was painted white with red knobs on the drawers, and on top of it was a lamp that had Thomas the Tank Engine for the base with more images of Thomas on the shade. Stacked neatly on one side were two piles of books. A quick scan of the spines showed several Dr. Seuss books, some fairy tales, a couple of popular modern-day children's books, and some coloring books. A box beside the books held an assortment of crayons and colored markers, as well as a set of watercolor paints and several brushes.

Something about the dresser triggered a physical sensation in me. Looking at the top of it didn't seem to bother me, but when my eyes settled on any of the drawers, I felt an odd sensation, as if something were pushing me away.

"I'm getting an odd sensation from this dresser," I told Duncan. "When I look at the drawers, it feels like something is pushing me away, or maybe blocking me. I'm not sure what it means, but I suspect those drawers were opened recently."

"Which of the drawers?"

I took a few seconds to let my eyes settle on each drawer, one at a time, before I answered. "I get the feeling when I look at every one of those drawers. I may be wrong, but I think all of them were opened."

Duncan walked over to the dresser and pulled open the top left drawer. Inside it was a collection of children's socks and little boy underwear. Modern-day superheroes and cartoon characters dominated the designs on them. I saw more of Thomas, plus Super-man, Batman, Spider-man, Transformers, SpongeBob SquarePants, and several *Sesame Street* characters including Oscar, Elmo, and Cookie Monster. Most of the socks were paired up but there were some singles in there as well. The socks and underwear along the far sides of the drawer were neatly folded and laid out, as if someone had tried to keep the drawer neat and organized. The rest of the drawer, however, was a jumbled pile of half-folded shirts and underwear. Looking at it gave me the sensation that I was wearing an ill-fitting hat, and that the hat was riddled with holes that allowed the wind and the heat to come through. This was a sensation I recognized because I'd experienced it a few times before when my father and I were playing games with my abilities.

"I think someone went through this drawer very recently and in a hurry," I told Duncan.

He nodded. "I would've come to that conclusion myself," he said with a smile. "Based on other things I've seen in the house, our victim is a very neat person. Things in the closets, the kitchen cabinets, and all the drawers are very precisely organized. She might have even had a touch of OCD. It looks as if this drawer was originally laid out in a similar fashion, but someone rummaged through it."

"Whoever did it either lacked finesse or they were in a big hurry. Maybe both."

"I suppose it could've been the kid," Duncan said.

"I don't think so," I said. I turned and looked behind us, across the room at the wooden toy box that sat beneath a window, its lid opened to reveal its contents. "I get the same sensation when I look at that toy box over there that I get when I look at this drawer," I explained. "Not only have things been hastily shoved around, there are some voids there."

"You mean things have been taken?"

"Yes."

"That may bode well for little Davey," Duncan said.

"How so?"

"Well, if whoever nabbed the kid took the time to gather clothes and toys for him, it suggests they have no intention of hurting him."

On the wall above the dresser, attached by a thumbtack, was another photograph of little Davey with the smiling woman I presumed was his mother. In every picture she was in, Belinda was looking at her son with obvious love and adoration in her eyes.

I turned to Duncan with tears burning behind my eyes. "If whoever took this child is hoping not to hurt him, they are too late," I said. "His life will never be the same."

Duncan sensed the depth of the emotion I was feeling. "If you need to take a break, we can do that," he said.

I shook my head and swiped at my eyes. "No, I'll be okay. I'm just angry and disappointed."

"Disappointed?"

"Yes, disappointed that our civilized society can be so uncivilized, that there are those in the world who can inflict such hurt, and pain, and cruelty on others with hardly a second thought."

Duncan walked over, took hold of me by my upper arms, and looked straight into my eyes. His touch made me feel lighter, as if I were floating above the ground. "There is a lot of beauty and love in the world, and you can't ever forget that, Mack," he said, making me taste sweet milk chocolate. "You have to hang on to the good stuff. If helping me do this kind of work is going to make you forget that, I don't want you to do it."

As I looked back at him, his face moved a hair's breadth closer to mine. I saw warmth, caring, and genuine affection in his eyes, and though I couldn't be sure, I got a strong sense that he wanted to kiss me at that moment. But then the reality of where we were, what had happened, and what lay in waiting for us in the other bedroom intruded. Duncan broke our shared gaze and looked down at his feet. His hands let go and he sighed long and heavy before turning away from me. He turned back to the open drawer of the dresser and, after taking a picture of its contents, he pushed it closed and opened the one beneath it.

I walked over and stood beside him, studying the contents. This drawer contained shorts and pants, and the same mix of organization and chaos that we had observed in the underwear drawer. Once again I sensed there were items missing. Duncan then opened the other two drawers, which held shirts and pajamas, and we saw that they were more of the same.

"You know, it seems odd to me that whoever took Davey gathered up clothes and toys for him, and yet they left behind his toothbrush," I said.

Duncan paused in his picture taking and gave me a quizzical look. "How so?"

"I don't know exactly," I said. "It's as if someone was gathering up items they would need to take care of the kid. And his toothbrush would be one of those things." I shrugged and shook my head. "Maybe it was just an oversight."

"A lucky one for us," Duncan said. "Toothbrushes are often good sources for DNA."

I assumed DNA would be needed only to identify a body and, as such, I shot him a horrified look. "You think he's going to end up dead?"

"Not necessarily," he said, seeing the expression on my face. "But the reality is that sometimes these kidnapping cases don't get solved for years, and kids change as they grow. DNA may be the only reliable method for identifying a living victim who's been missing for a long time."

After a few more minutes in little Davey's bedroom, Duncan prepared me for going into Belinda's room. "It isn't going to be pretty," he warned. "There's a lot of blood."

"I can tell from the smell," I told him. "Is she maimed in any way? Dismembered? Anything like that?"

"No."

"Then I think I'll be okay." I sucked in a deep breath and focused on mouth breathing, hoping to keep the smell from overpowering my other senses. Then I followed Duncan inside, to one of the saddest sights I've ever seen.

Chapter 15

We arrived back at the bar about an hour later. The weather outside was cold and gray, and the wind coming in off Lake Michigan split itself into icy tentacles that snaked their way down the streets and between the buildings of the city. There was definitely snow in the air; I could smell it, see it in the clouds, and feel it in my bones. I'd heard other people express similar sentiments often enough to suspect that these sensations were legitimate ones that others shared as well, but such is the nature of my disorder that I can never be sure. I can taste an oncoming snowstorm, something I've never heard anyone else mention, so I keep that one to myself. And I can often tell what kind of snow is coming from slight variations in the taste. Light, fluffy, dry snow tastes like white bread, whereas wet, heavy snow tastes like wheat bread.

Once inside, Duncan and I headed for my office, shedding our coats along the way. We waved several of my customers along to follow us: Cora, the Signoriello brothers, and Tad.

"We heard about some missing kid on the news,"

Frank said when we were behind closed doors. "They issued an Amber Alert and said he lives in the Halyard Park neighborhood. Is that where you guys were?"

I nodded, not saying anything. I was still struggling with my emotions.

"I could use a cup of coffee," Duncan said, reaching over and giving my shoulder a squeeze. "Can I fix you a drink? I've got something special in mind, an old family recipe. It will take me a few minutes because it requires some kitchen prep, but I promise you it will be worth it. And it's the perfect drink for a cold night like this one."

"Sure, thanks," I said, intrigued.

"Anyone else?" Duncan asked the others.

The Signoriello brothers were huge Pabst beer fans and they each had one in hand, most likely their second or third ones if history was any indication. Cora, who tended to live in my bar because she could conduct her business from anywhere there was Wi-Fi—and it was thanks to her that Mack's Bar had Wi-Fi—often nursed a single glass of Chardonnay for an hour or two. In typical fashion, she had half a glass that she had carried into the office with her.

Tad hadn't brought a drink with him and he quickly accepted Duncan's offer. I think the others might have passed had the offer been for any regular drink, but Duncan's preface had them intrigued. Eventually everyone accepted and Duncan left to go make his mystery drink.

I settled in at one end of my couch and the Signoriello brothers filled up the other. Cora claimed the work chair behind my desk and then went about setting up her laptop. Tad settled into the chair on the other side of the desk, meaning Duncan would have to stand when he came back.

These impromptu meetings had become something

of a regular event since the establishment of the Capone Club. A few people had emerged as "specialists" for the club, such as Cora for her computer and hacking skills, and Tad for his financial knowledge and contacts.

Another regular member—one whose "expertise" wasn't so obvious—was Kevin Baldwin, a single, thirty-something gentleman who has been out of town for a couple of weeks. He worked as a local trash collector—though he preferred the title "sanitation engineer"—and his primary value to the group was his access to people's trash. A lot of people don't realize that trash put out for collection can be gone through without a warrant by cops who are searching for information or evidence. The cops had asked Kevin a couple of times to set aside certain trash pickups on his route so they could search through them. Though the cops could legally confiscate someone's trash if they wanted to, they liked the idea of using Kevin to collect it for later inspection, because it kept the owner of the trash none the wiser.

The Signoriello brothers have little in the way of current expertise to offer, but they have an unbridled enthusiasm for the job, some great contacts in the insurance industry, and some keen insights on human nature gleaned from their combined 140-plus years of living.

Not surprisingly, the foursome in my office started pumping me for information almost immediately. I suspected they were hoping to get the scoop before Duncan came back, some juicy tidbit that he and the other cops investigating the case wouldn't want shared. But one thing Duncan and I had in common was a good understanding of human nature. As such, we had anticipated this and discussed it on the way back to the bar after leaving the Cooper house. Duncan had already told me what I could and couldn't share. Most of what I was allowed to tell was the same stuff the news people would get. Enterprising reporters monitor police scanners for bits of radio chatter that give away details, or they'll quiz neighbors, witnesses, or acquaintances for what they know. I've learned from Duncan that the cops are well aware of these information leaks and they expect that many of the details about the case will get out. But there are always a few things—sometimes seemingly insignificant things—that the cops try to keep under wraps so they can weed out false confessors and distinguish which of any similar crimes may be copycats.

In the Cooper case, one such bit of information was the fact that panty hose were found wrapped around Belinda's neck. The medical examiner who was there in the room with Duncan and me had determined—based on the amount of bruising around Belinda's neck and the amount of bleeding from her stab wounds—that the perpetrator had tried to strangle her with the panty hose prior to stabbing her. For whatever reason, the strangulation hadn't killed her, and after seeing the disarray in Belinda's bedroom, I guessed it was because Belinda put up too much of a fight. The ME did say he saw tissue under Belinda's fingernails—tissue we all hoped would belong to the perpetrator. But there were also deep scratches on the front of Belinda's neck, and the ME said that was a typical finding for someone who was being strangled from behind with something; victims typically clawed at the offending object in an effort to release the pressure on their throats and get some air into their lungs. The ME also said that while the strangulation might have rendered her unconscious, based on what we saw in that bedroom, it was clear that the stab wounds and the subsequent blood loss were the actual cause of death.

Beyond this bit of inside knowledge, Duncan had

told me to use my judgment. If information I was about to reveal was something the public would likely know or could easily find out, it was probably okay to share. Otherwise, I should keep it to myself. That he entrusted me with this knowledge and discretion made me feel good.

So when Frank started with, "What was it like?" and Joe jumped in right behind him with, "What did you see?" I was prepared to provide plenty of possibly helpful but hopefully harmless details.

I started by describing the scene outside when I first arrived. Then I told them about the foyer and the living room—how they looked, the stain on the carpet, the framed photos in the bookcase. After that, I briefly described the bathroom and the third bedroom that was used as a home office. Then Tad asked a question that tugged painfully at my heart and brought my impersonal descriptions to an end for the moment.

"That poor woman," he said. "What was she like?"

"She was pretty," I said, recalling the photos of her I had seen in the house rather than the blood-smeared death mask that had been Belinda's face. "She was also small. I bet she stood only five feet tall, which would have put her at a definite disadvantage against almost anyone, although she did have very muscular arms and legs, and that makes me think she worked out regularly. Given that, she might have surprised the killer by putting up more of a fight than they expected."

"Was there evidence of a struggle?" Joe asked.

"Some," I said. "But not as much as one might hope, at least not in terms of knocked-over furniture and that sort of thing. In fact, the house was impeccably neat. Things were very clean, and the cabinets and closets were all organized and very orderly."

Before I could explain further, Duncan walked in bearing a tray of six mugs. When he set it on the desk, I saw that one of the mugs had coffee in it. The other five were filled with a steaming, spicy-smelling, creamy-brown drink topped off with a cinnamon stick. Duncan doled them out to us, saving the coffee for himself.

"This is my granny's recipe for hot buttered rum," he told us as everyone sipped and moaned with delight. The drink was hot, creamy, and flavored with hints of nutmeg and cinnamon—the perfect hot toddy for a cold autumn night.

"Wow, this is good," I said, and then I took a second, longer taste. "You have to give me the recipe for this." I took another swallow and felt my muscles start to unwind and relax.

"I don't know if my granny would approve," Duncan said. "It's a closely guarded family secret. But I suppose if you're nice to me, I might be persuaded." There was more than a hint of innuendo in this comment and I saw the others in the room exchange looks.

Duncan took a sip from his coffee mug, and I wondered if he had souped it up with a shot of anything, or if he was drinking it straight. "What have you guys been discussing so far?"

"Mack was describing what the victim looked like," Frank said.

"And telling us how she was kind of a neat freak," Joe added. "Maybe she had OCD and had to see a shrink. You should check on her insurance claims and see if she had any psychiatric care. If she did, they might be able to give you some leads on the people or situations in her life that were problematic."

"Good idea," Duncan said, setting his coffee on a corner of the desk so he could scribble out some notes.

The brothers both smiled, looking very pleased with themselves and their contribution. I smiled, too. As retired insurance salesmen, they had a knack for inserting an insurance connection into every crime discussion we had. It might have been annoying—particularly since it had pointed a finger at me in Ginny's murder—if not for the fact that most of their ideas, like this one, were good ones.

"Mack was about to tell us about the sensations she picked up on," Cora said, her fingers poised above her laptop.

I looked over at Duncan and he gave me a subtle nod of his head, letting me know it was okay to continue. Everyone in the room understood that any information that was shared in my office was to be kept private.

"I got a definite sense of things missing from various parts of the house," I said. "Things like the little boy's clothing, and perhaps some of his toys. I even got a sense that something had recently been removed from the refrigerator."

Cora asked, "Can you tell me how many of each item was taken?"

I shook my head and frowned. "Based on the degree of the voids I felt with the clothes, I'm guessing it was multiples of everything, but I can't give you exact numbers."

Tad confirmed what Duncan had said earlier. "Taking that stuff makes me think they don't intend to kill the kid," he said. "I guess that's a positive."

"Yes," I agreed. "Particularly since I think it might have been some juice that was taken from the fridge. There were several other juice boxes lined up near where I felt the void, although there were also several yogurt containers there. But we didn't find any fresh, empty containers of either juice or yogurt in the trash."

Cora tapped away on her laptop keys. "It does sound like whoever took this kid is planning on long-term maintenance. Did they take any medicines, diapers, or the kid's toothbrush?"

I looked at Duncan, eyebrows raised. "Funny you should ask, because that's been bothering me," I told her. "Why wouldn't they take the toothbrush if they were grabbing things for the kid? It doesn't make much sense to me."

"It's a good question," Duncan said, and I could tell from the expressions on the faces of the others in the room that they were all curious as well. "Maybe they meant to take it and forgot. I'm sure they were anxious to get out of there. Or maybe they figured the toothbrush would be an easy thing to buy new without attracting any undue attention."

Joe Signoriello said, "I might be wrong, but the fact that they grabbed the stuff they did implies a lack of forethought to me, a level of unpreparedness. If taking the kid was something they had planned all along, wouldn't they already have stuff like that in place? I mean, come on, adults plan for kids in one way or another all the time, whether it be adoptions, or births, or even just visiting grandchildren. It's part of normal life and simple common sense. So if taking the kid was the main objective, I would think the kidnappers would already have all that stuff ready to go."

"Joe's right," Frank said. "Maybe taking the kid wasn't the main objective, but rather a by-product of his mother's death. Maybe that poor woman was killed because someone wanted her kid. Or maybe the kid got taken simply because he witnessed whoever killed his mother and the killer couldn't bring himself to kill a child."

"All good points," Duncan said. "Although I suspect

a two-year-old wouldn't be a huge concern as a witness. I suppose he could identify someone, but I doubt the testimony of a two-year-old would hold up in court. I'm leaning more toward the idea that taking the kid was the main objective."

"That poor boy," I said, shaking my head. I felt a hollow ache deep inside my chest and once again I wasn't sure if it was an emotional response or a synesthetic one. "I hope whoever took him did so because they want him, not because they want to make him disappear."

Several long seconds of morbid silence filled the room while everyone contemplated the various outcomes. Though for me, even silence is noisy. The various odors in the room—like Cora's perfume, the drinks we all had, the starch in Tad's shirt, and the steam from Duncan's coffee—each came with their own distinctive sound.

"Seems to me," Tad said, "that we need to figure out a motive. Once we understand why this woman was killed, it might help us find the correct pool of potential suspects. Now, granted I'm a little biased since I work in finance—but it does seem like money is often at the root of so many of these crimes. Any indication of that in this case?"

"Not so far," Duncan said, shooting me a look. I knew he was thinking of the earlier case we had.

"Either way, the kid must be scared to death," Cora said, looking concerned.

"I wonder if that's what caused that nasty taste I had there," I said.

The noisy silence I experience filled the room as everyone turned to stare at me with questioning expressions.

"What taste?" Cora asked.

"I wasn't sure if it was significant or not, and I didn't understand it, so I didn't mention it. It was a horrible, foul taste, like biting into meat that's gone bad. But I didn't have it all the time, only in certain areas. I first tasted it as we were approaching the house, when I was still outside. At first I thought it might have been connected to the blood smell, and a real taste. But it wasn't present in Belinda's bedroom and if it had been related to the blood smell, it should have been."

Cora scanned her computer screen and tapped a few keys. "So far when you've experienced a synesthetic taste, it's been triggered by either a touch or a sound. Were you touching anything when you had the taste?"

"I don't think so," I said, thinking back. "I was careful not to touch anything. Besides, Duncan made me put on gloves."

"Where in the house were you when you experienced the taste?" Cora asked.

"It was strongest in the boy's bedroom, the foyer, the hallway, and in the kitchen by the entrance from the hallway, next to the fridge. At first I thought it might be a smell from the fridge that was creating the funny taste, but Cora's right. A synesthetic taste is usually triggered by the lingering air waves from a sound, or from a touch. But when I notice strong smells, I have a tendency to mouth breathe to minimize them and that can lead to some odd tastes. Because of the blood smell, I was mouth breathing quite a bit and kept thinking that was causing the tastes."

"Seems like you experienced it in all of the places in the house where the kid would have been," Joe said, and his brother nodded in agreement.

"Maybe I smelled—and hence tasted—his fear," I said. "People tend to change how they smell with certain emotions."

"You mean, like pheromones?" Cora said.

"That, yes, but also just the way our body odor or our sweat smells when we're stressed, afraid, exhausted . . . that sort of thing. I don't know if it's the release of stress hormones that causes the change, or something else, but it exists. Plus, under those circumstances we tend to breathe harder and faster, emitting more of our smells into the air. If that little boy's fear left a distinctive smell in the air, I might've picked it up as both a smell and a taste since I was mouth breathing so much."

Still tapping away, Cora said, "If you tasted the kid's fear as well as smelled it, the taste would have manifested itself as a tactile sensation or sound for you. Did you notice any correlation between the taste and any sounds or sensations?"

"I did. I felt a chill, like a cold draft was blowing on me whenever I experienced that taste. It was as if I had suddenly stepped in front of a window air conditioner, or was standing in front of an open refrigerator door. Of course, I was doing exactly that at one point, and the entire experience was chilling, so it's hard to know if the cold sensation was synesthetic or real."

Still studying her computer, Cora said, "Emotional residue causes tactile sensations for you, too. So maybe the chill was caused by that."

"Maybe. It's hard for me to know." I turned and gave Duncan an exasperated look. "This is where I have my doubts about trying to help you. My confusion over these reactions may just muddle things even more for you."

"Give it time," Joe said. "The more practice you have with it, and the more things Cora can record, the easier it will get."

I cast a suspicious eye at him. "Has Duncan been priming you?"

Joe shook his head and, at the same time, Duncan threw his hands up and said, "Hey, I'm innocent here . . . for once."

"They're right, Mack," Cora said. "You have to give it time."

I knew in my heart that she and the others were right. But I also knew that there were lives at stake, and I didn't want to be responsible for anyone coming to harm. If I misinterpreted my reactions and led the police down the wrong trail, it might cost someone their life. It was a responsibility I wasn't sure I wanted to shoulder. Yet whenever Davey Cooper's smiling face flashed through my mind, I knew I had to do anything I could to help him. It left me in a dichotomous state of mind, one I feared I'd be living with for a long time to come.

Chapter 16

Over the next half hour, we continued to discuss the case and my experiences in the house, with Cora recording any new synesthetic reactions I had in the database, and occasionally looking up some that we'd already recorded. A couple of my staff members poked their heads in for a few minutes, including Debra Landers, who is affectionately referred to as Ann from time to time due to her last name and her propensity for doling out advice to coworkers and customers.

Debra is in her forties, with two teenaged sons and a husband she doesn't talk about much. She's been working here for the past three years, hoping to augment her kids' college funds. She is adored by patrons and coworkers alike, not only for her quick wit and down-to-earth advice, but because she loves to bake and is always bringing in the fruits of her labors to give away to anyone willing to sample her wares. And there is never any shortage of those. She's a valuable employee to me not only because of her abilities and personality, but because of her flexibility. She's willing to work any hours,

any days, and most times can come in at a moment's notice.

Everyone who poked their heads into my office knew
about the case we were working on. It was all over the
news because of the Amber Alert that had been issued.
While the media still didn't have all of the details, Belinda Cooper's murder and the disappearance of her
son was the top news story on every station.

No doubt Duncan and his cohorts were none too
happy about this since the cops had barely had time to
figure out who Belinda's next of kin were—her mother,
father, and a brother all lived in Ohio—and notify them
about her death before they heard about it on the news.
There was also an ex-husband, a man by the name of
Jamie Cooper, but so far no one had been able to find
him. Until he turned up, I felt confident he would be
suspect number one on Duncan's list. And Duncan was
willing to share information with us if it might help find
the guy.

"His driver's license still lists the house on Fourth
Street where Belinda lived and we can't find any other
known address for him, but the neighbors said he hasn't
lived there for nearly two years," he told the group.
"One neighbor said he thought the guy was floating between friends' houses, bunking wherever he could, and
another thought he'd left town. One thing they all
agreed on was that the divorce was a messy one that included a bitter custody battle over Davey."

"Belinda was given sole custody," Cora said, reading
from her laptop screen. "According to the court files,
there were some allegations of abuse from Jamie. Looks
like the cops were called to the Cooper residence a
number of times because Jamie beat up on Belinda."

Duncan stared at Cora with an expression I couldn't quite interpret. "How do you know all that?" he asked her.

She gave him an enigmatic smile. "Some of it is public information on the Circuit Court Access site," she said. "And if you know how to get past the public parts into the more private parts, it's amazing what you can find. And I'm *very* good at getting into the private parts," she added with a saucy tone and a flirtatious wink that made every man in the room squirm.

"How is it you can do that?" Duncan asked after a few seconds of awkward silence. The Signoriello brothers and Tad all looked to Cora, eager to see how she was going to answer the question. I was a little curious myself; would she stick with her double entendre, or answer Duncan seriously?

In the end, she did neither. "Do you really want me to answer that?" she asked in a teasing tone of voice.

Duncan narrowed his eyes in thought for a few seconds. "Come to think of it, no, I don't," he said finally. "I should probably maintain some level of plausible deniability in case you're ever busted."

"Smart man," Cora said, winking at him and making him blush. "But don't you worry. I'm very careful to never leave a trail." She waved a hand in front of her chest. "I promise you, this is the only bust I'll ever have to worry about."

Though I didn't look at any of them, I knew that at that precise moment, every male eye in the room was focused on Cora's ample chest.

Duncan cleared his throat and that seemed to knock the men out of their reverie. Out of the corner of my eye, I saw the Signoriello brothers both shake their heads and raise their drinks, and Tad suddenly developed a keen interest in the last dregs of his drink at the bottom of his otherwise empty mug.

Duncan said, "Do you think you can work any of that computer magic of yours and find out where Jamie Cooper might be, Cora?"

"I'll see what I can do."

With that, we broke up the little group in the office and headed back out to the main bar area, everyone except Duncan, who stayed in my office to make some phone calls and then left some ten minutes later.

The discounted drinks and the fun of trying to solve made-up or old crimes typically lent the place an air of joviality, but tonight, with the abduction of little Davey Cooper dominating the news, the crime solvers in the place had adopted a more serious attitude than usual.

After making rounds several times and assisting behind the bar for a while to be sure everyone was caught up and handling things okay, I made my way to a group that had congregated at the far end of the bar. Tad, Cora, and the Signoriello brothers were there, along with Holly, Carter, Alicia, and Sam. Included in the group were two uniformed cops, Steve and Mitch, who had just come in after finishing their shifts and were now fielding a barrage of questions from the group about the Cooper murder and kidnapping. Billy was leaning over the bar listening in, and Missy, though she tried to look like she was working, was hovering close by, eavesdropping as well.

The news about the Coopers had trumped the other murder that had occurred that day, that of Dan Thornton. That's partly because no one outside of the police and the ME's office knew Thornton's death was a murder, though now that the arrests had been made, I felt sure it would be in the newscasts later tonight and in the newspaper tomorrow morning. Still, the story of the Cooper boy and his mother would probably be more prominent.

"We think the person who took the kid is interested in keeping him alive," I heard Steve say to the others at his table. "So there's hope of a happy ending here."

"Assuming you can find him," Holly said. "These days, kids seem to disappear in the blink of an eye and if anyone ever sees them alive again, it's often a decade or so later. Look at those three girls who were kept inside that creep's house in Cleveland for ten years, or Elizabeth Smart and Jaycee Dugard. Those poor kids were there one minute and gone the next."

"There are some differences, " Billy said, swiping a towel inside a glass he'd been drying for several minutes so he'd look busy while he eavesdropped. "Age for one, and gender for another. Name one little boy who has disappeared and then resurfaced alive years later."

Several seconds of silence followed as everyone struggled to think of a single name or case. Finally Sam said, "There was one, a few years ago. But I can't recall his name. Shawn something, I think."

"What do you guys think was the motive behind all this?" Carter asked, heading down the same trail our smaller group had earlier. "Was killing the Cooper woman the main objective, making the kid an incidental that had to be taken care of, or was the main objective to get the kid, making the mother someone who had to be taken care of?"

"Good question," Holly said.

"Is there a husband in the picture?" Alicia asked. "Or was the Cooper woman single, like me?" With this last part, she looked over at Billy and gave him a sexy wink. Billy just smiled.

"There is an ex-husband," Mitch said. "A guy named Jamie Cooper. We found out he worked as a car salesman over in Brookfield up until a month ago. Apparently he got fired for showing up drunk to work. His boss gave us an address out in Glendale, an apartment he thought Cooper was staying at, but the roommate there, Jason, said he hasn't seen Cooper for the past week. Jason said Cooper went on a bit of a bender after getting fired, couldn't come up with his overdue rent money, and then disappeared. So far we haven't been able to find him. He wasn't scheduled to work today and he isn't at home. The roommate figured he'd found someone else to mooch off of for a while."

"Any idea who the new mooch victim might be?" Carter asked.

"Not sure," Mitch said. "The roommate told us Cooper had recently started talking about a girl he met named Valeria Barnes, but he doesn't know if the two are now living together or not."

Sam said, "Have you talked to this girl yet? It's not uncommon for a girlfriend to be jealous of the ex-wife and her connection to the ex because of their kid."

"We haven't been able to find her, " Mitch said. "There is no one with that name listed in the phone directories, the utility rosters, or with DMV. So either the name is one she made up, or she's someone who lives totally off the radar, which in this day and age is unlikely unless she's a homeless person. Based on the description of her that we got from the roommate, who only saw her once from a distance when she was outside waiting for Jamie, she is clean, well groomed, and nicely dressed. So I doubt she's homeless."

"So no one has seen the ex-husband or his girlfriend for a week," Carter summarized. "They sound like potential suspects to me."

"Yeah," Mitch said. "Until we can find them and question him, those two are at the top of our list."

"But why would they kill the mother and take the kid?" Sam asked. "What's the motive? Did the father want custody bad enough to do something like this?"

Steve and Mitch both shrugged. "Don't know," Mitch said, clearly the more talkative of the two cops. "We haven't had much time to work up a profile on the guy yet."

Cora shared what she'd discovered earlier from the public area of the Circuit Court Access site. "The divorce between Belinda and Jamie wasn't a pleasant one," she told the group. "They fought pretty bitterly over the kid and in the end Belinda got sole custody because of some allegations about a drinking problem and some abuse in Jamie's past."

Sam, still in his psychologist mode, pushed his idea a little further. "Were there any signs that whoever killed her knew her? Was her face covered up? Was she stabbed in places that might suggest the killer had issues with her?"

I watched both Steve and Mitch closely as they fielded this one, knowing that they likely knew, as did I, about the attempted strangulation. But they were good. Their expressions gave nothing away. Once again it was Mitch who provided an answer. "Most of the wounds were on her torso and she was stabbed from behind."

"Stabbed in the back?" Holly said with a grimace. "That might be a message."

I knew that was unlikely based on what Duncan had told me, but it was something I didn't share. When the killer had tried to strangle Belinda, he or she had come at her from behind with the panty hose. But Belinda had fought hard enough to make the stranglehold ineffective, forcing the killer to grab a pair of scissors and stab her instead. From the way it appeared, stabbing her in the back had been more a matter of desperation than any sort of diabolical message. The weapon of choice was one other tidbit of information that the cops were holding back for now, to weed out the crazies who might try to confess to the crime merely for attention. As it stood now, the media had said that Belinda Cooper was stabbed to death, and the presumption on the part of the public was that a knife was used.

Still searching for motives, Sam asked, "Is there any family money involved? Might someone have kidnapped the kid for ransom?"

"But why kill the mother if that's the case?" Holly posed. "Why not just take the kid? I mean, who's going to pay the ransom if the parent is dead?"

Carter said, "Maybe killing the mother is the kidnapper's way of telling the rest of the family that the perpetrators are deadly serious," Carter said. "It sends the message that they aren't fooling around. Meet their demands or else . . ."

The implied result made everyone in the group wince.

"So how about it, guys?" Sam asked the two cops. "Is there any family money?"

This time Steve answered. "We don't know, but it doesn't look like it. Based on what the cops in Ohio told us, Belinda's family appears to be average, lower- to middle-class folk. We don't know about Jamie's yet, but he can't be living high on the hog. His employer said he had the lowest sales of anyone on the payroll."

"Was the kid's mother dating or seeing anyone?"

"Not that we've found," Mitch said. "For all intents and purposes, her life revolved around her job and her kid. We haven't learned of any outside interests or activities she was involved in, nor does she have any family in the immediate area. Belinda and Davey Cooper pretty much kept to themselves."

"Where did she work?" Holly asked.

"At a day care center over on the west side of town," Mitch said. "She took her kid to work with her every day, so I'm guessing they weren't apart much."

"Well, they're apart now," I said, feeling sad as I recalled the adoring expression on Belinda's face in the photos. "Forever."

Chapter 17

Duncan returned just before closing, crooked a finger at me, and headed for my office. I excused myself from the others and headed that way. Once we were both inside with the door closed, Duncan said, "The task force on this case will be working all night, but so far all we've uncovered are a lot of dead ends. If they don't find the kid tonight, I'll need to canvass some of the Coopers' neighbors first thing in the morning, and I'd like you to come along, if you don't mind. Give me your take on what they say and how they say it."

"You want me to be a human lie detector?"

He shrugged and grinned. "Pretty much, yeah. I've seen you do it and frankly I think you're more reliable than the machines."

I frowned when he said this but it was more of a reflexive reaction than a reflection of actual feelings. To be honest, I kind of enjoyed that aspect of my abilities. When I was younger, I figured out early on that I had the ability to tell when my father was lying to me, and I also figured out that not all lies are bad. Sometimes he would tell me little white lies that were intended to make me feel better and, after exposing them as such, I realized that I hurt his feelings by doing so. I learned that my father's need to protect me, or at least feel like he was protecting me, was very important to him, so I started letting the white lies go by and pretending I bought into them.

It didn't take me long to realize that customers who came into the bar lied all the time. They lied to other customers, they lied to my father and me, they lied to our staff, and at times they lied to themselves, though these last ones were sometimes harder to pick up on. Occasionally, I would meet someone who never seemed to lie at all, and as I got older and savvier about people in general, I realized that these were the truly dangerous people, the sociopathic types who could lie without compunction. It was the guilt, that tiny sense of awkwardness most of us feel when we tell a lie, that allowed me to pick up on it. It's that underlying awareness that we're being deceptive, and the associated guilt that goes with it. It's the same thing that makes our pulse and blood pressure change, or our sweat glands produce a bit more, which is what a conventional lie detector detects. But those subtle little changes also affect the way our voices sound, and while most people aren't aware of these very minuscule changes, I am—not because I hear them but because I taste or see them.

Oddly enough, it's also how I can tell when a customer in the bar needs to be cut off. Speech is affected by one's degree of inebriation just as other bodily functions are, and I can see the change before others become aware of it via the person's slurred speech or other physical indicators like staggered steps.

I remember one customer in particular, a man named Rolly, who my father would often have me watch, because when Rolly drank too much, he became nasty and violent, trying to pick fights with other customers. Twice it resulted in disaster: once when Rolly picked a fight with another customer and the end result was Rolly's arrest and over a thousand dollars' worth of damage to our bar, and once when Rolly picked a fight with the wrong guy on a bus and ended up in the hospital with a broken arm, a broken nose, and a very bad concussion. Rolly was a pleasant enough soul when he was sober, or when he only had a few drinks under his belt. But there was a line he would sometimes cross and, when he went over it, all hell broke loose. I could tell when he was getting close to that line because Rolly's voice typically tasted like scrambled eggs to me—bland, boring, and ordinary. But the more Rolly drank, the spicier those eggs would get, as if they were seasoned with pepper, then onions. If he stopped at this point, he was generally okay, but if he continued to drink past the onion stage, his voice began to taste like someone had doused the eggs with Tabasco sauce. My job was to warn my father when Rolly's voice started tasting spicy so we could cut him off and send him home.

Everyone's voice triggers some sort of manifestation for me, but if I focused on them all the time my life would be a chaotic mess of smells, and occasionally images. I learned at a young age to mentally push these extra senses aside, much the same way one might try to ignore an itch they can't scratch for some reason. But if I choose to focus on them, they become crystal clear to me. And that's exactly what Duncan wanted me to do.

"I'm happy to try to help you," I told him, and then I added a caveat. "But remember, just because someone is lying, it doesn't mean they're guilty."

"Yes, I know," Duncan said in the sort of patronizing tone of voice one might use on a stupid child.

"I've spent more time with you today than I have with

my bar. If this is the way things are going to be, I'm going to have to set some limits. I can't spend the majority of my time helping you when I have a business to run, a business I depend upon for my livelihood."

"I realize that, and I promise you it won't be like this all the time. If I'd known that this Cooper thing was going to happen, I never would have involved you in the Dan Thornton case. I did that first one mostly to help you wet your feet, to give you a trial run at it."

"And you didn't really need me," I said. "You would have figured that one out on your own."

"Probably, eventually," Duncan agreed, albeit reluctantly. "But not as fast as we did. Still, it's water under the bridge now. I'm sorry the day turned out like it did, but I really do need your help with this latest one. We have to find that little boy, and time is of the essence."

I suspected he knew quite well that if he mentioned the missing child in his appeal, it would get to me. And it worked. I sighed and nodded my acquiescence.

"Thanks," he said in a tone that made it sound like a mere formality and left me feeling a little taken for granted. "Will you need to get or do anything before we head out in the morning?"

"My crystal ball, perhaps?" I shot back in a slightly irritated tone.

"Do you have one?"

"No, but if I did I'd be tempted to clobber you on the side of the head with it right about now."

"Then I'd have to arrest you," Duncan said, taking a step closer to me. His tone of voice changed dramatically, and its accompanying taste changed as well, shifting from smooth milky chocolate to something darker, spicier, exciting, and different. As he gazed down at me, I saw his pupils dilate.

"You would do that?"

"In a heartbeat," he said.

"Would you handcuff me?" I asked in a low, sultry voice.

Duncan sucked in his breath and the corners of his mouth twitched ever so slightly. He closed his eyes and sighed. I couldn't help but smile because I knew I'd gotten to him.

When he opened his eyes again, they looked different, softer. I wasn't sure I liked the change. "Let's talk about this," he said. We were back to that smooth milk chocolate.

"Talk about what? The case? What you want me to do?"

"No, this," he said, pointing a finger at first me, then himself. "This thing between the two of us."

"There's a thing between the two of us?" I said in a half-joking voice. "I thought you were just buttering me up to get me to like and open up to you. I took you for someone who flirts with all of your female suspects."

"I do," Duncan said with a wicked grin. "Flirt, that is, but I reserve that other part for the special women in my life."

"Women? Plural? Are there any others at the moment?"

His face darkened and his grin faded. "Only you, at the moment." Oddly, the chocolate turned bitter.

I wondered who had been in his life before me. As handsome and outgoing as he was, I imagined he must have had women lining up to date him. "Anyone special in your past?" I asked. "I don't know much about you. Have you ever been married?"

"No, but I came very close once."

"You mean you were engaged?"

"Closer than that, I'd say." That comment had me confused and it must have shown. "I was left at the altar."

"Oh, no," I said, genuinely shocked. "That must have been awful."

"It was one of the hardest things I've ever gone through. It's the main reason I moved here, so I could get a new start in a new place with no memories."

I found this news disturbing. If he was still recovering from a broken heart, I wasn't sure he was ready for any sort of long-term relationship with me. Then again, it was still early in our relationship and I needed to take things slow as much as he did. "If you need more time, maybe we should slow things down," I said.

"No, I'm good with where things are now."

I smiled, enjoying the closeness we shared, the heat I could feel radiating off his body. We weren't touching, but the electricity hovering in what little space existed between us felt like enough to light the entire city. "Now I understand why it took you so long to make a move," I told him. "You really did have me wondering there for a while."

"I didn't want to trespass on someone else's territory."

I had no idea what he meant by that and it was obvious from the confused look I gave him. "What are you talking about? Whose territory?"

"Zach's, of course."

"Zach? I haven't seen him in six weeks. We broke up back when you were investigating Ginny's murder."

"I didn't know that. You never said anything. Neither did anyone else."

I gaped at him in disbelief. "Seriously? You *are* a detective, aren't you? You didn't notice that Zach hasn't been around here for weeks, and that I haven't mentioned him at all? If you were curious, why didn't you just ask me, or anyone else for that matter?"

Duncan shrugged. "Just because I didn't see Zach

here didn't mean you weren't seeing him elsewhere. To be honest, I thought the reason you didn't mention him around me was because you thought it would be awkward. And I did ask someone else. I asked the Signoriello brothers, Debra, and Billy. They all shrugged and said they had no idea."

I smiled at that. "My employees and the customers who know me best are careful to protect me, because they know I tend to be a bit rabid on the subject of my privacy. They're my extended family; they look out for me. So until you make your intentions known, I don't think any of them will tell you much. Even then, I suspect they'll be pretty tight-lipped."

"I suppose it's nice that you have that with them," Duncan said, "though it certainly is a pain for me. I'm glad most of my suspects aren't as tight-lipped as your group of extended family, because if they were, I'd never solve a single case, even with your help." He paused and sighed, his breath gently rustling my hair. "And that brings me to my other concern."

The seriousness in both his tone and his expression caused me to take an involuntary step back, widening the space between us. "You have a concern?" I said, hating the faint tremble I heard in my voice and hoping he didn't pick up on it. I've always considered myself a strong woman and I hate looking or feeling vulnerable. It's one of the reasons I haven't had many romantic relationships so far in my life, and why the ones I have had were often limited. Opening myself up to someone else in that way doesn't come easily for me.

"It's more of a professional concern," Duncan said, and I breathed a hair easier. "I don't want my relationship with you to color your interpretation of things. Sometimes I jump to conclusions, and while I'm often right, sometimes I'm wrong. I don't want my assumptions or area of focus to interfere with your perceptions in any way, whether conscious or subconscious. Because, I believe in what you do, but I also believe that your interpretation of things can be subjective at times."

"Of course they're subjective," I said. "They're *my* experiences, *my* interpretations. No one else could possibly understand them, and sometimes I think people have trouble even comprehending what happens to me. I thought that by using Cora to log my reactions, we were taking steps toward objectifying things more."

"That's true, we are," Duncan admitted. "And so far your reactions have proven to be reliably repeatable for the most part, something I was skeptical about in the beginning. But I'm worried that you might want to please me, or try to give me the answers I want to hear, rather than what you're actually thinking, or feeling, or experiencing. How can I know that any feelings you have for me won't color the reactions you'll have down the road, the ones we haven't recorded?"

"You can't."

"You do have feelings for me, right?"

His question caught me off guard and he looked vulnerable and pensive as he stared down at me, awaiting my answer. I moved back toward him until I was close enough to again feel the heat radiating off his body.

"Yes, I do," I said, looking up into those dark brown eyes. "But I promise you I will never let those feelings color my interpretation of things, regardless of how our personal relationship plays out. I will never tell you what I think you want to hear to make you like me, or what I think you don't want to hear because I hate you. I will never manufacture reactions that support your theories, or to intentionally lead you astray. If I think you're full of crap, trust me, I will never hesitate to say so. And that starts right here, right now. If you think I'm incapable of maintaining professional objectivity during anything you ask me to do relative to a crime, simply because you're there and I feel something for you, you have a grossly overblown opinion of your manly charms."

"Ouch," Duncan said, smiling and jerking his head back as if he'd been slapped. "Point made."

"Good. Can we please move on then?"

"Absolutely."

"Although there is one more thing we need to settle."

"What's that?"

"I'll cut to the chase. They say that what's good for the goose is good for the gander. Nothing ventured, nothing gained. And turnabout is fair play." I realized then that I was babbling because of my nervousness, so I forced myself to stop. "Sheesh. Now that I've exhausted my repertoire of clichés, I have to ask . . . do you have feelings for me?"

In one swift second he closed the remaining gap between us by pulling me toward him. I was glad for his swift response because even that brief second of time felt like an eternity to me. Then his lips descended onto mine, and our bodies came into full frontal contact.

The next few minutes triggered the most sensational, wondrous manifestations my synesthesia has ever created. Though we were forced to break it off so we could head back out to the bar, our shared moment offered a delightful preview of what was to come.

It wasn't until much later that I realized he had never actually answered my question.

Chapter 18

Duncan stayed after the bar closed, and while I did the cleanup he stayed on his phone almost constantly, talking to other detectives and officers to get updates. I knew he was eager for someone to dig up some information on this Valeria Barnes woman. But by the time we headed upstairs to my apartment, I also knew that, so far, no one had had any luck in that regard.

Duncan slept with me, but we were both emotionally and physically drained. After a few passionate kisses, we fell asleep without taking things any further. Duncan awoke at eight, and though his movements awakened me when he got up, I was reluctant to get out of bed. It was Sunday, the one day when I get to sleep in because I don't open the bar until five in the evening. But Duncan gently nudged me out of bed, saying that he needed to relieve Jimmy and reminding me that I'd agreed to help him out for the day.

Over coffee he filled me in. There wasn't any relevant news to report, despite the fact that Jimmy and several other cops had spent all night manning phones for the hotline number that was listed in the Amber Alert for Davey Cooper.

Since Duncan seemed distracted and eager to get going, we didn't eat any breakfast. Instead, we took cups of coffee with us and headed down to the police station. A preview of the snow I'd sensed had come during the night, but it was only a smattering of wet slushy stuff that did little for the landscape other than make everything wet, cold, slippery, and messy.

When we arrived at the police station, we found Jimmy in a conference room with nine other police officers and detectives, all of whom were sitting around a huge table. A half-dozen hardwired phones were on the table and all but one of them were being used. The sixth one rang as we entered the room and the officer who answered it said, "Cooper hotline."

The officers who weren't manning the hotline phones were using cells to make phone calls of their own. Duncan caught Jimmy's eye and gestured toward the hallway with a sideways nod of his head. Jimmy, who was manning a hotline phone at the moment, gave him a couple of nods in return to let him know he understood. We stepped back out into the hallway to wait, and Duncan left me there to go fetch some more coffee.

Jimmy came out before Duncan returned and he seemed surprised to see me standing there alone. "Where's Duncan?" he asked, and I could sense his discomfort with me. It wasn't an out and out dislike—at least I didn't think it was—but rather something that felt almost like fear. I wasn't sure if it stemmed from his doubts about my abilities or his belief in them. Did he think I was a big hoax, or was he afraid I'd find out something about him that he'd rather keep hidden?

"He went to grab some more coffee," I said.

"That's surprising," Jimmy said. "I didn't think he'd ever drink our cop house stuff again after tasting yours."

From the tone of his voice, I wasn't sure if he meant this as a compliment or not, so I ignored it. "Made any progress on the Cooper case?"

Jimmy gave me an odd look and said, "Let's wait for Duncan."

Jimmy's voice triggered the taste of oranges, but it was a fizzy taste, like orange soda. The amount of the fizz varied from one encounter to another, and at the moment it was as if the orange flavor was exploding in my mouth. I wasn't sure what that meant but guessed it had something to do with the level of tension Jimmy felt, which was reflected in his voice. The big question for me was what was creating the tension, me or the case?

After a minute or so of Jimmy and me standing in the hallway staring at our shoes, Duncan returned. "Anything new?" he asked.

"Maybe. We got a possible lead from one of Belinda's coworkers," Jimmy said, his voice fizz lessened now. "She said Belinda had a new man in her life, someone she met at the grocery store. Apparently they bonded over a salad bar the store puts up. It's a popular singles spot."

"Really?" I said. "That's the new meeting place?"

Jimmy shrugged. "Safer than your typical bar pickup, I imagine. People don't tend to loosen their morals or their tastes over lettuce the way they do over booze." I sensed there might have been a slight dig directed toward me in his comment, but I couldn't be sure. Then, as if he'd suddenly realized what he'd said, he shot me an apologetic look. "Sorry, Mack. Your bar's a nice enough place, but not all of them are. And it's kind of a crapshoot when it comes to finding dates in a bar."

"No offense taken," I said, though I could feel the lie in my own voice.

"Anyway," Jimmy went on, seeming content with my comment, "it doesn't sound like things were very serious yet between this guy and Belinda. They only met a week ago and, according to the coworker, all they did was meet once for lunch and go to a movie together. But the movie date happened Friday night, which means this guy is a suspect. Unfortunately, all we know about him at this point is his first name: Edwin."

"That shouldn't be too hard to follow up on," Duncan said. "We find out where Belinda shopped—I'm assuming it's a store near her house—and then we canvass the store employees and the neighborhood for anyone named Edwin. Most likely he lives in the same neighborhood or close by if he's using that grocery store. Edwin isn't that common of a name, assuming he doesn't use a nickname like Ed or Eddie, so maybe someone will know him."

"That's assuming Edwin is his real name," I said. "I've seen both men and women give out false names to members of the opposite sex in my bar when they first meet. I imagine the same thing must happen elsewhere."

"Maybe, but let's hope not," Duncan said. "We can search the neighborhood property tax records for the name Edwin, too."

"If we do any neighborhood-based searches, we'll have to include more than just the victim's," Jimmy said. "We scanned her bank statements and it looks like the store she shopped at the most is one called Corner Foods. It's in Riverwest but close enough to parts of

Brewer's Hill and Harambee that I imagine it pulls customers from those neighborhoods, too."

Duncan said, "Well, we were going to help with the canvassing. That's why I brought Mack along. But maybe we should start with the store instead."

"If Belinda went to a movie with this guy, she had to have found a babysitter," I said. "Maybe she used a neighbor."

"Good point," Duncan said.

Jimmy glanced at his watch. "I already have guys knocking on doors around the victim's neighborhood to see if anyone saw or heard anything."

"Did they?"

Jimmy shook his head, looking grim. "One neighbor saw Belinda out playing in the yard with Davey for a little while during the day, around lunchtime, but it got dark around five-thirty, and no one saw anything after that. You know how it is right after the clocks go back and the first winter darkness sets in. Everybody crawls into their caves for the night and they don't come out again until morning."

"Do we know for sure what Belinda's time of death was?" I asked.

Jimmy shot me an annoyed look, as if it perturbed him that I would even ask such a question. And he didn't answer it, Duncan did.

"The ME said it was around seven last night." He turned back to Jimmy. "Do you know who Belinda Cooper used as a babysitter?"

"I don't, but one of the other guys might. I'll check into it and let you know."

With that, Duncan turned back to me. "Need some groceries for the bar?"

"I can always use some fresh veggies," I said with a shrug.

"Then let's go shopping."

The Corner Foods store clearly got its name from its location. It had an entrance on one street and an exit on another, spanning the corner where the two streets met. Parking was a little dicey as the lot behind the store was small, but due to the early hour, we were able to find a spot on the street not too far from the entrance.

Though the store wasn't huge, I was impressed with the variety of stuff it had to offer. Shoppers wouldn't find a lot of choices when it came to brand-name products, but the produce section boasted plenty of fresh fruits and vegetables and there was a meat counter at the back of the store manned by a butcher who would provide personalized cuts of meat for the asking. It was a cozy neighborhood store, a place to get items that ranged from daily basics like milk and eggs, to more obscure and less-used items like shoe polish and hair dye. The staff was friendly and helpful and while Duncan went to talk with the cashiers, I scoped out the salad bar where Belinda had supposedly met her new man.

The salad bar wasn't set up yet because of the hour, so I wandered into the nearby produce section and started scouting out the fruits and vegetables. I was standing on one side of a middle-of-the-aisle display of berries when a male voice across from me said, "Hi there." I looked up and saw a thirty-something blond man watching me from the other side of the display. He was relatively attractive, of average height, with blue eyes and a slightly chunky build. His voice tasted like a sweet red apple.

"Hello," I said in return, smiling.

"Are you new here?" he asked. "A face as pretty as yours, with that red hair, it's memorable. I come here a lot and I'm sure I haven't seen you before."

"No, I've never been here before," I answered with a smile. "But I have heard a good pick-up line or two in my time. Yours is a little old."

He flashed me a beguiling, bashful smile that revealed a deep dimple in each cheek. "Yeah, I'm not much of an expert when it comes to this dating stuff. In fact, I'm a full-fledged dork. Ten years of marriage to my college sweetheart didn't give me much experience. And now that I'm on my own, I'm at a bit of a loss, I'm afraid."

"Divorced?"

"No, she was killed last year in a car accident. Pregnant with our first child at the time."

"Geez, I'm so sorry."

"Sometimes crap happens," he said. "It hasn't been easy. How about you? I don't see a ring on your hand. Are you single?"

"I am," I said, reaching over the berry display and extending my hand. "My name is Mack. Mack Dalton."

"It's a true pleasure to meet you, Mack Dalton," he said, taking my hand in his. He gave it a quick shake and I noticed that the flavor of his voice had turned tart. "I'm Edwin Winters."

I yanked my hand back so fast that I knocked one of the containers of blueberries clean off the display and onto the floor. The plastic container popped open and the berries rolled every which way. As I stepped back, I squished several of them with my foot and their smell wafted up to me, making me hear harp music. The smell of blueberries always sounds like harp music to me, but these were very juicy and ripe and, if the music was any indication, also sweet.

"Geez," Edwin said, looking at me as if I were a creature he'd never seen before, "what the heck was that?"

I didn't answer him right away, but I didn't want to scare him off, either. So I flashed him an apologetic smile and shrugged my shoulders. "I'm sorry," I said. "I can explain."

Edwin stared at me, and then made a little shrugging gesture as if to say, *Then go on, explain.*

I didn't, mainly because I wasn't sure where to begin. Then I heard Duncan call out my name. He was standing twenty or thirty feet away, amidst a group of cashiers. "Is everything okay over there?" he asked.

Edwin shot me a look of disgust. "Why didn't you tell me you had a boyfriend in here? Why did you lead me on like that?" His voice raised several notches in conjunction with his anger, turning the apple taste even tarter and attracting everyone's attention.

When Duncan heard the ruckus, he left the circle of cashiers and hurried over toward me, giving Edwin the stink-eye. "What's going on over here?"

I nodded my head toward the other side of the display and said, "Edwin here was just introducing himself to me."

"Edwin?" Duncan repeated. "Your name is Edwin?"

"It is," Edwin said irritably. "What of it?" He folded his arms over his chest, adopting a defensive stature. His voice now was a mix of tart apple with just a hint of rot.

"Do you know a woman by the name of Belinda Cooper?" Duncan asked.

"Is that what this is about?" Edwin said with an air of disbelief. "What are you, some family member of hers, like a brother or something?"

"Or something," Duncan said. He pulled out his badge and flashed it.

"Oh, crap," Edwin said. "Look, just because I lead some of these ladies along so I can have a little fun, that doesn't make me a criminal . . . unless serial dating is a crime." He punctuated that with an awkward little laugh, looking from Duncan to me and then back to Duncan again. When he saw that we weren't laughing with him, his own smile disappeared and he said, "What the hell, dude."

"When was the last time you saw Belinda Cooper?" Duncan asked.

"Friday night," Edwin said. "We went to the movies together and saw the seven o'clock showing of that new chick flick that's out. After that, I took her home. I wanted to stay over, but she wouldn't let me. Said she couldn't do that with her kid in the house. To be honest, I had no plans for seeing her again. She moved way too slow for me."

"She didn't want to put out, eh?" Duncan said. His expression had relaxed and his voice had taken on a friendly, jovial tone.

Edwin fell for it. "Frigid as can be," he said with a little laugh. A second later, he looked as if he wanted to suck that laugh—and his words—back in, but he realized it was too late.

"Is that why you killed her?" I asked him.

He shot me a bemused look and took an involuntary step back. "What? Killed her? Belinda's dead?"

"Don't you watch TV?" Duncan asked him. "It's been all over the news."

"I use my TV for gaming. I don't have cable and there isn't anything on the regular stations worth watching." His voice was still tart and I realized it had changed to that taste when he'd told me his name. That's when I knew he'd been lying to me, though I wasn't sure if it was only now and when he'd given me his name, or the whole time. But I had an idea.

"All that stuff you said about your wife and her death, none of that was true, was it?" I asked him.

At least he had the decency to look embarrassed and ashamed of his behavior.

"No," he admitted, his voice still tart. "But I learned long ago that it works to get chicks. If you tell them you're divorced, they're always wary, worried about the ex-wife coming back into your life, or wondering why she dumped you. And if you tell them you've never been married, they start wondering why, figuring there must be something seriously wrong with you. But a grieving widower, that's irresistible to women."

I shot him a look of disgust, though my feelings were directed at myself as much as they were at him. I'd fallen for his stupid shtick and it ticked me off.

"So far, you're one of the last people to see Belinda Cooper alive," Duncan said. "I think you're lying to us. I think you did stay with her Friday night and when she didn't put out for you then or the next morning, you got real mad. I mean, hell, you wasted all that time and money on her, and for what?"

"I didn't kill her, if that's what you're implying," Edwin said, backing up several more steps.

"Prove it," Duncan said. "Where were you yesterday evening between the hours of six and eight?"

Judging from the scared expression on Edwin's face, I guessed that he wasn't anywhere that was going to provide him with a solid alibi. I guessed right.

"I was home, alone, like I am most of the time," he grumbled. "It was Saturday and I didn't have to work, so

I slept in and then kicked back to play some video games. I live alone so I didn't even bother to get dressed."

"Is there anyone who can verify that you were there?" Duncan asked.

"I just told you I live alone."

"Were you logged on to any gaming sites?"

He shook his head, looking quite glum. "I don't play those interactive games. I'm mostly into football and Mario Brothers."

"Where do you work?"

"I'm a collection specialist for the Debukey law firm."

"A collection specialist?" Duncan said, looking puzzled.

"Overdue bills and that sort of stuff," Edwin explained with a look of chagrin. "It's not a popular job. I spend most of my day getting screamed at and threatened by people who can't pay their bills. It's not the best way to meet women. That's why I come here."

"Tell me about Friday night, when you took Belinda home. What happened?"

Edwin let out a little *pfft*. "Nothing happened. I didn't even get inside her house. She said she didn't want to risk waking up her kid. We shared a peck of a kiss and said good-bye in my car. I watched her walk inside the house and then I left."

"So her son was there, as far as you know?"

Edwin nodded. "Yeah, she said she had a babysitter who was watching him, a neighbor kid or something like that. That was one of the reasons she needed to get home early."

"And you didn't come back on Saturday evening for another run at her?"

"I just told you I didn't." He was clearly perturbed now.

"Give me your full name, your address, and your home and work phone numbers, including any cells," Duncan said. Edwin grudgingly complied and Duncan wrote it all down in the little notebook he always carries with him. When he was done, he flipped the notebook closed and tucked it back into his shirt pocket. "You can go for now," he told Edwin. "But I might want to talk to you again, so if you have any plans to leave town, let me know first."

Edwin nodded so hard and fast, it looked like a spasm. "No problem," he muttered; then he hightailed it for the door.

"Damn it!" I said to Duncan. "That guy totally had me fooled."

"What do you mean?"

"When you were over there talking to the cashiers, he walked up and used this stupid pick-up line on me and managed to get me feeling all flattered and friendly toward him. And it was all a lie."

"So, you fell for a smooth operator's lines. Some of them are very good. It's nothing to be ashamed of. Heck, you fell for my lines."

I could tell this last part was his attempt to levy some humor into the situation, but I wasn't going for it. "It's not that, Duncan. It's this . . ." I waved my hand around in the air to indicate the general area of the store. "It's this thing I'm doing for you. I should have picked up on the fact that that Edwin guy was being dishonest, or at least deceptive, but I didn't. He was so practiced and smooth with his lies and his pretend vulnerabilities that he never gave himself away. It wasn't until you made him nervous that the taste of his voice changed enough for me to tell whether or not he was being honest. Or at least I think that's what it was telling me." I ran a hand through my hair and gave Duncan a worried look.

"One mistake doesn't negate all of what you're doing," he said.

"But what *am* I doing? I'm not sure my reactions are reliable enough for what you need. You were right; it's all so subjective. I'm interpreting my reactions, but I'm also making assumptions to arrive at those interpretations. It was all fun and games when I played hide-and-seek as a kid with my dad, but there's a little boy's life at stake here, Duncan. What if my assumptions are wrong?"

"You're just upset over that guy's ability to fool you. And I'll bet if you think back and analyze everything you experienced during your chat with him, you'll find something that was telling you he wasn't on the up-and-up."

He was right, of course, but that didn't make me feel any better.

Duncan put his hands on my shoulders. "I have faith in you, Mack. You got it right every time these past few weeks when I tested you. You always knew when someone was lying."

"But that was with people I know—people like Cora and Tad and the Signoriello brothers. What if knowing someone and being familiar with that person's norms is necessary for me to be able to pick up on the lies?"

"You think you have to know someone in order for your reactions to be reliable?"

"Yes . . . no . . . I don't know . . . maybe." I waved his question away, getting more and more impatient with his insistence. "That Edwin guy's voice tasted sweet to me, until he gave me his name. Then it turned tart and sour. Normally I would have interpreted such a taste change as a lie and I would have thought this guy was lying when he told me his name, simply because it made the taste of his voice change into something more sour and more uncomfortable. But his honest voice is the sour one, and I think that's because lying is his norm. Most people are a little uncomfortable when they lie, even if it's a subconscious thing, and I think that's what alters their voice reactions for me. But when you have someone like Edwin, who is more comfortable with the lie than the truth, it's the exact opposite. And if I don't know that about him, I'm not going to interpret things correctly."

"So you make a mistake now and then. No big deal," Duncan said. "You got it right with the Stratford and Weber gang. Evidence of all kinds can be misleading from time to time."

"But this isn't about just the evidence, Duncan. It's about me. I don't want the guilt of knowing I sent you guys off on a wild goose chase. If things turn out bad for that little boy, and I do anything to delay the investigation in any way, I don't think I could live with myself."

"I think you're overreacting."

"Well, I don't. It seemed like fun when it was all imaginary crimes with no real victims, but now it's not so much fun anymore. I'm sorry to say this, Duncan, but I quit."

Chapter 19

I turned away and walked out of the store, eager to escape Duncan and all the evil in the world that I now associated with him. Unfortunately, I couldn't run very far because he was the one who drove us here, and I didn't even have my purse with me. I leaned against his car to wait for him and felt a little annoyed by how slowly he followed, taking his time as he walked down the sidewalk. He was talking on his phone, and while I realized that might be part of why he was taking his time, I also suspected that he knew I had nowhere to go and he hoped that having a little time to cool myself down might make me change my mind.

Duncan wasn't saying much on his phone, but he was listening intently. His expression looked serious and he ambled along the sidewalk a bit crookedly, as if all his attention was so focused on what he was hearing that there was little left over for the rest of his body. When he was a few feet away, he looked up, saw me leaning against his car, and stopped where he was. Aside from what I suspected was a grunt of acknowledgment, he said nothing. For the next minute or so he just stood there, listening. Then he hung up his phone without even saying good-bye.

He turned and stepped out into the street, heading for the driver's side of the car, unlocking the doors with his key fob as he went. As soon as I heard the locks pop up, I opened my door, got in, and fastened my seat belt.

The inside of the car smelled like Duncan, a clean smell that brought to mind line-dried sheets on a sunny day, which I found odd since I'd never actually smelled a line-dried sheet. I suppose I associated that smell with line-dried sheets because I had bought a couple of candles that smelled similar and were labeled as such. Plus, I use those dryer sheets that supposedly smell like "outdoor freshness." The smell typically triggers a sound like very fine sandpaper being rubbed over smooth wood, and as I sat in the car, I noticed that sound was louder inside than it had been outside. That's when it hit me. Belinda Cooper had a garage attached to her house.

"Did Belinda Cooper own a car?" I asked.

Duncan nodded.

"Is it at her house?"

"I believe so," Duncan said. "Why?"

"I want to see it."

"I thought you were done. I thought you didn't want to do this anymore."

"I know. I'm sorry." I looked over at him, fighting back tears. "I'm afraid, Duncan. I'm afraid of saying something, or misinterpreting something and causing someone harm."

He reached over and gave my shoulder a reassuring squeeze. "I understand," he said. "I have that fear all the time. None of this is pure science, Mack. None of it is guaranteed. We cops make assumptions all the time based on gut instincts and the way we read people. Your ability is no different, really. And I promise you it won't make me dismiss any actions we would take based on the more normal evidence we get. So all your input will do is help. It may lead us down a path we would have taken anyway, or it might suggest paths we hadn't considered. But I promise you I won't let it detract from our normal processes and procedures. Okay?"

I nodded, unable to speak for the moment. My emotions had a strangle hold on my throat.

Traffic was light so it didn't take long to get to Belinda Cooper's house. Crime scene techs were still on-site processing the place. We ducked under some crime scene tape strung up on the front porch and entered through the front door. The door to the garage was off the living room and after Duncan explained to the officer in charge what we wanted to do, he led us out there.

Belinda's car was an older model Volvo sedan, and I wondered if she chose the make of the car with an eye to its safety reputation, or if it just happened to be the car she could afford at the time.

"What is it you want to do?" Duncan asked.

"I want to get inside the car."

The vehicle wasn't locked, and after donning gloves, Duncan opened the passenger-side door since it was closest and then went to open the back door.

"Don't open that," I said. "Can I sit in the front seat?"

"Sure. Hal said they haven't processed it yet. They'll probably have it towed in to the lab for further analysis, but as long as I document that you were in the car, it should be fine."

I settled in the front passenger seat and shut the door. First I closed my eyes and let my senses absorb what they could. I picked up on several familiar and identifiable smells, including one that took me a moment to place. Unlike the other smells, this one was not one I expected to find. After processing the smells, sounds, and feel of the car, I opened my eyes and looked around the interior space. When I turned and looked in the backseat, something struck me right away. I opened the door and got out.

"There's no car seat in here," I said. "Given little Davey's age, there should be one. Did you find one in the house anywhere?"

"I don't know. I'll have to check with the techs."

"If the person who took Davey made the effort to take toys and clothes along, odds are they might have come for the car seat, too. They would have needed one to transport him."

"You're right."

"The reason I wanted to get inside the car is because it's a perfect trap for smells and sounds," I told Duncan. "They stay confined inside for the most part. They don't dissipate as quickly as those in the open air."

"So did you pick up on something in Belinda's car?"

"I did. I picked up the smell of bleach or chlorine, which triggers a squeaking sound, kind of like a mouse, or like rubbing your finger on glass. The sound is loudest, meaning the smell is strongest, toward the back seat. I noticed it in the house earlier, too, but I didn't put much importance on it there because it's something you'd expect to find, especially since Belinda seemed to be a very clean-conscious person. But it doesn't make as much sense in the car."

"Bleach," Duncan said, squinting in thought.

"If the person who took Davey came out here and took his car seat, they might well have had that smell on them for some reason. Maybe they work as a maid at a motel, or they clean houses or something like that."

Duncan was writing in his little notebook. "This is good, Mack. If we can verify that there was a car seat in here, this is a good, solid lead." He closed his notebook and reached over to give my shoulder another one of those squeezes, but this time his hand lingered, his fingertips touching the base of my neck. It triggered an electric zip that went from my shoulder into my groin, a sensation that was discomfiting and pleasant at the same time. When he finally withdrew his hand, I felt relieved yet disappointed.

We went back inside and Duncan did a search of the kitchen and bathroom, looking for any bleach or cleaners containing bleach. Belinda Cooper had tons of cleaners in the house, but the only thing we found with any sort of bleach in it was a powdered, color-safe laundry detergent and some toilet bowl cleaner. Both of these had other things in them and their smells were different from the one in the car, as was the sound that accompanied each one. Just to be sure, I sniffed the other cleaners to see if they sounded like the smell in the car had, but none of them did.

After we'd made sure there wasn't a car seat in the house anywhere, I stood by and listened as Duncan called Jimmy. I gathered from Duncan's end of the conversation that no one had thought to ask about whether or not there was usually a car seat in Belinda's car, and no one had yet noticed that there wasn't one, because they hadn't processed the car yet.

When he hung up the call, Duncan glanced at his watch and said, "One of the guys canvassing the neighborhood gave me the name and address for the babysitter. Her name is Christine Wolff and she lives a few doors down. I don't want you to do anything that makes you uncomfortable, but I'd like it if you'd come along."

I felt renewed and restored after my success with the car, and it wasn't likely I'd see anything gross, so I agreed.

Five minutes later we were standing on the front

porch of a house four doors away. The place resembled Belinda's house, though it didn't look to be in need of quite as many repairs. There was a large picture window in the front and, though it was covered with curtains that kept us from seeing inside, the glow of a TV shone through. We could hear what sounded like some kind of shoot-'em-up playing inside.

Duncan rang the doorbell and the sound from the TV stopped. We heard footsteps and then a female voice yelled through the door, "Who is it?"

"Milwaukee Police Department," Duncan yelled back. He held his badge up so it could be seen through the peephole.

"You've already been here," the woman yelled back.

"Yes, ma'am, but we have some additional questions, if you don't mind. It won't take long."

A moment later a thin, fortyish-looking woman wearing a terrycloth bathrobe with a flannel nightgown beneath it opened the door a crack and peered out at us.

"I already told the police everything I know," she said, eyeing me curiously.

"Yes, ma'am," Duncan said. "I'm sorry to bother you again, but there are some additional questions we need to ask. You're Mrs. Wolff?"

"I am."

"I understand you have a daughter named Christine who often babysat for Belinda. Is that true?"

"It is," she said, clearly impatient. "But she has nothing to do with any of this and I don't want her involved. We don't know who did this, or what they might do to keep people quiet."

"I understand your concern," Duncan said. "The questions I want to ask your daughter aren't directly related to the crime itself. I'm more interested in finding out some things about Belinda's day-to-day life."

Mrs. Wolff chewed the inside of her cheek, still holding the door and looking impatient. "I'll need to talk to my husband first," she said.

"That's fine," Duncan said. "I'll be happy to talk to him. Is he here?"

"He's at work," she said. "If you want to talk to him, you can come back this evening."

She started to close the door when another hand appeared from somewhere behind her, the fingers wrapping around the door's edge and preventing Mrs. Wolff from closing it. Then we heard another female voice. "Let me talk to them, Mom."

"Go back to your room," Mrs. Wolff said, never taking her eyes off us.

"Davey is missing," the other female voice said. "I want to do whatever I can to make sure he's okay."

Mrs. Wolff hung onto the door and glared at us, as if her daughter's willingness to help was somehow our fault. After several seconds of indecision, she finally stepped back and let her daughter open the door wider. Christine Wolff was tall and thin, and she had a stud through her nose, a dog collar around her neck, and shoulder-length, black hair with a streak of electric blue in it. She, like her mother, was wearing a flannel nightgown and a robe—clearly not early risers or churchgoers, at least not this Sunday. I idly wondered if Christine slept with that collar on.

Duncan quickly stepped inside, and I guessed it was because he didn't want to give Mrs. Wolff a chance to change her mind. I followed him and, once we were in, Mrs. Wolff closed the door to the cold. We were standing in a small foyer with dark wood wainscoting on the walls and oak hardwood floors. Mrs. Wolff not only didn't invite us deeper into the house, she stood in the doorway to the living room with her arms folded over her chest, her jaw firmly set, making it clear to us that we were not welcome to venture any farther.

Duncan got straight to the point. "We just have a couple of quick questions for you, Christine. To start with, did you babysit for Belinda Friday night?"

Christine nodded. "I already told one of the other cops that, Belinda had a date with some guy she met at the grocery store. Apparently it didn't go as well as she hoped. She said he seemed pissed that she wouldn't hop right into bed with him, or let him come in and stay."

Apparently Edwin had shown his true colors that night. Had Belinda's reaction pissed him off? Was he not just a serial dater, but a killer? I shook my head as if to break that thought loose. My imagination was getting the better of me, probably because I still stung from the humiliation of my own experience with Edwin.

"Did Belinda date very often?" Duncan asked.

"No," Christine said. "She hardly did anything like that. Once in a while she would go out with some women friends from work to a movie or something, but I don't think she's been dating anyone since she split from her husband."

"Does he ever come by?"

Christine looked momentarily confused. "Does who come by? Her ex-husband?"

Duncan nodded.

"I don't think so, but I really didn't see that much of Belinda. She never had much need for a sitter. She works at a day care and takes Davey with her every day. And, like I said, her social life was the pits."

Mrs. Wolff piped up then. "I think that ex of hers stopped by once or twice right after they split, but that was awhile ago and he never stayed long."

"Do you know if the ex-husband ever took Davey with him?"

"Not a chance," Mrs. Wolff said. "Belinda was very protective of that boy and I think she won full custody. I talked to her once or twice, just an occasional chat when we ran into one another on the street. I've been trying to lose some weight, so I do a thirty-minute walk every morning and every evening here in the neighborhood. Occasionally Belinda would be outside with Davey and we'd strike up a chat. She didn't come right out and say so, but she hinted that her ex had a drinking problem and had gotten physical with her. I think that's why she got full custody. And you can say what you want about that woman, but one thing was very clear: she loved that little boy. She'd never let her ex get his hands on him."

"Did you take a walk on Saturday night?" Duncan asked Mrs. Wolff.

"I did."

"Did you see anyone at Belinda's house? Or anyone in the neighborhood who didn't belong?"

Mrs. Wolff shook her head. "I went around east that night and Belinda's house is to the west. I like to alternate my route so it doesn't get too boring."

Duncan was scribbling notes, and there was a pause of several seconds while he finished what he was writing and formulated his next question. "You said Belinda took Davey with her to work every day." Both Christine and Mrs. Wolff nodded, but they stopped and took on puzzled expressions when Duncan asked his next question. "How did she do it?"

"What do you mean?" Christine said.

"How did Davey ride in the car?"

"In the backseat, in one of them kid seats," Mrs. Wolff said. "Why are you asking about that?"

"Do either of you know what the car seat looked like?"

"Yeah," Christine said. "It's gray plastic with a blue plaid lining—bright blue, like my hair." She grabbed the blue strand and pulled it forward to show us, as if we might miss it somehow.

"Did Belinda use the car seat for anything else?" Duncan asked. "Did she ever take it out of the car?"

"I don't think so," Christine said. "As far as I know, it stayed in the car all the time, but like I said, I didn't see that much of her."

"Anytime I saw her driving around, she had Davey in the car seat," Mrs. Wolff said.

As I stood listening to this Q and A, I heard a constant squeaking noise that I recognized as a synesthetic sound. I leaned over and whispered into Duncan's ear.

He nodded when I was done and then said to the two women, "One more thing. Do either of you ladies use bleach for anything?"

"Sure," Christine's mother said with a shrug. "Nothing kills germs better than bleach. I use it to clean my bathrooms all the time. In fact, I used it just this morning. Why do you ask?"

Chapter 20

Not long after, we left the Wolff house and headed back to my bar. Mrs. Wolff had been very patient in letting us question her daughter, but when Duncan asked if she would let us look around her house, she drew the line.

"I'm not letting you do that until I can talk to my husband," she said. "It's my understanding that you can't do it without a warrant unless we let you. Is that right?"

"It is," Duncan said slowly, "but if you don't have anything to hide, there's no reason not to let us look around."

"The hell there isn't," Mrs. Wolff said. "I watch enough of those crime shows on TV to know that innocent people get railroaded all the time. Just because my daughter has a connection to the Coopers, you want to try to blame this thing on her."

"No, ma'am," Duncan said. "I assure you that's not what we're here for."

"Look," Mrs. Wolff said, walking over and opening her front door, "I'm real sorry about what happened to Belinda, and I hope her little boy is okay and you find him. But I've seen and heard about enough cases where the government or the police overstepped their bounds and an innocent person paid the price. You cops get your eyes on a target and it's like you have blinders on. I'm not letting you do that to my daughter. I would like you to leave now."

We all stood there in silence for several seconds, and the cold air wafting into the foyer triggered a cold, tart, sour taste in my mouth, as if I were sucking on a frozen lime. Christine looked spooked and I thought her mother's words had probably scared her.

Without another word, we turned and left, and when we got back in the car I could tell Duncan was in a foul mood.

"She's kind of right, you know," I said. "There have been plenty of cases where the cops zero in on a certain suspect and then devote all of their efforts to proving that person's guilt. Look at that poor man who was a suspect in the bombing at the Atlanta Olympics."

"We aren't focusing all of our efforts on one person," Duncan grumbled.

"I didn't say you were. I'm just saying that it's understandable that people are reluctant to simply invite the cops into their homes."

"Usually it's the guilty ones who are reluctant."

"If you really think one of them is guilty, you can get one of those search warrant thingies, right?"

Duncan glanced over at me and smiled. "Search warrant thingies?"

"Hey," I said with a shrug, "I don't do this for a living. The tricks of your trade are as foreign to me as the ingredients in a Macktini were to you the first time you came into my bar."

"I know. I'm just ribbing you a bit. And let me educate you. I'm not going to be able to get a search warrant based on the fact that someone, namely you, thought you smelled bleach in the victim's car, and Mrs. Wolff admitted to using bleach. Now, if you'd smelled some very rare and uncommon substance that isn't likely to be found in every house in the city, I might have better luck. Though we sometimes wish it were the case, we can't get a search warrant just because we want to. There has to be probable cause, a reasonable suspicion, or some sort of specific evidence we're looking for, like a particular weapon."

"Thanks for the education."

Duncan sighed and, as we pulled up in front of my bar, he said, "Tell you what. We're both tired and a little cranky. How about I drop you off here and let you have a break. I'll go back to the station, sift through the evidence we have so far and do a few background checks, and if I have anything that I think you can help with, I'll let you know, okay?"

"Fine," I said. Without another word, I got out of the car and went inside the bar. Duncan waited until I was inside and had locked the door behind me before he pulled away. I went upstairs to my apartment and fixed myself something to eat—some toast and scrambled eggs—and then, after setting my alarm, I went back to bed.

The alarm woke me at three and I got up, showered, and headed downstairs to begin my bar prep. Debra and Billy showed up a little after four to help, and at five o'clock, Missy and my new cook, Jon, came in, too, and we opened the doors. Almost immediately the place began to fill up.

As usual, a group of people gathered in one corner,

pushing several tables together near the end of the bar. Within an hour, all of the usual, expected regulars were there: Cora, Tad, Sam, Carter, Alicia, Holly, Joe, and Frank. Soon a new guy came in and joined the group, someone I didn't recognize, a massive hulk of a man who stood at least six-foot-six and probably weighed somewhere around three-fifty. He had long, blond hair pulled back into a ponytail and incredibly blue eyes that reminded me of morning glories. Cora introduced everyone to the newcomer.

"This is Tiny Gruber. He's working on a construction site a few blocks over and I invited him to come in for a drink tonight."

"Hey, dere," Tiny said, marking himself as a born and bred Wisconsinite. I knew from that little bit of speech that Tiny was someone who would travel *up Nort'* and come in for a drink because he was *t'irsty* and couldn't find a *bubbler*, a term I'd learned is unique to Wisconsin. When I went to my first Bar Owners Association meeting out east, the blank stares I got from folks when I asked where the bubbler was clued me in. Turns out everyone else calls them drinking fountains.

I smiled at the newcomer and said, "Tiny? That seems like the perfect name for you . . . not!"

He smiled back at me and made a funny face. "Yeah, I know it's silly, but I've been called dat since I was a kid. Even den I was huge." He shrugged. "I used to hate it, but I've gotten used to da name."

His voice, with its strong Midwestern cadence and a tone as deep and rumbling as thunder, gave me a fizzy taste on my tongue that was like a mix of dark ale and coffee. It wasn't a particularly pleasant taste but it wasn't terrible, either. It was just unusual.

Cora, who I suspected had marked Tiny as her next

romantic conquest, said, "Tiny is intrigued by the crime-solving stuff we do here and he brings a unique history to the table."

"What is that?" I asked.

"His sister was murdered and the case has never been solved."

"I'm so sorry," I said to Tiny. "I know how that feels."

Tiny shrugged. "It's been twelve years now, so I don't have much hope of anyone ever solving it, but I heard about da group here and thought maybe something someone said, or did, would give me some new insight into Lori's case."

"Lori? That was your sister's name?" I asked, and Tiny nodded. "How old was she when she died?"

A couple of the people in the group squirmed when I asked this question, I suspect because it was so blunt. But having been there myself, I know how frustrating it can be to have people tiptoeing around the subject. It was always refreshing for me when someone just said it like it was: murdered . . . dead . . . killed . . . whatever. The euphemisms, like *passed*, *gone*, and *departed*, drove me crazy. And I figured that twelve years of separation from the events would have left Tiny with enough distance to deal with the rawer words.

"She was fourteen," he said, and the rest of the group winced, though I'm not sure if it was because they hadn't known this fact already or just because it was so awful to hear of anyone so young meeting such a tragic end. "She was wit' her friend and dey went to da store on the corner to get a soda. Needer of dem was ever seen alive again. The police found dere bodies two months later."

"Your sister's name was Sharon Gruber?" Joe asked.

Tiny nodded and said, "Her friend was Anna Hermann."

"I remember that case," Joe said. He nudged his brother with an elbow. "You remember, don't you, Frank?"

Frank nodded solemnly.

"Did the cops have any ideas about what happened?" Tad asked.

Tiny shrugged and shook his head. "No one saw a t'ing," he said. "Least not as dey were sayin'."

"I'll mention it to my detective friend, Duncan," I said. "He told me once that he likes to work on cold cases, so maybe he'll take a look at it for you."

"T'anks," Tiny said. He had a very childlike smile that didn't quite fit with his appearance and voice. Despite the incongruences, I liked him.

"Well, welcome to the group," Frank said, and the rest of us nodded our agreement. Frank was holding an unlit cigar, a prop both of the brothers used from time to time. It was their way of mourning their inability to smoke inside the bar now that there were laws against it. "Our group likes to try to figure out crimes, and sometimes we make them up for practice." He turned and looked at me. "Mack here, in particular, needs the practice, and Tad and Cora have developed a new case for us to work on."

"Oh, I don't know, guys," I said, shaking my head and making a face. "I'm not sure I'm up for a game right now. It's been a long day. And kind of a rough one."

"Then you need something that's fun and relaxed to help you unwind," Frank insisted.

"Yeah, let us have our fun," Tad said. "You still don't think like a cop and if you're going to be of any help to Duncan, you need to be able to. These games will help."

"I don't think they have so far," I said.

"You figured out the last one," Cora pointed out. I

suspected there was a double meaning behind her remark—a reference to Dan Thornton's case—that only a few of the people in the group would get.

"Probably just luck," I posed.

"I don't think so," Frank said. "Practice makes perfect." Then he pushed his glasses up on his nose, stuck the cigar in his mouth, and did his Groucho Marx impression. "It's like getting older . . . you just have to live long enough." It was a bit I'd seen a hundred times over the years, but it always made me laugh. Both of the brothers did Groucho impressions because they both bore a resemblance to the man. Personally, I thought Frank looked more like Super Mario than Groucho, but he had Groucho's voice and mannerisms down pat enough that the impression generally worked.

"All right," I said, resigned to my fate. "But first I want to get myself a drink." I headed behind the bar and, while I was prepping my drink, Duncan came in, saw me behind the bar, and joined me.

"How are you doing?" he asked.

"I feel better after taking a nap."

"I'm jealous. And I feel bad about the way we left things earlier. Are we okay?"

I shrugged. "Sure."

Duncan poured himself a cup of coffee and asked, "Who's the new guy?"

"That's Tiny," I told him, and he smiled at the incongruous name. "He's someone Cora brought in, and I suspect she has him targeted as her next paramour. He seems like a nice enough guy and he has a special interest in the Capone Club." I then filled him in on Tiny's story about his sister and her friend.

Duncan wrote down the girls' names in his little notebook. "I'll see what I can dig up once we resolve this current case," he said, tucking the notebook away.

"I can introduce you if you want. The Capone Club has a new crime they want to run out tonight and they're ready to get started. They seem to think I need more practice. Care to join us?"

"I can't now, but I will another time. I have to get back to the station and keep working on this case. You're going to join them?"

"I am."

"Good, because they're right. If you practice at thinking like a detective, it will help you, which in turn will help me."

"I don't know," I said, still hesitant. "It's hard to get my mind off the Davey Cooper case."

"I know, but there's nothing you can do right now anyway. I'll let you know if there's any news. In the meantime, take care of your bar and yourself. If something comes up that I need your help with, I'll call you. I promise. Otherwise I'll see you in the morning. I have a suspicion that it's going to be a late night."

"Okay."

"What time do you think you'll be up?"

"I'm always up by nine so I can have a cup of coffee and check the morning news before I come down and start prepping for my opening. Debra and Pete have offered to do that stuff for me now and I've agreed to let them come in early, but apparently my body isn't aware of the new arrangement yet. I wake up every morning at the same time whether I want to or not."

"Maybe you need practice with that, too," Duncan said. "Tell you what. On the off chance that you can sleep in a little, I'll either call or come by at ten then. Does that sound okay?"

"Sure."

Duncan frowned and said, "Are you sure we're okay here?"

I sighed. "We are. I'm just in a funk worrying about that little boy."

"That's understandable. I think we've all been affected by this one." He leaned down then and kissed me, not on the lips, but on my temple. It could have been a brother's kiss, or a father's, but it was the first time Duncan had kissed me at all in public and it had a powerful effect on me, triggering an odd image of chocolate-colored fireworks and hot bursts of chocolate flavor in my mouth. "See ya, Mack," he said. And then he left.

The kiss had not gone unnoticed by the group at the Capone Club table.

"My, things certainly appear to have moved in a new direction," Cora said.

"It's about time you two quit dancing around one another," Joe said.

"Yeah," Frank said, agreeing with his brother.

"Can we please stop focusing on my love life and get back to tonight's test case?" I said, settling into an empty chair with my drink.

I had to admit that I liked having the financial freedom to hire enough employees so I could sit with my customers and enjoy some fun time. Prior to Ginny's inheritance money, I barely had time to eat, work, and sleep. But while I was enjoying my newfound downtime, I also knew I would never give up my bartending duties altogether. I loved being behind the bar, mixing drinks, hearing snippets of conversations, getting to know my customers' trials and tribulations, offering up suggestions or advice whenever someone asked. And invariably someone would. Some bartenders I know are reluctant to give out advice of any kind, but I've never been bothered by the idea. I'm a firm believer in free will and if I offer up a suggestion to someone, they have the power to accept or reject it. And after so many years behind the bar, I think I've seen and heard enough about life and all its ups and downs to build a decent base of knowledge regarding others' experiences, and human nature in general.

Unfortunately, that knowledge didn't help me much in figuring out that night's crime puzzle. I think I was too focused on the real case and Davey's smiling, innocent, cherubic face. Unless we found him soon, I had a feeling little Davey Cooper would be haunting my dreams for a long time to come.

Chapter 21

After a few minutes of whispered consultation between Tad Amundsen and Cora, it was Tad who presented the night's case. But before he did so, Cora prepped us.

"This case is designed to see if you can pick out the killer or killers from a limited number of suspects, based on the facts that we give you. You are allowed to ask questions. Tad and I are the only ones who know the answer. So the rest of you are all welcome to play."

Cora looked over toward Tad and gave him a little nod. He nodded back, looked at the sheaf of papers in his hands, and began describing the night's crime scene.

"Listen very carefully to the details I'm about to give you," he told us. "You may want to take notes so you can remember everything, because all the knowledge you need to solve this crime is in what I'm about to tell you."

Everyone at the table had pens and paper of some sort to write on. I, however, did not and didn't get any. I don't know if it's because of my synesthesia or if it's just a random trait of mine, but I have an excellent memory.

"You are welcome to ask questions at any point if you want to further clarify things," Tad went on. "Are we ready?" He looked around the table and we all either nodded or mumbled some form of assent. "Okay then, here we go. It's a cold, frigid evening in February when the police are called to the home of a successful, wealthy novelist."

Carter scoffed and rolled his eyes. I suspect that at this point in Carter's writing career, the idea of a financially successful novelist seemed like an unreachable dream. Tad ignored Carter's nonverbal commentary and continued.

"We'll call our novelist Harvey Winters. Harvey's second wife, Patricia, is hosting a dinner at their house for a group of her friends, all of whom are struggling, undiscovered artists. The police are called to the house by Patricia a mere half hour after the gathering is underway because she and the other attendees heard a gunshot coming from Harvey's study and found the door was locked from the inside. After knocking and calling out to Harvey without any answer, Patricia heads outside to see if she can look or get in through any of the windows to the study. But all of the curtains are closed and none of the windows are open and, after returning to the house, Patricia calls the police.

"Patricia tells the police when they arrive that Harvey often locked his study door from the inside with a keyless dead bolt, to keep her from barging in on him uninvited, because he needed uninterrupted focus in order to produce his bestselling works. What's more, she said that sometimes Harvey would stay in there for days at a time without coming out. The study had its own bathroom, a comfortable couch for sleeping, and a kitchenette that could provide Harvey with plenty of food and drink during his epic lock-ins.

"Patricia tells the police that on this particular night, Harvey had gone into his study just before the first guest arrived, though he had gone to hide as much as he had to write, since he didn't like his wife's friends and wanted nothing to do with them or the dinner. Patricia assumes Harvey used the dead bolt to make sure none of the guests would inadvertently wander in on him.

"The police break down the door and discover that the dead bolt had, in fact, been thrown. Inside, they find Harvey sitting in a chair behind his desk, dead. There is one bullet hole in his forehead, and the desk chair, which swivels, is turned at a ninety-degree angle so that the man's left side is leaning against the desk and his right side is facing a wall behind the desk. The desk is situated several feet in front of this wall and faces the opposing wall, which has a fireplace built into it. The fireplace is located directly across from the desk and there is a fire burning in it. Patricia tells the police that Harvey always lit the fireplace in the wintertime, claiming that staring into the flames often helped his creative process. In fact, she had laid the wood for tonight's fire herself, as a goodwill gesture to Harvey for letting her have her friends over. Hanging over the fireplace is a portrait of Harvey that was painted by a professional artist.

"The police are quite puzzled since it's obvious Harvey was shot, but there is no gun anywhere near the body, nor are they able to find one anywhere else in the room. All the windows are locked from the inside and there is no other way in or out of the room."

Joe Signoriello interrupted at this point and asked,

"What about the chimney? Could someone have gone in or out using the chimney?"

Tad shook his head. "Good question, but the answer is no. The only opening in the fireplace is at the top of the firebox and it's a damper that covers a pipe too small for anyone to use as a point of egress. Plus, there is a fire burning in the fireplace and, upon closer examination, it appears the fire has been burning for some time because there is a bed of hot cinders beneath the logs on the grate.

"From the angle of the shot, the police are able to determine that the bullet was fired from somewhere in front of Harvey and that it had a slight upward trajectory. But because the chair Harvey is sitting in swivels very easily, and there is no exit wound, they can't be sure what direction Harvey was facing at the time he was shot. They realize the chair might well have turned simply from the energy of the shot hitting Harvey, or from the slumping of his body. The shot might also have been fired while Harvey was standing in front of the chair, causing him to fall into it. Therefore the police cannot tell with any certainty from where in the room the shot was fired."

"A classic locked-room mystery," Carter said with a smile. "I like it. And if the solution is a believable, logical one, I might want to steal it and use it in one of my books."

"First you have to solve it," Cora said. "But when you do, I think you'll agree that the solution is a logical one. We fed this scenario into the crime-solving computer program my company has been working on and asked it to come up with some probable suspects. The program posed certain questions about possible experiences, knowledge, and characteristics any of the suspects might have that would fit with plausible explanations for the scenario. We then used those details to develop a list of suspects."

"Interesting," Carter said. "If that program of yours doesn't work for solving real crimes, I might want to borrow it for creating some fake ones for my books."

"It will cost you," Cora said with an enigmatic smile.

Tiny, who up until now had simply been sitting quietly and listening, leaned across the table and pinned Cora with his eyes. "You have a computer program dat can help solve crimes?" he asked.

"Sort of," Cora said. "It's still being developed and it has a lot of quirks. Right now it's better at reverse engineering a scenario like the one we're using here tonight. When we've tried to use it on real crimes, the results have been iffy, to say the least."

"How much psychological information have you plugged into it?" Sam asked.

"Not much," Cora admitted. "So far my programmer has spent most of his time working on the analysis of evidence and the proximity any of the potential suspects have to the crime scene and any collected evidence. We have also played around with motive, to some extent, but, to be honest, that's an area that's largely lacking at the moment . . . that, and the emotions that might color a potential suspect's motivations. So far, the program is very scientific and analytical in the way it conducts its calculations. It could use a human touch."

"I'd be happy to help with that," Sam offered. "Most of my work has been focused on criminal and other types of abnormal psychology."

"That would be great," Cora said with enthusiasm. "That could be just the piece we need to make this program complete."

"It will cost you, of course," Sam added with a wink, "though I suppose we could work out a trade of some sort, one that would include my writer friend Carter here."

Cora gave him a crooked, grudging smile. "Well played," she said. "Well played indeed. I'm sure we can work something out."

Tiny said, "Do you t'ink dis program of yours could help me solve my sister's murder?"

Cora gave him an apologetic look. "We can try, Tiny, but I don't want you to get your hopes up too high. When we tried to use it to solve the murder of that woman whose body was found in the alley behind the bar a few weeks ago, the lead suspect by a large margin was Mack. And several of us at this table were on that list as well, so I don't think it's very reliable yet."

"But will you try?" Tiny asked. "I'll give you all the information I have. I've spent twelve years looking for her killer, and I have a t'ick file full of suspects, evidence, time frames, dates . . . all dat dere kind of stuff. If we plug it into your program, who knows what might pop out."

"Sure," Cora said, smiling at Tiny. "We'll do it. Bring me your file tomorrow and we'll get started on it right away. Maybe Mack here can talk her new detective boyfriend into sharing some evidence from the old police file, too."

After casting a malevolent glare at Cora for her boyfriend remark, I gave Tiny's arm a gentle squeeze. I knew all too well the frustration and anger he was feeling. "I talked to Detective Albright about it already," I told him. "He's pretty tied up with his current case, but he said he'd look into it the first chance he gets."

"We'll all help in any way we can," Sam offered, and everyone else at the table nodded their agreement.

"T'ank you," Tiny said. There was the hint of a crack in his voice, as if his emotions were about to get the better of him. Interestingly, I saw that hint of emotion quite literally in an image that flashed through my mind: a pilsner glass filled with some dark brown liquid, which suddenly cracked in half, spilling its contents.

"Great," Tad said with a smile. "Now that that's settled, can we get back to the case at hand?"

"Sorry I sidetracked ya," Tiny said.

"No problem," Tad assured him. "Okay, back to the crime scene and our list of suspects. After interrogating all of the guests at the house, the police determine that the killer has to be someone who was in the house at the time of the murder. There is fresh snow on the ground outside and, other than the footprints leading from the cars parked in the circular driveway up to the front door and Patricia's footprints outside the windows of Harvey's study, there is no evidence of anyone being anywhere else outside the house. Everyone present for the dinner heard the shot and while they generally agree on when it occurred, there are some slight variations—no more than a minute or two—in the actual times given by each suspect. The guests were all enjoying a cocktail hour when they heard the shot and hadn't yet sat down to eat. Because none of them had ever been to the rather grand house before, they were all milling about taking self-guided tours or doing other things, as you'll soon see.

"The first suspect is Patricia, who stands to inherit Harvey's fortune. The police learn when they talk to some of the other guests that Harvey and Patricia's relationship has been very strained of late and there is a rumor that Patricia has taken a lover. Patricia fancies herself an artist, although her works, which are sculptures done in wood and clay, have thus far not struck a chord with the buying public. She has no job experience or talents, just her looks and figure, which won her the role of the victim's trophy wife. Patricia states she was in the living room at the time of the shot, showing some of her own art pieces to two of the guests.

"One of those two guests is Michael, a divorced, fortyish gentleman who is an unpublished novelist. He owns a store that sells magic tricks, costumes, and party favors, and he sometimes does magic shows at parties. The police learn that Michael has a motive when they discover that he accused Harvey of stealing one of his stories and publishing it as his own after Michael sent Harvey one of his manuscripts for evaluation. Michael sued Harvey but was eventually forced to drop the suit because he could no longer afford the legal fees after Harvey's lawyers filed a slew of paperwork that would have meant hours and hours of legal representation for Michael.

"The second guest who was reportedly with Patricia is a woman named Angela who the police discover also has a reason to want Harvey dead. Patricia tells the police that Harvey thought most of her artist friends were hacks, including Patricia herself, and despite Patricia's requests, he refused to underwrite any of them, including his own wife. But then Angela tells the police that Harvey had approached her in secret a year ago and told her that, unlike the others in the group, he thought her watercolor paintings had promise. He offered to set her up with the owner of a gallery in New York that he knew, and to sponsor her for a year while she worked on creating more pieces. Based on that, Angela quit her job and spent what little savings she had on more art supplies in preparation for her year of work. But at the last minute, she discovered that Harvey's real goal had been to get her in bed with him. Once she'd slept with him a couple of times, he swore he'd never promised her anything and told her that her art was crap. He then dumped her like a load of stinky trash. She hasn't been able to get another job, which has led to her falling behind on her mortgage, and now the bank is foreclosing on her house."

"Sounds like Harvey was a creep who deserved to die," Frank said.

"No one deserves to die," Tiny said, and the group fell silent for several seconds.

Finally Holly said, "Even if the guy was a creep, it doesn't give anyone the right to kill him."

"Let's remember that this is a made-up scenario," I cautioned, flashing back on the look Cindy Whitaker had given me yesterday. Did she deserve to die for what she had done? The woman had ruined one life and taken another, all in the name of selfish greed. Was Hammurabi's Code the way to handle things? Should the old rule of an eye for an eye, a tooth for a tooth determine one's fate? Should one's life be forfeited for the taking of another's, assuming it's done out of greed or some other selfish motive as opposed to self-defense? I realized that my own answer to that question had changed after my father was killed, at least for a while. During those first few months, I was filled with anger and an overwhelming desire for revenge. If I had known at the time who killed him, would I have taken justice into my own hands? I couldn't be 100 percent sure, but I feared I might have, and that scared the hell out of me. I shoved those thoughts aside and shifted my focus back to Tad and the suspects in our made-up case.

"Another suspect present at the dinner party is a single woman named Christa who paints landscapes in oils," Tad went on. "The police learn she was having an affair with Harvey up until a week ago when he reportedly dumped her. This happened very publicly in a local restaurant, and Christa vowed in front of several people that she would make Harvey pay. When asked where she was at the time the shot was heard, she says she was in the bathroom that is located just off the foyer, but no one can verify that.

"Another attendee and suspect is a single, thirty-something gentleman named Paul, a part-time mechanical engineer, who minored in chemistry. He puts his knowledge to use in his art by creating metal sculptures. He says he was alone in the kitchen at the time of the shot, refilling both his glass and Christa's with wine. At first, Paul doesn't appear to have any motive, but the cops later catch him and Patricia sharing a very intimate moment that gives credence to the rumor about Patricia having an affair. Realizing Paul might want Harvey out of the way so he and Patricia can be together, the cops add him to the suspect list.

"Next we have Harvey's twenty-four-year-old daughter, Dona, from a previous marriage, who was in the house at the time of the incident but who swears she was in her bedroom watching TV. The cops learn that she recently had a big argument with her father about money, a fight that resulted in her father cutting her off from her usual allowance. The daughter is dating Freddie, a man in his early thirties who was recently discharged from the military where he was an expert marksman. He is currently unemployed, and he is also the basis of the argument Dona had with her father, since she was using her allowance to support Freddie.

"Finally, we have Freddie, who was in the house when the police got there, but who swears he must have entered the house after the gunshot because he never heard it. None of the other suspects can recall seeing Freddie come in or head upstairs to Dona's bedroom, which is where he was found when the police arrived. Freddie says Dona called him on his cell to tell him that the front door was unlocked and that her father and stepmother were both busy elsewhere, so to just come on in and head upstairs. Freddie swears that's what he did."

Tad set down the papers he was holding, removed his glasses, and looked out at the group. "That's it, folks. You have seven potential suspects. Now figure out who killed Harvey and how it was done."

Chapter 22

Not surprisingly, Carter was the first one to start putting forth questions and scenarios. "Is it possible that the sound of the shot wasn't the actual shot? Could it have been a recording and the actual shot was fired before the guests arrived?"

"Interesting idea," Tad said. "But even if that was true, how did the killer then get Harvey inside his study and lock the door and all the windows from the inside without getting trapped in there his- or herself? There is no key access to the lock from the other side of the door."

"Hmm, I don't know," Carter said, frowning and studying his notes some more.

"What about heat vents or air ducts?" Billy asked. He had been eavesdropping on the story while he was making drinks. "Could the bullet have been fired that way somehow? Like from the daughter's bedroom?"

"Another interesting idea," Tad said. "But then, how could the person firing the gun have aimed?"

"Was the daughter's bedroom located above the

study, with a shared vent between the two, one in the bedroom floor and one in the study ceiling?" Billy posed.

"Good idea, but no," Tad told him.

"What about an air duct in the walls that was big enough for someone to have fit into?" Billy tried, not yet willing to give up on his theory.

Tad shook his head, making Billy frown. "Nope. Anyone else?"

The group pondered the situation for another ten minutes or so, sharing notes about the individual suspects. Joe, Frank, Holly, Billy, and Carter all liked a different suspect for different reasons, and I watched Sam watch them with an inquisitive expression. I wondered if he was analyzing them in his mind, trying to decipher what psychological aspect or quirk led each of them to the suspect they picked.

I was stumped and offered nothing in the way of assistance. Eventually, I got up and started helping out around the bar, occasionally coming by the group to check on their progress.

Over the next couple of hours, they debated and discussed, posing different theories and then shooting them down. The discussion pulled in several other customers, some of whom were new to me and to the bar, others who were semiregulars. Among the semiregulars was Dr. Karen Tannenbaum, an ER doctor who worked at a nearby hospital, and who had heard about the Capone Club both via the news and through some of her coworkers who came in to the bar regularly. She had stopped by after her shifts several times to join the group, stating that she liked the puzzle aspect of the game because it was much like approaching a patient with mysterious symptoms and trying to come up with a viable diagnosis. During one of her first visits, she explained to us how med school teaches its students an old adage that when you hear the sound of hoof beats, think of horses, not zebras.

"It means we should first look for the more common, obvious diseases and disorders that fit the symptoms as opposed to the rarer, more exotic ones," she had explained. "But I like looking for zebras. That's why I like this group. It gives me a chance to find them." She had been coming in several times a week since then, and her knowledge of medicine and the human body had proven key in figuring out solutions to some of the cases.

As the night wore on, the group struggled to come up with a solution. The Signoriello brothers eventually got tired and went home, after soliciting a promise from the others that they would be told the solution the next time they came in. The brothers were quickly replaced by other customers who were listening in and wanted to participate. But, despite the changing and growing crowd, it was looking as if this one wasn't going to be solved. That's when Dr. Tannenbaum—or Dr. T, as she had become known to the group—threw up her hands and jokingly said, "This case is too complicated. I need a consult."

Carter said, "Dr. T, that's brilliant! Two heads are better than one. So far, we've been looking at this more from the perspective of there being one culprit, but what if it was more than one? Maybe two or more of the suspects put their heads and talents together and figured out a way to get the deed done."

"You're on the right track," Tad said.

"So who would logically be paired up?" Sam asked.

"The daughter and her boyfriend," Dr. T offered.

"Or Patricia and Paul," Holly added.

Tad, most likely realizing the hour was late and the bar would be closing soon, said, "If you want, I'll tell you who the culprits were and then you guys can figure out how they did it."

"No, don't do that yet," Carter said. "Let's think this through. In addition to the *who*, we need to figure out the *how*. And I think the how rules out the daughter and her boyfriend. I can't see any way they could have done it. Yes, Freddie is an expert marksman, but there was no way for him to see his target. In fact," he said, his voice growing more excited, "no one could see the target. Therefore, the culprits had to leave part of this up to chance."

"How so?" Sam asked, looking confused, as did all the others at the table.

"Think about it," Carter said. "Where was Harvey most likely to be while he was locked away in his study?"

"At his desk," I said.

"Right!" Carter said. "And the culprits had to hope that was the case."

I was seeing the light now. "And assuming he was seated behind his desk, the shot had to have come from directly in front of him," I said.

"The fireplace," Holly offered, and the others at the table all nodded and murmured their agreement.

Carter continued, "Patricia's artistic talent was sculpting . . . wood and clay. What is the fireplace full of?"

"Wood," came a chorus of voices around the table.

"And Paul was also a sculptor," Carter said.

"With metal," Holly said with a frown. She looked back at her notes for a few seconds and then her face lit up. "But he was also a mechanical engineer!" she added excitedly.

"Yes!" Carter agreed. The excitement around the table became palpable, and for me that meant quite literally. "I think I have it figured out," Carter said. "Patricia and Paul put their heads and their talents together. Patricia cored out part of the center of a log, using wood that is slow burning. They then placed a bullet inside the resultant tunnel, with the tapered end pointing out. Using Paul's engineering skills, they calculated how to aim their special log so that the bullet would fire in the right trajectory to hit Harvey. They would have had to lay the fire ahead of time, which Patricia had told the police that she did, and they might have stacked the wood in a special way to create the right type of burn on the altered log. But once Harvey lit the fire and the bullet was heated enough, it would have fired."

"You got it!" Tad said.

"Bravo!" Cora said, clapping her hands.

"Well done," I said to Carter. "For winning tonight's game, you get a drink and your meal of choice from my menu for free. But since we're closing in about ten minutes, I'll let you have it the next time you come in, okay?"

"Works for me," Carter said. "Free beer and pizza tomorrow night."

With that, the crowd began to disperse as everyone headed home. My employees and I began the clean-up work and by a little after three, the place was locked up for the night and I was upstairs preparing to go to bed. When I went to brush my teeth, I got all fumble fingered and dropped my toothbrush into the toilet. Cursing under my breath, I fished it out, tossed it, and washed my hands. Fortunately, I had a spare, one I had bought the last time I traveled, intending to take it with me. But I had forgotten it and it had been sitting in a drawer in the bathroom ever since. As I took the new toothbrush out and opened it, I remembered the trip I'd bought it for, a bartenders' convention that had been held in Boston. The night I returned from that trip was the night my father was murdered.

I held the toothbrush a moment, feeling a tightening in my throat as I flashed back to that night and the horror of finding my father shot and dying in the alley behind the bar. The pain was still relatively fresh, and I made a mental effort to push the memories aside, shoving them into a deep, dark corner of my mind where I could lock them away. It was a trick I'd learned over the ten months since his death, my way of getting through the day—or night—without breaking down.

I focused on the fate of Davey Cooper instead, giving myself something else to think about. As I tossed the wrapper from the toothbrush into the trash, I realized my throat still had that odd tight feeling. And something in my mind clicked. I raised the toothbrush up closer to my face, sniffed, and the tight sensation increased. Just to be sure, I opened the drawer I had taken it from and tossed it back in there. As soon as I closed the drawer, the tight sensation dissipated. I opened the drawer and picked up the toothbrush again, and as soon as I did, that tight sensation returned.

At first I wasn't sure what significance my little test had, but then I remembered Duncan's remarks from earlier and a thought jelled in my mind. Excited, I went to the phone and dialed Duncan's number.

Chapter 23

Duncan's voice was all sleepy and sexy when he answered and I felt both guilty for waking him and disappointed that he wasn't by my side.

"Duncan, it's Mack."

"What's wrong? Are you okay?" His voice had quickly become more alert.

"I'm fine, but I had a bit of an epiphany just now about the Cooper case." I then told him about my experiment with the toothbrush. He listened in silence and I tried to imagine what his expression was as I relayed my tale. I concluded by saying, "I'm fairly certain that the tightness in my throat was a reaction to the smell of the brand-new toothbrush, maybe the plastic it comes in or something used to make it. When I think back to other times I've bought a new one, I can remember having that same tightening sensation. It's one of those reactions that was subtle enough and seemed meaningless enough that I basically ignored it all those times. But I had the same tightening thing happen when we were looking at Davey Cooper's toothbrush."

Either Duncan was more tired than I realized or I hadn't clued him in well enough to where my thoughts had led me. "So Davey's toothbrush was new. What of it?"

"There was no package for a toothbrush in the trash anywhere," I said. "And I remember you saying that the toothbrush would be a good source of DNA. Even *I* know that from watching crime shows on TV from time to time. I think it's safe to assume that whoever took Davey might have realized that, too. So they took his old toothbrush and replaced it with a new, unused one so there wouldn't be any DNA to test in case anyone wanted to match it against a child."

"But there was DNA on the toothbrush," Duncan said, and for a moment, my hopes were dashed. Then I had another epiphany.

"How can you be sure that the DNA on that brush is Davey's?"

My question was met with silence and I could tell Duncan was thinking through the ramifications. I took advantage of the moment to extend my theory. "And that hairbrush that was there by the sink, it had one short brown hair in it . . . just one. Don't you think that's odd? The assumption, of course, is that it's Davey's hair, since Belinda's was blond. But what if it was placed there knowing that anyone investigating his disappearance would make that assumption?"

"Interesting," Duncan said, and I could hear sounds that told me he was now out of bed and moving around. "We did collect both the hair and the toothbrush. And you're right. Normally we would have assumed any DNA we could extract would be Davey's."

"How can you know for sure if you don't have him to get a sample from?"

"We can't match it to him directly, but we could do a

mitochondrial DNA comparison, and, given what you've just told me, I think I'll get the lab on it right away."

"What will that tell you?"

"Mitochondrial DNA is found outside the nucleus of a cell and it's DNA that comes solely from the mother. So we can determine if any DNA we find is Davey's by matching it to Belinda's DNA." He paused, and sighed. "This is very helpful, Mack. Nice work."

"Thanks."

"Now try to get some rest. I'll call you in the morning."

I mumbled some agreement to this directive, knowing that sleep wasn't going to come easily. And I was right. It was nearly five in the morning before I finally drifted off, and then my sleep was plagued with images of that little boy, crying and hollering in terror for his mommy while some vague human shape carried him away. I had the same dream several times and each time it woke me just as Davey was being carried out the door of his house. And each time I awoke, I had a foul taste in my mouth. I was too sleepy to make the connection the first few times, but eventually I recognized the taste as the same one that had come to me when I was walking through the Cooper house.

I was excited and eager to tell Duncan about it, but when he called me a little before ten, I soon learned that he had bigger news.

"We dug up some information on Jamie Cooper." Duncan sounded as tired as I felt. "We found an old DUI arrest from five years ago and a woman by the name of Peggy Smith posted Jamie's bail in cash. She was working as an attorney at the time but there's no record of her on file as an attorney for the past four years. We're trying to find her, but it's a common name and, aside from the DUI, we haven't been able to establish any other connections between her and either Jamie or Belinda.

"I also had the lab expedite the mitochondrial DNA comparison between Belinda Cooper and the hair we found in the brush at her house. I don't have a full report yet, but they were able to tell me enough to show that you were absolutely right, Mack. Either Davey Cooper isn't Belinda's natural child or someone substituted a hair in the brush to mislead us."

"What about the toothbrush?"

"It's still being processed. We'll be able to get a full profile from that sample, but it takes longer. I hope to have something in the next day or so."

"It sounds like you're up against someone who is smarter than the average criminal," I said, thinking Duncan must have been up most of the night if he had the DNA info already. "That's kind of scary."

"Yeah, and it also confirms the theory that taking the kid was the primary goal here. I don't know if killing Belinda was part of the original plan or not, but clearly whoever did this put some serious thought into it. Fortunately, I have a secret weapon they don't know about."

"What's that?"

Duncan chuckled. "You, silly. You're my secret weapon."

While his words made me feel good, my feelings on the matter remained mixed. There was a part of me that knew I couldn't turn my back on someone like Davey Cooper if I was able to help in any way. But the danger—not to mention the type of people and environments—it exposed me to still left me feeling reluctant. And that made the praise a bit uncomfortable for me.

"Is there anything I can do to help?" I asked.

"Not now," he said, and, as I felt my spirits sink, I realized I was hoping he would say yes. "If we manage to track down the ex-husband or this mystery girlfriend of his, I'd like you to listen in on any interviews we do, like you did on Saturday with that group from Stratford and Weber. Or if we find any new evidence, I might want you to take a look at it. Otherwise, you're free to return to your life as a bar owner for today."

"Gee, thanks for the permission," I said, knowing my disappointment could be heard in my tone.

"I didn't mean it to sound that way," Duncan said, his voice all apologetic.

"I know. I'm sorry. I didn't sleep well last night and that's left me tired and cranky this morning."

"Don't worry, something will turn up. I'm manning the call lines and fielding any leads from those right now, and we've got officers and detectives out canvassing still. I'll stop by later to update you on things, okay? I'm going to need a cup of your marvelous coffee before too long. This cop-house stuff tastes like battery acid."

"Do you know that because you've tasted battery acid, or is there a little bit of the synesthete in you, too?"

"Neither. I'm just exercising some poetic license. Out of curiosity, how does coffee taste to you?"

"Happy," I told him, "assuming it's the right kind of blend. Otherwise, it might taste irritable, or angry, or indifferent, or obstinate."

Duncan laughed. "I'm sorry I asked. Now, I'll probably be haunted by nightmares where coffee beans with deviant personalities chase me down."

That made me laugh, too, and when I hung up a moment later, I felt better than I had before he called. By the time I dressed and headed downstairs to start prepping for the bar to open, I was in a good mood. Debra and Pete came in to help, and I enjoyed having a little time to partake in something as simple as good friends and easy conversation. No mention of death or missing children or murder had come up by the time we unlocked the doors, and I had to admit that I found the respite refreshing.

It didn't last long. Cora came in at eleven-fifteen to order lunch and she was followed a short while later by the Signoriello brothers and Carter, all of whom joined her. At noon, Holly and Alicia came in for their lunch break and pushed a table over to join the others. A few minutes after that, Dr. T came in to grab a bite to eat before she went on duty at three.

Of course, the talk of the table was the Cooper case and I was barraged with requests for new information. I didn't share any, not knowing if Duncan would want me to. The newscasts on TV kept showing that same picture of little Davey that I'd seen in the house, asking viewers to call if they had any knowledge of his whereabouts. Added to the plea was a picture of Jamie Cooper, Davey's father, and a request to call the police if anyone had any knowledge of the whereabouts of this "person of interest" in the case.

I wondered if they would try to put together a sketch of the mystery girlfriend, Valeria, and get that out to the public, too. After what Duncan had told me earlier, I got curious and switched over to a Chicago-based channel. Sure enough, the same Amber Alert was showing on that station at the top of every hour.

Since there was little in the way of new information on the case, the group decided to do another one of their own cases. In honor of Fraud Monday, it was half price for the drink of the day, a Sneaky Pete. Since Holly, Alicia, and Dr. T all had to report to work upon leaving the bar, I made them a virgin version by using a

shot of chilled espresso, an ounce of simple syrup, a teaspoon of vanilla flavoring, and a few drops of maple flavoring.

Carter had a case he wanted to present, so he told it
to all of us with the caveat that we pass it along as the
day went on and others came into the bar. We agreed
and he started his tale.

"For this one we're going back to the sixties . . . the
1860s that is. It's August of 1863, the early days of the
Gold Rush, and one day, this prospector comes walking
into a saloon in Arizona. His face, arms, neck, and
hands are deeply tanned and his hair is sun bleached
nearly white. He claims he has just struck it rich and
found the mother lode. He tells the others he's been out
in the desert looking for gold and went out with a burro
laden with barrels of water and some satchels packed with
hardtack and jerky. After about two months, he found a
cave whose walls were filled with veins of gold. But he did-
n't have the necessary equipment to mine it so he
chipped out a few surface nuggets with his hammer and
knife, and then decided to head back to town. But, by
then, his food and water were nearly gone. With his
water rations running low, he had to quit sharing it with
the burro, so it died a few days later. He tells the men in
the saloon how he had to eat some of the meat from the
burro to survive, and when his water ran out, he managed to get enough liquid to keep going by cutting
open some barrel cacti and squeezing the moisture out
of the inside pulp by twisting it inside his bandana. He
thought he was a goner, he tells them, but he finally
managed to make it back to town.

"To celebrate, he booked himself a hotel room, took
a much-needed bath, and then visited the local barber
shop. It was a challenge, he says, because no one wanted
to feed him or house him looking the way he did when

he first got to town, all filthy and smelly, with a big bushy beard and hair grown well below his collar. 'But I convinced them when I showed them these,' he says, and then he takes out a handkerchief, unfolds it, and drops two small gold nuggets onto the bar. He tells the others, 'I cashed one nugget in already—the biggest one—to pay for my room and all, and these may not look like much, but that vein I found has enough gold in it to make twenty men filthy rich. Problem is, it will require some blasting and hauling work to get the rest loose, and I'm flat broke. All I have left for money is these gold nuggets right here. So I'm willing to share my good fortune with anyone who wants a part of it, because I can't get the gold out alone. And, believe me, there's plenty to go around. Would any of you good fellows be interested in a stake?' "

Carter paused to take a sip of his drink and I looked around the table at the others. He had their undivided attention and had he paused much longer, I'm sure there would have been a loud protest.

"So that's the guy's story," Carter continued. "After he is done with it, several of the men in the saloon walk over and examine the nuggets the prospector has dropped onto the bar. One of the men suggests they might be fool's gold, but another fellow, one who knows how to tell real gold from the fake stuff, assures them the nuggets are real. With that assurance, several men take money out in preparation for buying a stake in the prospector's mine. But the barmaid, who happens to be the bartender's wife, tells them to put their money away because it's obvious the prospector is lying. How does she know?"

With that, Carter leaned back in his chair and took another swig from his drink, a self-satisfied smile on his face.

Dr. T was the first person to venture a guess. "Was the guy who said the gold was real in on it with the prospector?"

"Nope," Carter said. "No consults this time, Dr. T. The prospector is alone."

No one else said anything for a minute or so, and then Holly snapped her fingers and said, "I got it! You said his face was tanned . . . the whole thing?"

Carter smiled and nodded.

"Then clearly the man was lying. If he'd been out in the desert for months and had to shave when he got to town, the lower part of his face that was covered by the beard wouldn't have been tanned."

"Excellent!" Carter said.

"Just in time for me to head back to work," Holly said, beaming.

"Good work, Holly," I said. "Since you've already had and paid for your lunch, the next time you come in, you can have a meal on the house."

"I'll be back tonight after work," she said. "I want to know what's going on with that poor little boy."

"Me, too," Alicia said, and then the two of them got up and left.

The next hour or so was blissfully normal, an ordinary day in the bar. It felt good to be away from all the death and mystery, but we all had one ear tuned to the TV the entire time, waiting to see if there were any updates on the search for Davey Cooper. There weren't, but just before three o'clock, Duncan called me.

"I need your help," he said.

I had mixed feelings about the request, because I was eager to see him and hoped it would be some good news about the Cooper case, but I also feared the news might be bad.

"What's up?" I asked, and then I held my breath waiting for the answer.

"We found Jamie Cooper," he said. "In fact, we had him the whole time and didn't know it. He spent the wee hours of Sunday morning in the drunk tank, plastered out of his mind after he was arrested outside a local bar. Apparently he had been on one hell of a bender and when the bartender cut him off, he got mad and started trashing the place. He left before the cops got there, but some public ambassadors found him curled up in an alley around four in the morning. He didn't have any ID on him—we think somebody rolled him—so he was listed as a John Doe. When he woke up yesterday afternoon, they moved him to the jail pending an arraignment today and he didn't give us his name until just a little while ago. We have him here at the station now and we're getting ready to question him. Would you mind listening in?"

I breathed a sigh of relief that it wasn't bad news and felt a sense of renewed hope. Maybe Jamie Cooper would help us find his son. "Sure," I said. "I'd be happy to."

"Great," Duncan said. "I have a patrol car waiting out front to bring you here."

His presumptuousness annoyed me, but not enough to change my mind or my mood. So I told him I'd see him shortly and then made arrangements with my staff to cover things while I was gone.

The same two cops who drove me to the Coopers' house were waiting out front and they greeted me like old friends. I had mixed feelings when Tyrese declared me a member of their cop family and the district's secret weapon.

When we arrived at the station, they dropped me off out front and I went inside, where I was buzzed into the inner sanctum. Duncan greeted me in the hallway and escorted me back to the same room I'd been in when he interrogated the suspects in Dan Thornton's murder. I settled in and turned on the room speaker and then waited while Duncan went to fetch Jamie Cooper.

When Duncan brought Jamie Cooper into the room, it was easy to see why no one had recognized him despite all the appeals on TV. He didn't look anything like the picture that had been broadcast with the Amber Alert. His dark hair was greasy looking and messy, he had several days' worth of scraggly beard growth, his eyes were sunken and bloodshot, and his overall color was pasty. He also looked much thinner in the face than he had in the picture I'd seen.

Duncan steered him, shuffling, to a chair, which Jamie dropped into like a sack of wet towels. Jamie then leaned forward, elbows on the table, head in his hands. Duncan left then, which had me puzzled for a minute, and I watched to see what Jamie might do. He didn't budge until Duncan returned bearing a cup of hot coffee. Jamie cupped it in his hands like it was the most precious thing he'd ever held.

Jamie took a sip of the coffee and, judging from the grimace on his face, it either tasted bad or was scalding hot . . . maybe both.

"Mr. Cooper, I need to talk to you about Davey and Belinda," Duncan began.

"What's the bitch want to do to me now?" Jamie grumbled, his speech sloppy. His voice tasted like sour soup that was too hot, making me want to spit. "I told them I can't pay child support if I don't have a frigging job. What the hell do they expect from me?"

"You seem to have been able to afford to buy booze," Duncan observed, and Jamie shot him a mean glare. "When did you last see Belinda?"

"I don't know . . . a few weeks ago?"

"Where have you been for the past two days?"

Jamie snorted with amusement. "I don't know. Can't remember much," he said. "Why?"

"When was the last time you were at Belinda's house?" Duncan asked, ignoring Jamie's question.

"I haven't set foot in that place in . . ." He grimaced as he tried to think, as if it hurt. I suspected it did. "Long time ago," he said finally.

"Your ex-wife Belinda was found dead Saturday night," Duncan said.

Jamie stared at him a moment with a half smile on his face while his brain tried to process the information. Then he let out a big belly laugh. "Good one!" he said, slapping a hand on the tabletop. "You cops are a riot."

Duncan said nothing; he just sat in his chair, leaning back and staring intently. Jamie shook his head and continued to chuckle to himself for a few more seconds. But when Duncan's demeanor and expression didn't change, Jamie's expression sobered up. "You're just messing with me, right?" he asked with hope in his voice.

"No, I'm not," Duncan said very matter-of-factly. "We found her dead in her bedroom Saturday night."

It took Jamie several seconds to digest this bit of information. He shook his head once as if to rattle something loose, and the action made him moan and then massage his temples.

I knew the moment things clicked for him. His shoulders straightened and he sat up rigid in his chair. He dropped his hands and looked back at Duncan. "What happened to her?" he asked, and the soupy flavor of his voice turned to a beefy strong taste that was no longer too hot. "And where's Davey?"

"Let's not play games, Mr. Cooper," Duncan said. "I think you know very well what happened to her."

"I do?" Jamie said, looking thoroughly confused, and when the beefy taste didn't change, I felt his confusion was genuine. But whether it was due to his innocence or his inability to recall past events due to whatever drunken state he'd been in, I couldn't be sure. "Where's Davey?" he repeated.

"Don't you know?"

"How would I know?"

"Mr. Cooper, your ex-wife was murdered."

Jamie just stared at him, gape jawed. I half expected Duncan to fill the silence that followed—it felt as if it lasted for a full minute or more—but he remained silent, and the two men engaged in a stare-off. I don't think either one of them blinked once the entire time, but while Duncan was clearly focused on Jamie Cooper, Jamie didn't appear to be looking at anything in particular. I got the sense he was trying to digest the news that had just been delivered.

It was Jamie who eventually broke the silence, finally focusing his disconcerted stare on Duncan. "Someone killed Belinda? Why? I mean, sure, she was a bitch to me, but hell, I deserved it. She never hurt anybody . . . never bothered anybody. And she didn't have much. Why would anyone want to hurt her?"

"I understand you hurt her yourself a time or two when the two of you were married," Duncan said.

Jamie looked as if he was about to object, but instead he snapped his mouth closed and hung his head in shame. "I know . . . I did some stupid stuff. I'm still doing stupid stuff. It's the damned booze. It makes me mean, but I can't seem to stop." He threw his head back then and sighed heavily. For a few seconds he sat that way, staring at the ceiling, and then I think the reality of his situation suddenly dawned on him. He moaned, rubbed his stomach, lifted his head back up, and stared at Duncan. "You think I killed her, don't you?"

"Did you?"

Whether it was the motion of his head, the hard hit of reality, or some combination of the two, I don't know. But the next thing to come out of Jamie Cooper's mouth was vomit. Duncan shot back with his chair just in time to avoid the splatter as it hit the edge of the table and the floor. Duncan muttered some choice words that made his chocolate voice taste like it had jalapeños in it, and then he got up and left the room.

He entered the room I was in a few seconds later. "Well, wasn't that just dandy," he said, clearly disgusted.

"At least you avoided the puke bomb," I said, trying to hide my amusement because I sensed Duncan wouldn't appreciate it. Vomit has never really bothered me, as I've been around it my entire life. You can't work in a bar for any length of time and not be exposed to it on a somewhat regular basis. I suppose I've become inured to it the same way medical professionals often do.

We watched as an officer took Jamie out of the room and a maintenance worker came in to clean up the mess. "When he's cleaned up, I'll take another go at him," Duncan told me. "What's your take so far?"

"He seems genuinely befuddled by it all, but it's hard to tell if that's because he doesn't know anything or if it's because he just doesn't remember. It looks like he went on quite the bender."

"Yeah, he still reeks of alcohol, and that was before he barfed."

"Do you think he could have killed his wife and done something with the kid in such a bad state of drunkenness that he truly doesn't remember any of it?"

Duncan shrugged and frowned, watching the maintenance guy, who was sprinkling some kind of powder on the mess in the interrogation room. "Serious drunks have blackouts all the time, so who knows? The killing did seem kind of clumsy and maybe that's because he was so drunk he couldn't function normally."

"Maybe," I said doubtfully, and Duncan didn't miss my hesitation.

"What? You have another idea?"

I shrugged. "Jamie's a big guy and Belinda Cooper was a small woman. Even drunk out of his mind, I would think he could overpower her easily."

"You're right," Duncan admitted grudgingly. "We had hoped to find some blood or tissue from the killer under Belinda Cooper's fingernails. We did find tissue, along with some nylon fibers, but the tissue was her own, from pulling at the panty hose that were wrapped around her neck."

"Unlike the kidnapping, Belinda's murder didn't seem well planned," I said. "The panty hose, were they hers?"

"They could have been. They matched others we found in her bedroom, but they're a standard brand that half the women in Milwaukee probably have, so I don't know if that's any help. I have the lab techs analyzing some skin cells we found in them, so it would appear they had been worn. Maybe we'll get lucky."

"Well, I don't see any killer taking the time to take off their own panty hose to strangle the woman, so I'm betting they're Belinda Cooper's."

Duncan looked at me then and smiled.

"What?" I said.

"You're getting the hang of this. You're starting to think like a cop."

"Is that a good thing?"

"I think so. I always knew you'd make a good barstool detective."

The door to one of the other interrogation rooms opened and an officer escorted Jamie Cooper inside. He still looked haggard, but his face was clean and his hair was wet and looked as if a comb had been run through it.

"Okay, here we go again," Duncan said. "Show me what you can do, Mack." With that, he gave me a peck on the cheek and headed in for round two with Jamie Cooper.

Chapter 24

I switched the speaker knob over to the new room and sat back to listen to round two of Jamie's interrogation.

"Sorry about that," Jamie said when Duncan entered the room and sat catty-corner from him. "My head is spinning and that coffee didn't sit too well."

"You'd be surprised how many cops react the same way. We're not known for the quality of our coffee here." Duncan's demeanor was relaxed and easy, I presumed to set Jamie at ease. "Mr. Cooper, your ex-wife is dead . . . murdered . . . and we need to know where you were between the hours of six and eight on Saturday evening so we can rule you out."

"She really is dead?" Jamie said, looking sad and pathetic. Duncan nodded. "I was hoping you were just messing with me, trying to rattle me or something by saying that."

"Can you tell me where you were?"

Jamie screwed his face up and I couldn't tell if he was having an emotional reaction to the news, trying to remember where he was during the time in question, or in some kind of pain.

"I suppose you could check at the places I normally hang out," he said finally. Then he named two bars located not far from mine. "What about Davey?" he asked then. The concern and worry on his face looked genuine.

"We don't know where your son is," Duncan said. "He's missing."

"Then he's not dead, too?" His relief also seemed genuine, though Duncan's next words made it short-lived.

"We don't know. There's no evidence at the house that he was harmed in any way, but we have no idea where he is or who he's with."

Jamie Cooper leaned forward, put his arms on the table and his head on his arms. Then he began to sob.

Duncan waited patiently for a minute or so, then he grabbed a box of tissues on the table and slid it toward Jamie, nudging his arm with the box. "What can you tell me about Valeria Barnes?" he asked gently.

Jamie raised his head, grabbed a tissue from the box, and blew his nose noisily. When he was done, he said, "Val? I just met her like a month ago. She introduced herself one night when I was at one of the bars I go to. She likes to party and she was willing to buy me drinks, so we kind of hit it off. "

"Are the two of you lovers?"

Jamie made a face that I couldn't quite read. "No, but it wasn't from lack of trying. It seemed like she always had an excuse." He paused and ran a hand through his damp hair. "And when I drink, I sometimes . . . I have trouble . . . you know?" He looked at Duncan with a sad, embarrassed expression.

"Your roommate said you haven't been there in a while. Are you staying at Valeria's place?"

Jamie nodded. "I was. She has a camper that she lives in and she invited me to stay in it at night with her. It was nice in a way because she would arrange to meet me somewhere each night we got together and we could park the thing somewhere close to a bar and then spend the night in the camper if we wanted to and not have to drive. Though, most of the time Val would move us during the night, because in the morning when I woke up, we'd be somewhere else." He shot Duncan a worried look and then shrugged. "I suppose you already know I have several DUIs and lost my license awhile back." Duncan nodded. "That's why I lost my job. It's hard to be a car salesman if you can't drive."

"You're not living with Valeria anymore?"

Jamie shook his head and then blew his nose again. "I didn't live with her, exactly, just spent some nights. She always kicked me out early in the morning, around seven. She'd drop me off someplace, arrange to meet me somewhere at a bar that evening, and then take off. She said she had to get to work."

"Where does she work?"

"I don't know," he said, wincing and rubbing his forehead. "I don't think I ever asked her. I don't process too well in the mornings."

"Where is she now?"

Jamie sighed. "I have no idea. Friday night when we were at the bar, she said she was going to the bathroom and she never came back. I thought maybe she'd gotten sick or something and had gone to lie down. But when I went outside to try to find her, the camper was gone." He paused and sighed. "I really thought she was into me," he said. "She even acted jealous whenever I talked about Belinda."

Duncan perked up at that. "Did you talk about Belinda a lot when you were around her?"

"I guess. It seemed like Val was always asking about her and Davey. She wanted to know where Belinda worked, what her hours were, what they did for fun, that kind of stuff. And she was always asking me if I was going to go over there to see them, like she was worried that Belinda and I might hook up again or something."

I had a strong suspicion that Valeria's interest in Belinda and Davey stemmed from something else altogether, and judging from the look Duncan gave me through the window, so did he.

"Did Valeria have a favorite place where she liked to park the camper most of the time?" Duncan asked.

"There's a Target over on Miller Park Way and she parked in their lot quite often since no one bothered us there. And they're open from eight in the morning till like eleven, I think, so it was convenient if we needed something, or had to use a bathroom."

"When was the last time you were parked there?"

Jamie screwed his face up in thought. "What day is it now?"

"It's Monday."

"I think it was Friday night." He thought a moment and then nodded. "Yeah, I remember her saying something about how we needed to kick off the weekend. That was the night she disappeared."

"And you haven't seen or heard from her since then?"

Jamie shook his head, but not with much conviction. "I remember going outside and back to where we parked the camper. When I saw it was gone, I went back to the bar. I thought maybe she'd come back, but she never did. I remember the bartender telling me I had to leave at some point, but I don't remember much after that."

"Obviously you kept drinking," Duncan said. "How did you pay for the stuff?"

"I had money Val gave to me. She always let me carry the cash so I could pay for the drinks."

"Did she ever use a credit card?"

"Not that I can remember," Jamie said, and Duncan's shoulders sagged. "Val always had a ton of cash around, wads of it."

"What does Valeria look like?"

Jamie gave us a description, more detailed than the others we'd heard, but matching in the basic characteristics: about five-two, slender but a little full in the hips, pouty lips, long brown hair, dark brown eyes, Hispanic. "She had that sultry, sexy Latina accent, you know?" Jamie said at one point, momentarily lost in some bit of reverie.

"What does her camper look like?" Duncan asked next.

Jamie gave him a description of that, too, stating that it was a white camper with gold trim mounted on an old Ford pickup, a dark blue F-150.

"Do you have somewhere to stay?" Duncan asked.

Jamie shook his head. "I don't have enough money to pay my back rent on the apartment I was staying at. I spent too much on the booze. And, to be honest, I don't think my roommate, Jason, would take me back anyway. I've burned a lot of bridges. Booze has a way of making your friends disappear."

"Where have you been staying during the day for the past week or so?"

Jamie frowned and scratched his head. "I've been wandering around. For a couple of days, I stayed at the house of some guy I met in a bar, but then his girlfriend booted me. Probably a good thing. They were into drugs a lot. The other days I spent wherever I could. There are enough indoor walkways downtown to stay in out of the cold, and sometimes in the mornings I'd sleep for a while in a public restroom or something and then try to clean myself up a little. I had a backpack with some clothes and stuff in it, but I don't know what happened to it."

What he said about the downtown area is true. There are a number of buildings along the riverfront region that are connected by a maze of indoor corridors.

"What about family?"

Jamie huffed at that suggestion, and then his expression turned terribly sad. "My sister was killed in a car accident seven years ago. I was driving."

"Were you drunk?" Duncan asked.

Jamie let out a humorless laugh. "No, I wasn't. In fact, prior to that I hardly ever touched the stuff. I'd have the occasional beer with the guys, but that was it. I didn't start drinking hard until about a year after her death."

"What about your parents?"

Jamie shuddered. "They're both dead."

I didn't want to feel sorry for Jamie. His drunken, abusive behavior had made him easy to dislike initially. But upon hearing about his history, I found myself feeling some pity for the man. The fates had certainly not been kind to him and while it didn't mitigate his behavior and wrongdoings, it did make them a little easier to understand.

Duncan told Jamie they were going to hold him for now under charges of public drunkenness, loitering, destruction of property, and a battery charge being filed by the bar's bouncer. In addition, Duncan told him that he was considered a potential suspect in Belinda's murder. Jamie didn't protest, which surprised me at first, but then I figured that with nowhere else to go, spending a day or two in a jail cell with three squares might seem like a good deal.

"Do you think Valeria had something to do with this?" Jamie asked Duncan.

"I don't know. Do you?"

"If she was still with me, I might think so," Jamie said. "I could see her going off on some jealous rampage and killing Belinda. But . . ." He left the obvious conclusion unstated, and instead asked, "Do you think my boy is okay?" He looked more haggard and forlorn now than when I first saw him.

"I certainly hope so," Duncan said, and I could tell he felt a little sorry for the man.

"I need to get my life together," Jamie said. "I need to beat this damned booze habit."

Duncan went over to the interrogation room door and had an officer come in and take Jamie away. Then he joined me in the listening room. "I think he's telling the truth," he said.

"So do I. I was hoping he might help us solve this and find the kid."

"I don't think he knows where Davey is or who killed Belinda, but he did give me some information that might be useful. I'm pretty sure that Target store has cameras on their lot, so we might be able to get a visual and maybe even a plate from that camper. This Valeria Barnes woman is a ghost so far—no DMV records, no arrest history, nothing. I'm pretty sure the name is a phony, but if that camper was licensed at some point, it at least gives us a starting point."

"Do you think he's okay?"

"Who, Jamie?"

"No, Davey."

"I don't know. The evidence suggests that whoever took him meant him no harm, but people do crazy things when they think they might go to prison. To be honest, the fact that we haven't found him yet doesn't bode well."

"But we think they took clothes and toys for him," I said, unwilling to accept his doom-and-gloom prediction. "Doesn't that imply that the person who took him intends to keep him?"

"It would suggest that, yes. But the question is, for how long? If this Valeria Barnes is a finder for a child molester, or a child pornography ring, or some foreign kidnappers who intend to sell the kid abroad, then they won't keep him for long."

Those outcomes hadn't crossed my radar yet and hearing them depressed me.

Duncan reached over and cupped his hand around the back of my neck. Then he pulled me to him and gave me a kiss that made me forget everything else . . . at least temporarily. When he pulled his lips away from mine, it nearly made me moan. He leaned down, touched his forehead to mine, and spoke in a low, intimate tone.

"I was really hoping to solve this case so we could spend a little time together, but I have to get back to work. I expect it's going to be a late night again, and another early start in the morning. So is it okay if I have the guys take you back to the bar and give you a call sometime tomorrow?"

Hell no! After that kiss we just shared, I wanted more than anything to take him somewhere quiet and alone, somewhere the ugly rest of the world could be temporarily shut away, somewhere we could focus only on us. But I knew that couldn't happen. What's more, I realized that the future would probably be like this fairly often, with Duncan's job—and mine, though less so—interfering with our time together.

"Of course it's okay," I said, wondering if he could tell I was lying.

After one more kiss that made me rethink my answer, we both parted with heavy sighs.

Thirty minutes later I was back at my bar, feeling like I was walking into another world.

The Capone Club group was gathered in their usual spot, and also as usual, Cora was there at the center. I went over and greeted everyone, and then I fielded questions about Davey Cooper. Everyone was wondering what, if any, progress had been made in finding the boy. I told them there wasn't much in the way of new information, but that the boy's father had been found and it didn't appear as if he was involved. There was a palpable sense of depression amongst the group with this news and I felt bad about bringing them down. After I was done with the questions, I asked Cora if she would meet me in my office. Once we were inside, she asked me how everything had gone and I gave her more in-depth information than I had shared with the others. I knew from my prior discussions with both her and Duncan that Duncan trusted Cora to keep certain information to herself. In exchange, Cora shared any dirt she dug up using her phenomenal computer skills.

"I have someone new for you to look up," I told her. "Jamie Cooper had a very short-term girlfriend who was asking a lot of questions about Belinda and little Davey. She was living out of a camper, and Jamie was sharing it with her for a while. I don't have any kind of license plates and, besides, the police can look that up if they get them, and I already know from Duncan that they haven't been able to find any information about her in their usual searches."

"It doesn't sound promising," Cora said, tapping away on her laptop. "I'll see what I can do. Give me a name."

I gave her Valeria Barnes's name, and then we spent a few minutes adding my reactions to Jamie Cooper into the database she was keeping for me. It wasn't a lot, and none of it seemed particularly helpful.

When we were done, Cora stared at me for a moment and then said, "Are you doing okay with all of this?"

"I guess so." Even I could tell I didn't sound very convincing. "I think it's just going to take me a little while to get used to all this sadness and death."

"How are things going with you and Duncan?"

"Pretty good, I think," I said with a smile. "I was hoping we would get to spend some time together tonight, but he needs to work on the case. It was a bit of an eye-opener for me. I realize that if I hope to have a relationship with him, I'm going to have to share him with his job."

"He pretty much has to share you with your job, too," Cora pointed out.

"I suppose so. But I just spent all this money to expand the bar, and I set things up so I could have more free time and some semblance of a life outside the bar. And then I go and hook myself up with someone who has even less spare time than I did before I made the changes. I have this sinking feeling that I'm going to end up spending a lot of my newfound free time alone."

"You'll never be alone, Mack," Cora said, closing her laptop and preparing to leave the office. "You've got us. Besides, I'm a pretty good judge of men, if I do say so myself, and I'm betting Duncan Albright will find a way to spend as much time with you as he can."

"I hope you're right, although I'm afraid that most of that time will be spent helping him investigate cases. And I don't know if I want a relationship that revolves around so much death and despair."

Cora was at the door to my office and had her hand on the knob, ready to leave. She turned to me and said, "If I recall correctly, the death and despair found you before Duncan did, when your father and Ginny were both murdered. In fact, it was that very death and despair that brought him to you. It was fate."

With that she left the office, leaving me alone with my somber thoughts. I couldn't deny that I was enjoying my relationship with Duncan, but on some level it bothered me. For one, I couldn't quite shake the feeling that it was a relationship of convenience for him, that my ability to help him solve these cases had a lot to do with his interest in me. I realized that my life prior to my father's murder had been a very insular and protected one. Maybe Cora was right. Maybe everything had happened for a reason. Maybe it was fate. Maybe it was fate's way of telling me it was time to step out of my shell, to be a little less safe, to take some risks with the hope of a happy outcome.

If Davey Cooper was never found—or worse yet, was found dead—I wasn't sure I could continue helping Duncan. But I also knew that until this case was resolved, whatever its outcome, I would feel obligated to help. Little Davey Cooper's picture was too firmly planted in my mind.

Chapter 25

It snowed again during the night, an inch or so of light, powdery stuff that dusted the city. Tuesday morning dawned bright and sunny, but the weather forecast was calling for clouds to move in later in the day, bringing with it three to five inches of lake effect snow. It was the week before Thanksgiving, and I knew this first major snowfall of the season would be welcomed by most. Unlike the snows in January and February, the snows of November and December often put people in a holiday mood.

I woke just before my alarm was set to go off at nine-thirty, and had only been up for a few minutes when my phone rang. When I saw from the caller ID that it was Duncan, hope surged that he was calling with some good news about Davey Cooper.

"Good morning, sunshine," Duncan greeted when I answered. "I have a deal for you."

"What's that?"

"I've got some bagels and cream cheese that I'm willing to share in exchange for some of your wonderful coffee."

"Sounds yummy. I think we can work something out. Any news on Davey Cooper?"

"Some," Duncan said. "I'll tell you when I see you."

"And when will that be?"

"That depends on how long it takes you to come downstairs and let me in the door."

"You mean you're here already?"

"I am. And it's cold out here. How long are you going to keep me waiting?"

"I'm on my way." I disconnected the call and headed downstairs to let him in through the bar's front door. He came in along with a blast of frigid, cold air that made me shiver. As soon as I closed and locked the door, he grabbed me by one of my arms, spun me around, and gave me a very nice good-morning kiss.

When he finally released me, I laughed and said, "If you keep that up we won't have time to eat."

"That's okay with me," he said, his voice laced with the taste of dark chocolate. And then he led me up the stairs to my apartment.

Twenty minutes later, I said, "That was a very nice appetizer, but I still want my bagel and cream cheese."

He laughed and said, "And I still want my coffee."

When we were both dressed and sitting at my table, I finally broached the subject uppermost in my mind. "What's the latest on the Cooper case?"

"Well, we got lucky with the camera footage from the Target parking lot. Not only were we able to get a good look at the camper, we were also able to get a license plate number. We got a shot of the mysterious Valeria Barnes, too, but it's from too far away and it's too fuzzy to be of much use."

"And?" I urged, spreading a thick layer of cream cheese on a garlic-encrusted bagel that smelled wonderful and made my neck feel hot and prickly. I made a mental note to have Cora add this sensation to our database, though I had my doubts as to how useful my synesthetic reaction to garlic would be. Biting into the slathered bagel turned that hot, prickly sensation into something much more satisfying, like a just-scratched itch.

"I'm afraid the license plate number was a bit of a dead end. The plates were stolen. We canvassed the bars that Jamie Cooper mentioned, and they verified his story, including the one that he was in on Friday night when Valeria ditched him. But we can't find the friend Jamie supposedly stayed with for a couple of days, because Jamie can't seem to recall a name or an address. We were able to get a sketch done up of our Ms. Barnes, however."

He showed me the sketch, which looked like a generic late-twenties or thirty-something Hispanic woman. "It's not very specific," I said, feeling depressed. "I know at least two women who resemble this sketch."

"Still, it's progress," Duncan countered, dabbing at some cream cheese at the corner of his mouth and then licking it off his finger. "It seems pretty clear to me that this Valeria woman is involved somehow. Her timely appearance in Jamie's life, all of her questions to him about Belinda and Davey and their day-to-day lives, and her unfortunately successful attempts to remain under the radar all point to someone who's complicit in this whole thing. So at least now we have a better idea of what direction to take, whereas before we were sort of floundering."

I didn't comment, partly because it didn't sound like much progress to me, and partly because Duncan's phone rang just as he finished talking. I sat quietly, eating my bagel and watching him as he took the call, trying to guess from his facial expression if the news was good or bad. But despite my supposed abilities and my best attempts to eavesdrop, I couldn't discern if the call was even relevant to the Cooper case. Turned out it was.

"Well, this is an interesting development," Duncan said when he disconnected the call. "We've found Valeria Barnes's camper." He punctuated the news with a bite of bagel.

"That's great!"

"Not really," Duncan said with a mouthful of cream cheese and bagel. I waited impatiently for him to swallow so he could continue. "The only thing that's left of it is a burned-out hull. Someone called in a fire in an abandoned lot in West Allis and by the time the fire department responded, the thing was totally engulfed."

"Sheesh, it's like you can't catch a break with this case."

"It seems that way, I know, but you never know when some seemingly unhelpful evidence will suddenly provide a valuable clue. We're going to air the Amber Alert again this evening and include a sketch of this Valeria woman this time. Maybe someone will recognize her. In the meantime, can I talk you into coming with me to look at what's left of the camper?"

"Why? If the thing is burned up, I don't think I'll be much help."

"You won't know if you don't try."

I caved to his request but with a caveat. I insisted on staying at the bar long enough to greet my morning staff and ask them to prep for opening. Duncan agreed—it wasn't like he had much choice, short of dragging me along with him—and we headed downstairs. Pete and Debra showed up minutes later and I told them I was leaving for a while. Then Duncan headed the two of us to the West Allis site where they'd found the burned-out camper.

The air outside tasted like white bread and I told Duncan the snow that was coming would be the light, fluffy stuff. He gave me an amused look but said nothing. It took us nearly twenty minutes to get to the abandoned lot where the camper was. The entire thing was cordoned off, along with fifty feet or so of ground in either direction, and there was a team of evidence techs along with some arson investigators scouring over the area and what was left of the truck and camper. Duncan made some introductions and then walked me over closer to the camper.

The stench of burnt plastic and other materials filled the air. There was a coat of white foam on top of the camper's remains and the sight of it made my hands and arms feel sticky. I had a host of other reactions to the smells, the sounds of the crew working, and the various things I looked at, but none of them offered up anything unusual or different that I thought would be of any help.

Duncan spent some time talking to the detectives and arson investigators, leaving me alone in a far corner of the taped-off area around the scene. When he came back to me, he said, "The arson boys said it looks like she used—"

"Gasoline," I said. "I can tell from the sound. The smell of gasoline sounds like rustling leaves."

Duncan smiled. "I'm not going to tell them you knew that. They've spent a lot of time and money perfecting their ability to examine and analyze fire scenes, only to come up with the same conclusion. Your nose could put them all out of a job."

I shrugged. "It's not like it's very useful information," I said. "I imagine gasoline is a pretty common thing used to set fires, and anyone can buy it at any one of dozens of gas stations."

"At least it doesn't appear that there are any bodies in the camper or the truck," Duncan said. "We were able to get a VIN number off the truck, but when the guys traced it, they found out that the last registered owner is an older gentleman who lives in Waukesha. He says he sold the camper a little over a month ago to a woman named Carlotta Solis. But we can't find a Carlotta Solis anywhere and the truck was never registered after the sale."

"Do you think this Carlotta woman is Valeria Barnes?"

"Probably, but it's likely another false identity. The man who sold the truck said the woman paid in cash so he didn't ask any questions."

"So we're still no closer to finding the kid."

"Nope." He paused and looked at me hopefully. "Unless you have some great revelation to share."

I shook my head and gave him an apologetic look. His phone rang then, and when he glanced at the caller ID, he said, "It's Cora. Maybe she's found something."

In typical Duncan fashion, he answered the call and then spent most of his time just listening. He didn't say much beyond an occasional grunt or other noise of acknowledgment. When he was done, he thanked Cora, disconnected the call, and said, "Cora went searching through some genealogy sites and found a Valeria Barnes."

"That's great!"

"Not really. This Valeria Barnes was born in Milwaukee thirty-two years ago and she died six months later of pneumonia."

I pondered this information for a moment. "Do you think our Valeria stole the identity of that one?"

"More than likely."

"Bummer."

"Yeah," Duncan said, looking disappointed. "Another dead end."

"No pun intended, I take it?"

Duncan smiled, but there was no real humor to it. "This doesn't seem to be helping, so if you want, I'll take you back to the bar."

"That would be great."

Twenty minutes later, I was back home. Duncan came inside with me for a few minutes to grab a cup of coffee to go. There was a good-sized lunch crowd by the time we got back, and once again we had to field questions about any updates on the Cooper case. Unfortunately, we left the group disappointed.

I worked for a couple of hours behind the bar, and during the late afternoon the predicted snow started to fall. The crime-solving group waxed and waned. Holly and Alicia came in for lunch just after one o'clock. Sam hadn't come in at all, but Carter showed up around noon and joined Cora and the Signoriello brothers, all of whom had been parked in the bar since it opened, according to Debra. Dr. T was there, too, though she said she once again had to be at work by three. The group also had a couple of newcomers, two male students from nearby Marquette University—Rob and Allen—who said they were business majors. Everyone was trying to solve today's riddle, which came from Frank and Joe Signoriello. And it was literally that—a riddle.

I wasn't in the mood for games—little Davey Cooper had consumed all my thoughts and interest—so I wasn't going to get involved. But when the Signoriello brothers urged me to play and told me that the answer to the riddle had a tie-in with the Cooper case, my interest was piqued. Besides, the brothers were so excited over their contribution to the group, I didn't have the heart to snub them.

"It's Tuesday, which means it's Vandalism Day," Joe said.

"That means Bad Attitudes are half price," I said. "Who wants one?"

The Signoriellos took me up on the offer, as did Carter, Rob, and Allen. Dr. T, Alicia, and Holly all opted for a virgin version of the drink, which was made using coconut-flavored coffee syrup, some rum flavoring mixed with a little simple syrup, and then equal portions of ginger ale and pineapple juice, topped off with a touch of cloves in place of the spiced rum.

Cora, who seemed distracted by something she was doing on her laptop, had her usual glass of Chardonnay.

When everyone had their drinks and food, Joe said, "In honor of Vandalism Day, we came up with a bit of graffiti in the form of a riddle. In order to solve the case and find the perpetrator, or at least get a lead on him, you'll have to solve the riddle."

"Listen carefully," Frank said. "Five hundred begins it, five hundred ends it, five in the middle is seen. First of all figures and the first of all letters take up their stations between. Join all together, and you bring before you the name of an eminent king."

The group got busy with Allen writing on a napkin, and they started by jotting down the number five hundred twice with the number five in the middle: 5005500.

"Is it a phone number?" Allen asked.

The Signoriello brothers, both of whom were looking smug, shook their heads in unison.

"You have to add the rest of the riddle in," Carter said. Then he wrote down the numbers on a different napkin. "The first of all figures is one, right?" he said.

"What about zero?" Rob posed.

"Hmm, good point," Carter said. He then wrote down 50050500 and the group stared at it for a minute or so without anyone offering up a guess.

"If the fives were ones, I'd think it was some kind of binary code," Allen said.

"We still need to add in the rest of the riddle," Carter reminded the group. "The first of all letters is the letter *A*." A new napkin appeared and this time he wrote down two lines of figures. The first one was 50050A500 and the second one was 50051A500.

Once again the group stared at the figures in silence, occasionally turning the napkin around and staring at the answer sideways and upside down. I did so as well and told the group, "The colors are all wrong." They all looked at me as if I'd said the sky was pink, so I tried to explain. "Numbers and letters all have colors when I see them, and these don't work. The letter is blue, but the numbers are red and yellow."

I could tell from the looks I was getting that the entire group was confused by my comment. Allen and Rob probably thought I was off my rocker totally, since they were new to the bar and didn't know about my synesthesia. I shrugged and said, "Welcome to my world."

There was some more discussion about the figures, and guesses were put forth that they represented an address of some type, or a shipping container, or an identification number of some sort. The Signoriello brothers promptly shot each proposed solution down.

I was about to give up and go back to working the bar

when I remembered Joe saying that the answer had a
tie-in with the Cooper case. That's when it hit me. In my
mind, the numbers changed and the colors suddenly
worked. "I got it!" I said. Not wanting to spoil it for the
rest of the group, I walked over and whispered my answer in Joe's ear.

Joe gave me a respectful look and said, "She figured
it out."

There was a chorus of moans from the others. "I'm
not going to tell you," I said. "I'll let the rest of you figure it out so someone can win a free meal."

"Can you at least give us a hint?" Holly said.

I looked at the brothers and they shrugged in unison. "Okay, here's a clue. Think about who came up
with this riddle and where they're from."

There were several seconds of silence, and then
Carter said, "You guys are Italian, right?"

The brothers nodded.

More silence followed as the group tried to figure
out how the brothers' ethnicity tied into it—everyone
except Cora, who was still occupied by whatever she was
doing on her computer. Then Allen snapped his fingers
and said, "I got it. The numbers are Roman numerals."

As soon as he said this, the group grabbed another
napkin and started interpreting the riddle using this
idea. It took some discussion to agree on what the
Roman numeral for five hundred was because some in
the group thought it was a *C*, and others thought it was
an *M* or an *L*. Eventually, they all agreed on *D*, and after
a few seconds of rearranging things, they came up with
the answer: DAVID.

Since Allen was the one who figured out the hint, I
awarded him a free meal. Everyone congratulated the

brothers on coming up with such a clever riddle, and it did my heart good to see them both basking in the praise.

That was when Cora finally looked up from whatever she was doing and said, "I have something. I need to call Duncan right away."

Chapter 26

I led Cora, carrying her laptop, into my office and we used the bar phone to call Duncan. I was dying to ask Cora what it was she had found, but I held back, figuring I'd get clued in when she told Duncan.

After a brief greeting, she said, "I found the death certificate for Valeria Barnes and it listed Milwaukee Memorial as the hospital where she was born and where she died. That got me to thinking that whoever used her identity might have had access to her medical records. So I started searching for other people who had died at that same hospital at a very young age and then I started researching the names. Some of them were too common to be of much use, but I remembered you saying that Valeria looked and sounded Hispanic, so I focused on any names that sounded like they were of Mexican or Spanish origin and I found something interesting. Several names of babies and children who died young during the seventies and eighties came up as names with current IDs. And they didn't exist anywhere that I could find up until the past two or three years, when they suddenly appeared in utility billing records, welfare applications, and with DMV."

She paused and listened for a minute or two, and then said, "Do you really want me to answer that, Duncan? We've been down this road before. You know that what I do isn't one hundred percent legal, so it might be better if you don't know. Plausible deniability and all that, remember?"

She listened again and then said, "Yes, I realize it's an issue for you from an evidence standpoint, but at least it gives you a lead. I'm thinking that the person who created Valeria Barnes, or perhaps even Valeria herself, might have access to those old hospital and death records. It's worth a look."

Over the next few minutes, I sat and listened as Cora read off the names she had found. When she was done, she said, "Yes, she's sitting right here across from me. Do you want to talk to her?" She then handed me the phone.

"Hi," I said. "This is good news, isn't it?"

"It might be," Duncan said. "Unfortunately, I can't use the information she gave me to search the hospital records. No one will give me a search warrant based on some coincidental name similarities."

"My mother was in Milwaukee Memorial Hospital when she died," I told him. "It's also where I was born. What if I went there and asked for a copy of her death certificate? The accident that resulted in my mother's coma was a hit and run. The driver of the car was never found, so you could even say you were investigating it as a cold case or something, couldn't you?"

"I suppose, but what good will that do?"

"It might get us into the medical records area at least," I said. "We can get a look at how they do things and find out who has access."

"I guess it's worth a try," Duncan said, though he didn't sound hopeful. "And it's all we have for now, so let's do it. I can come by and pick you up in fifteen."

"I'll be waiting."

Milwaukee Memorial Hospital was a sprawling affair that covered several city blocks. By the time we figured out which building we had to go to for medical records, it was nearing five o'clock and Duncan was afraid they would be closed.

They weren't, but the receptionist who greeted us—who, according to her ID badge, was named Lisa—said that even though the department was open twenty-four hours a day, access for the general public did stop at five, a mere eight minutes from our arrival time.

"What is it you need?" Lisa asked.

"I want a copy of my mother's ER report," I told her. "She died here on June eighth of 1980."

"Nineteen-eighty?" Lisa said, rolling her eyes. "That's not going to be easy to find. It's probably been sent to storage on microfiche. Can you come back tomorrow?" she asked with a pointed glance at her watch.

"I'm afraid this is a very urgent matter," Duncan said, flashing his badge. If he hoped it would intimidate the woman, he was sorely disappointed.

"Why is an ER report from thirty-some years ago so urgent?"

Duncan started to say something, but I beat him to it. "My mother died as a result of a car accident. She was hit by someone who fled the scene and was never caught. She was pregnant with me at the time and the doctors kept her alive long enough for her to deliver me. Then they removed the life support."

Lisa's expression finally softened, so I surged on—

ward, not wanting to lose any momentum I had gained from my sob story. I never knew my mother, but that didn't mean I didn't grieve for her. I summoned up all the emotion I could and managed to get a few tears to well up in my eyes.

"Someone has come forth and said they know who the driver was," I told her, letting my voice break. "So the cops are reopening the case. But if the person who hit her knows the cops are looking into it again, he or she might try to disappear. Please," I pleaded, swiping at my eyes, "can't you help me?"

Lisa frowned, and sighed. "Even if I can find the record, I can only release it to the cops if I have a release signed by the next of kin."

"That would be me," I said. "My father died nearly a year ago and I'm the only one left. Maybe you heard about his death? He was shot in the alley behind the bar we owned."

Dawning spread across her face. "You mean Mack Dalton?" she said, and I nodded. "I remember hearing about that. I used to go to his bar when I was in college. There was something in the paper about it a few weeks back, wasn't there? You finally caught the guy who did it?"

I nodded.

Lisa took one more look at my tear-stained face and her shoulders sagged. That's when I knew I had her. "Okay, I'll take a look," she said. She shoved a clipboard at me. "Fill out this form and then sign it at the bottom. I assume you have some proof that you're next of kin?"

"I have a driver's license," I said.

"That will do. Give me her name and date of birth and I'll go see what I can find while you fill out the form."

I gave her the information she needed and, after instructing us to wait where we were, she disappeared through a door off to one side after swiping her badge in front of a security-card reader. As she disappeared through the door, we got a brief glimpse of a cubicle-filled back office area.

"This isn't going to get us anywhere," Duncan grumbled. "We need to get into that back area and have a look around."

No sooner had he said this than the door opened. I expected to see Lisa, and was about to object at how quickly she had returned, thinking she had given up on the search. But instead it was a group of four women who came out, all of them carrying coats and purses that told me they had just finished their shift and were headed home.

Both Duncan and I watched the group as they left, chattering among themselves. One person in the group in particular caught my eye: a dark-haired, dark-eyed woman who looked to be around thirty years old. She looked a lot like the sketch Duncan had shown me, but then I felt certain there were dozens of other women in Milwaukee who would also fit the bill.

It wasn't her looks, per se, that had snagged my attention. As she walked by us, I heard a distinctive squeaking sound, as if someone was rubbing a finger on a piece of glass. "Did you see that woman?" I said to Duncan as soon as the group had left.

"I did."

"She smells like bleach. It's faint, but it's there. I heard the same squeaky sound when she walked by that I heard when we were in Belinda Cooper's car."

Duncan stared for several seconds at the door the women had just gone out. Then he said, "Come on. Let's see where she goes."

We left the office—I could only imagine how puzzled Lisa would be when she returned to her desk and found us gone—and trailed behind the group of women through the halls and out of the hospital, eventually entering a parking garage. I cursed under my breath and said, "Dang it, we won't be able to follow her out of here because you parked several blocks away on the street."

"Perhaps not, but we can at least get a make and model of car, and a license plate number."

We continued trailing behind the women, up a flight of stairs in the garage. Then they began to say their good-byes and gradually split off. Finally, the dark-haired woman was walking alone. We stayed a good ways behind her and when she took her car keys out, Duncan grabbed me and pulled me in between two parked cars.

"Squat down," he said, and I did so alongside him. We heard the sound of the woman getting into her car and shutting the door, then the sound of the engine roaring to life. In a low voice, Duncan said, "She'll have to drive right by us in order to exit the garage. Stay down until I say so."

A moment later, the car went past us. Duncan stood then and looked from behind as it drove away. "Got it!" he said. He took out his little notebook and wrote. Then he grabbed me again and we hurried back to his car.

Chapter 27

When we got back to Duncan's car, he drove straight to the police station. I followed him inside and into an office where he sat behind one of four desks. He then woke up the computer on the desk and started typing. I pulled up a nearby vacant chair and scooted in beside him to watch.

After a few seconds he said, "Bingo!" and typed in some more information. Then he turned around and kissed me on the nose. "I love your nose," he said.

It wasn't a declaration of love, but for now I supposed it was as close as I was going to get. I took it and smiled.

Once again he took me by the hand and led me back outside. "Come on, let's go visit Alberto Alvarez."

"Is that who the car is registered to?"

"It is."

We headed into the south side of Milwaukee, fighting the rush hour traffic as we went. Eventually, we pulled up in front of a red brick bungalow in the Layton Park neighborhood on Thirtieth Street. It was a quaint neighborhood with older model bungalows set close together, all of them with small but well-manicured front lawns leading out to a sidewalk.

Duncan parked behind an older model blue sedan; then he nodded toward it and said, "That's the car."

He turned off the engine and we got out. As I looked at the house, I saw a curtain move in a front window and knew our arrival had not gone unnoticed. I followed Duncan up a sidewalk that divided the postage stamp–size front yard in two. Duncan rang the doorbell and knocked on the door.

At first I thought no one was going to answer, but just as Duncan was about to knock again, the wooden front door swung open, revealing the same woman we had seen at the hospital.

"Can I help you?" she said, looking puzzled but wearing a smile.

She had a distinct Latina accent and a scent wafted toward me that made me hear that squeaking noise again. I felt my heart begin to race, though I couldn't tell for sure if it was a reaction to some sensory input, or a physical response to the excitement I felt.

"Mrs. Alvarez? I'm Detective Albright with the Milwaukee Police Department. I'd like to ask you a few questions, if you don't mind."

"What about?" Her voice remained calm and curious, but I caught the tiniest flinch of a muscle above her left eye that made me think she was nervous. I also noticed that she didn't correct Duncan when he referred to her as Mrs. Alvarez.

"What is your first name?"

She hesitated a second and I could tell she didn't want to reveal it. "Juanita," she said finally.

"I'm looking into the abduction of a little boy named Davey Cooper. Does the name ring a bell with you?"

"No," she said much too quickly. She seemed to realize her denial had been abrupt because she added, "I mean, I've seen the TV reports and all, so I heard of him that way, but I don't know the child."

"Is your husband home?"

Her smile faded and she seemed to bristle at the question. She came back with one of her own. "No, he is not. Can I ask why you are here at my house?"

"I'm just following up on a lead," Duncan said.

"And what lead is that, exactly?" Any hint of welcome and cooperation was now gone.

"I'm not at liberty to say," Duncan responded, continuing the game of cat and mouse.

"Then neither am I," she said, with a decidedly unfriendly smile. She started to close the door but Duncan stopped her.

"What about the name Valeria Barnes? Does that sound familiar to you at all?"

The woman paled noticeably, answering the question without intending to. "I do not have to speak to you," she said. "I know how you cops can be. I've had too many friends who were arrested for no reason. You think just because our skin is darker than that lily white color you have, that we all must be crooks. So if you want to speak to me, you can do it through my lawyer."

At that point, a little girl with dark brown hair, who looked to be around four years old, appeared behind Mrs. Alvarez. "Who is it, Mommy?" she asked.

"Go back inside, Sofia," Mrs. Alvarez commanded. The little girl pouted but retreated.

Once again, Mrs. Alvarez tried to close the door and Duncan again stopped her. "Mrs. Alvarez, if you are involved in any way with the murder of Belinda Cooper and the disappearance of her son, I can promise you that I will see you put away for the rest of your life."

This time she succeeded in closing the door; actually, she slammed it.

"Well, that was certainly interesting," he said.

"She knows something," I told him.

"Yeah, even I know that and I don't have your superpowers. Did you hear the squeaking sound again?"

"I did. It's faint, but it's there. "

We turned away and walked back to the car. Once we were seated inside, Duncan started the engine and we drove down the street and around the corner. He cruised around the block and then parked on a cross street, out of immediate sight but in a spot where we could see the blue sedan.

"Now we wait," Duncan said.

"For what?"

"If we get lucky, maybe the husband will come home. But I'm betting not. I think Mrs. Alvarez will call him and head him off. And I wouldn't be surprised if she tries to leave here and hook up with him somewhere else."

We sat in silence for several minutes, staring at the car. I tried to will Mrs. Alvarez out of her house, but there was no action other than a neighbor who pulled up and parked in the spot we had just vacated, and then entered the house next door. At one point, Duncan got on his phone and asked someone to look into the name Juanita Alvarez and call him back. He also asked to have a DMV photo of her pulled and have it shown to Jamie Cooper, to see if he recognized her as Valeria Barnes.

"I didn't know that your mother's accident was never solved," Duncan said after he disconnected his call.

"I didn't know myself until I was a teenager. That's when my dad told me."

"It must have been hard for you growing up without a mother."

I shrugged. "There were times in school when the other kids teased me about it, and I suppose if I'd ever known my mother, the loss might have had more of an effect. But my dad did a great job of raising me and whenever he needed a female point of view on things, he would hit up one of our regular customers. There was a lady named Genevieve who used to come in all the time and she taught me what to do once I started my periods. And whenever I had boy troubles, I would sometimes confide in the women who came into the bar. I had a lot of temporary aunts and uncles, people who were regulars for a number of years and then moved on for whatever reason. Some of them moved away, some of them got a life that cut down on their bar and drinking time, some of them died. So, while I realized that I was different from all the kids who had a mother, and I grieved over the fact that I never knew her, it was a different kind of grief, I think. Sometimes I felt guilty that I didn't feel more, especially when I would find my dad all red eyed and sad, looking at the old pictures of the two of them."

"Do you still have those pictures?"

"I do. They're in an album stuffed in a closet."

"Do you ever look at them?"

"Occasionally, but I haven't for a long time. My dad used to sit with me and go through the pictures often when I was little. He said he wanted me to know my mother as much as I could even though I never got to spend any time with her. I think the sessions were as much for him as they were for me. Sometimes he would talk to her as if she were in the room with us. It was sweet but also kind of creepy."

"Don't you have any real aunts and uncles, or cousins, or grandparents?"

"My mother had a brother and a sister, but her

brother died when he was little and the sister lives over in France. I never hear from her. Apparently, she thought my dad wasn't a good match for my mother and she was angry that she married him. Then she blamed him for her death. My mother's parents died in a plane crash about two years before I was born. My grandfather was the pilot and they think he had a stroke or something. My dad was an only child and his mom was a single parent who died of cancer years ago. So I suppose I might have a grandfather out there somewhere, but my grandmother never told anyone his name and no one has ever come forward. I'm not sure the guy even knew he was a father."

"I'm sorry," Duncan said.

I shrugged again. "I'll manage. I miss my dad something fierce but, in a way, I have a family with some of my employees and the customers who come in to the bar all the time. The Signoriello brothers are like uncles to me, and Debra has been like a sister. Cora has been a good friend, too."

Duncan straightened up suddenly and stared out the window. "It looks like Mrs. Alvarez is on the move." He started up the car and we waited as the woman got the little girl situated and then slid behind the wheel. When she pulled out, so did Duncan, trying to keep a discreet distance behind her. He let a couple of cars get between us but kept the blue sedan in sight.

"Well, either Davey Cooper isn't in the Alvarez house or she left him there alone," I said.

"I don't think he's there. But, with any luck, Mrs. Alvarez will take us to him."

We tailed her car through city streets for five minutes or so, Duncan deftly dodging in and out of traffic. She got onto Interstate 94, and exited from there onto Interstate 43 heading north a few miles later.

"Do you think she's making a run for it?" I asked Duncan.

"I don't know what the hell she's doing. But she's playing it smart, staying just under the speed limit and driving carefully. I don't even have a reason to pull her over. So I guess we'll have to see where she takes us."

We followed her past the communities of Shorewood and Whitefish Bay, bastions of the rich and well-to-do. After about seven miles, she exited and followed several more roads, making a couple of turns. When she finally reached her destination, it was a place neither of us had anticipated and it brought our pursuit to a grinding halt.

Chapter 28

"I never would have guessed she was coming here," I said as we sat outside the gates of an elite country club. "How can she afford a membership?"

"Maybe her husband works in the place." Duncan pulled up to the gate and flashed his badge at the guard, who looked duly unimpressed. "I'm looking for a Mr. Alvarez," Duncan said.

"Are you a member here, sir?"

"No."

"Then I'll be happy to let Mr. Alvarez know you were asking for him. Your name?"

I could tell Duncan was fuming. "Mr. Alvarez is a person of interest in a case I'm investigating involving both a murder and a kidnapping. I need to speak with him."

"As I said, I'll let Mr. Alvarez know. Would you like to leave a contact phone number?"

"Listen, you jack donkey," Duncan said irritably, jumping out of the car and getting in the guard's face. "A little boy is missing and his mother has been murdered. If anything happens to that little boy because you are jerking me around and pretending you have some kind of authority, I'll personally see to it that you are brought up on obstruction charges." He glanced down at the guard's name badge and then added, "So think very carefully about this, Roger."

Roger did. I could see the indecision stamped on his face. "If I let you in here, I could lose my job," he said.

"If you don't let me in, I'll see to it that you lose your job."

Roger was stuck between the proverbial rock and hard place and he began to sweat despite the chill in the air. I understood his dilemma. No one wants to lose their job, but this was the maddest I'd ever seen Duncan and it was a scary sight. Finally, Roger made his decision.

"Fine," he said. "Go on in."

"Where can I find Mr. Alvarez?"

"He works in the fitness building. You'll probably find him there."

After getting some brief directions from Roger, Duncan got back in the car. Once Roger opened the gates, we drove onto the compound and followed the signs to the fitness building. We knew we were in the right area when we saw Mrs. Alvarez's car in the parking lot. I expected the guard to call and warn the Alvarezes that we were coming, but either he hadn't or he wasn't able to get through in time.

We found Mr. Alvarez and his wife, along with the little girl we had seen at the house, standing off to one side in a large open fitness area that was furnished with all the latest in workout machinery. Two men and four women were on the treadmills nearby, the women all dressed in trendy, expensive workout wear. There were also a few men working a circuit of the other equipment in the room.

Fortunately, Mrs. Alvarez had her back to us. Had

she seen us coming, I suspect she might have tried to make a run for it. As it was, we were able to catch her completely unaware and when she turned around and saw us, her eyes shot daggers at us. "What are you doing here?" she shrieked. "You can't come in here."

A tall, blond Adonis-type wearing tight-fitting white shorts and a green T-shirt that was a size or two too small for him—presumably to show off his assets—quickly approached.

"Is there a problem here, Alberto?"

Juanita Alvarez didn't give her husband a chance to answer, something I suspect happened a lot at home. "These people don't belong here," she said to the Adonis. "They are harassing us."

Adonis gave us a calm but questioning look and Duncan flashed his badge at the man.

"I'm here on official police business," Duncan said, and Adonis shifted his inquiring gaze back to the Alvarezes.

"We have nothing to say to you," Juanita said, her voice laced with venom. She pointed her finger at us in a jabbing motion as she spoke.

"Juanita, please," Alberto said. "Do not make a scene."

While I was focused on the action going on before me, I also noticed something else that piqued my attention: a very loud squeaking sound identical to the one I had heard in the backseat of Belinda Cooper's car.

"How can I help you, Officer?" Alberto asked.

"I am looking into the death of Belinda Cooper and the kidnapping of her two-year-old son, Davey."

Alberto squinted in thought and then said, "Are you talking about that missing child on the television this weekend?"

"Alberto, don't talk to them," Juanita harangued.

Then she whirled on Duncan. "We have nothing to say to you."

I looked around and saw that we had attracted the attention of the other people in the room. Adonis—who seemed far more interested in having this little tête-à-tête take place somewhere out of eye and earshot of the members in the room than he did in the fate of the little boy—said, "Might I suggest that you discuss this matter elsewhere, somewhere private?"

"I don't see how we can help you, Officer," Alberto said. "Why would we know anything about this death or the little boy?"

Duncan shifted his attention to Juanita. "Does your husband know about all the late nights you spent with Jamie Cooper?"

Juanita paled. Alberto looked over at his wife with a confused expression. "What is he talking about?" The little girl, who had been hiding behind her mother's legs, started to cry.

"Nothing, Alberto. I told you, don't talk to the cops. They always make innocent people like us look guilty."

"You have been working during those nights you were gone, right?" Alberto said. "You said the hospital needed some help on the night shifts."

"Of course," Juanita snapped. "How else would I be able to make the extra money?"

Adonis, who was shifting his weight nervously from one foot to the other, said, "You really need to take this discussion somewhere else."

I looked at Alberto and asked, "What is your daughter's name?"

"Sofia," he said.

At the same time, Juanita said, "None of your business." Apparently, she had forgotten that she had said the name earlier when we were at her house. At least now we knew the name she had used then wasn't a made-up one.

I ignored Juanita and once again addressed her husband. "Alberto, tell me your daughter's name is something else. I want you to lie to me."

He gave me a puzzled look. "You want me to lie? Why?"

"Please, I know it sounds like an odd request, but please indulge me."

"Damn it, Alberto," Juanita said. "Stop talking to these people. You are going to get us into some kind of trouble."

Alberto eyed his wife with the first hint of suspicion. He shifted his gaze to me and said, "My daughter's name is Lolita." With this statement his voice, which up until now had tasted like peppery cinnamon, switched to a bland pasty taste, as if I'd just eaten a teaspoonful of wet flour. "What is this all about?" he asked, looking worried. He was back to peppery cinnamon. "Why are you focusing on my family for this?"

I leaned over and whispered into Duncan's ear. "I don't think he knows."

Duncan nodded and stood there for several seconds, thinking. Adonis was even more agitated now, eager to make all of us go away. Most of the people who were exercising had given up the pretense of not listening. They had stopped what they were doing and their attention was now completely focused on us. Then Duncan's phone buzzed. He took it out, looked at the caller ID, and said, "Excuse me a second. I need to take this."

He answered the call, said, "Albright," and then listened. I could hear the buzz of a voice in the background and I had a slight metallic taste in my mouth, which I knew from past experience was a synesthetic response to the faint metallic tones I could hear coming over the line. I heard enough to tell that it was a man on the other end, but I couldn't make out any words. Duncan said nothing, but his expression changed suddenly. He squeezed his eyes closed, grimaced, and sighed. Then he said, "Thanks," and disconnected the call.

Juanita had turned to Alberto and rattled off something in Spanish while Duncan was taking the call. I wasn't able to understand most of it, but I could tell she was pleading with him and I heard the word *abogado*. This sounded enough like the Italian word *avvocato*—which I knew from hanging with the Signoriello brothers meant lawyer or attorney—that I guessed what the gist of Juanita's plea was.

Alberto seemed to sense that maybe it was time to be less forthcoming because he then said, "I wish to speak with an attorney before answering any more questions."

Juanita was obviously pleased by this and she shot us a look of victory.

Duncan sighed, clearly disappointed. "Then I suggest you obtain an attorney at your earliest convenience because we will be talking to you again. And do not try to leave town. We will be watching you."

We turned to go, leaving a shell-shocked-looking Alberto and a frightened-looking Juanita behind.

"Aren't you going to take her to the station or something?" I asked when we were out of earshot. "You can't just let her go."

"I don't have much choice. I don't have anything to hold her on and I'm betting she won't come down to the station willingly. Even if she did, I'm sure she'll lawyer up and clam up."

"What about showing her picture to Jamie Cooper? Wouldn't that give you something to use against her if he identifies her as Valeria Barnes?"

"That's not going to work."

I started to object some more but a sign I saw stopped me in my tracks as a realization hit me. "Hold on," I said, grabbing Duncan's arm. "I want to check on something." I steered him down a hallway to a door with a window in the top of it. I peered through the window and saw a large indoor swimming pool on the other side. I opened the door and went inside, Duncan following.

"This is the smell," I said, breathing in the warm, humid, chlorine-scented air. There were three people in the pool swimming laps and they either didn't know we were there or didn't care. "The squeaky finger sound is very loud in here."

"You mean the chlorine smell?"

I nodded.

"If Alberto tends to or uses the pool, it would make sense that he would smell of chlorine, but what about Juanita?"

"Who's to say she doesn't use it?" I said. "Or, I suppose the smell could carry from him to her, especially if he spends a lot of time handling pool chemicals. That might be why the smell was fainter on her."

"They're tied up in this thing somehow, at least she is," Duncan said. "My gut knows."

"I agree. That's why I can't believe you're just letting them go. Can't you at least set up someone to watch them?"

"With all the overtime we have in on this case already, I doubt they'll approve a surveillance team just because you said the woman smells like bleach and bears a resemblance to our sketch, especially since we haven't seen any sign of Davey."

"But what about Jamie Cooper? If he identifies Juanita as Valeria, won't that be enough?"

Before he could answer, Adonis came in. "Is there anything else I can help you folks with?" he asked with curt politeness. "I don't want to disturb our guests any more than we already have."

"There is one thing," Duncan said. "Who's responsible for maintaining this pool? You know . . . the chemicals and all that stuff?"

"That would be Mr. Alvarez," Adonis said. "Anything else?" Clearly he wanted us gone.

"No, thank you," Duncan said. "We'll be going now." He took hold of my hand and steered me out of the pool room and toward the exit. Once we were outside and safely out of earshot of Adonis, I said, "You didn't answer me on the Jamie thing."

"That's not going to work out like we hoped," he said. "Jamie Cooper is dead."

Chapter 29

As Duncan drove us back to town, I sat in the car in stunned silence and listened as he told me what had happened.

"When someone went to show Jamie Cooper the picture of Juanita Alvarez, they found him dead in his jail cell, a victim of aspiration. The working theory—at least until an investigation and autopsy can be done—is that he vomited again and then had a seizure, or perhaps he vomited while he was having a seizure. The seizure was most likely a by-product of his withdrawal from alcohol and he choked on his own vomit." Duncan's tone was a mixture of frustration, sadness, and anger.

We rode the rest of the way in silence, each of us lost in our own morbid thoughts. When we got back to the bar, Duncan dropped me off out front, saying that he might stop in later, but for now he wanted to focus on the case and dig up what he could about Alberto and Juanita Alvarez.

The bar was busy and I saw that the Capone Club table had expanded to twice its usual size. There were a lot of new faces along with several of my regulars, and I was delighted to see food and drinks in front of all of them.

Debra was still working because, she informed me, Missy had called in sick. She also told me how the Signoriello brothers' riddle for the day had been a big hit with everyone and had been told several times so that new arrivals could take a crack at solving it. The brothers had stayed in the bar all day long and they were still there, enjoying their starring role in the day's puzzle.

After meeting and greeting the folks at the Capone table, I caught Cora's eye and nodded toward my office. She gathered up her laptop and joined me there a few minutes later. I filled her in on what we had discovered and she beamed with pride when she realized that her sleuthing abilities may have helped us get a leg up on the case.

"There was something Juanita said to her husband when he asked her if she really had been working at night," I told Cora. "She said, of course she had been, otherwise how would she have been able to make the extra money. I don't suppose you have any way to look into their finances."

"Give me a little time," she said. "I'll pull a credit report on them, see what accounts they have in their names, and take it from there. But if the money was kept as cash, I might not be able to find anything."

After telling her the sad news about Jamie Cooper, I left Cora to do her thing and headed back out to the bar. A group of off-duty cops had come in and they were seated at the Capone table, working on the Signoriello riddle. I offered breaks to the employees who were on duty, and told Debra she could go home if she wanted and I would fill her place. Debra thanked me, but then opted to stay, stating that her teenaged boys were eating her out of house and home and she could use the money to augment her five-hundred-dollar-a-week grocery bill.

At a little after seven, Kevin Baldwin came in and his arrival was greeted with a chorus of welcomes from the Capone Club table. He'd been gone for a couple of weeks because his mother had passed away and after he was done fielding all the greetings and condolences from everyone at the table, I offered him a drink and asked him if he would step into my office for a couple of minutes.

"I don't know, Mack," he said, looking wary. "The last time you invited me into your office, it didn't go so well for me." Kevin, like me and several of the patrons of my bar, had been a suspect in Ginny's murder. As such, he had undergone an intense interrogation in my office when Duncan was investigating the case.

"I know, and I'm sorry," I said to him. "But this is nothing like that. I promise."

Once I had him in the office and Cora had done her share of the greeting-and-condolences thing, I told him about the Cooper case and our suspicions about the Alvarez family. "I was thinking that it might be helpful to get a look at their trash," I said to him. "To see if there is anything in it that suggests that little boy has been or might still be with them."

"Where do they live?"

I gave him the address.

"That should be easy," he said. "The trash gets picked up in that neighborhood tomorrow. I'll call the guys who have that route and ask them to keep the Alvarez trash separate from the rest."

"Thanks, Kevin. I owe you one."

With that, Kevin went back out to join the others and I returned to my overseeing duties. Though the next few hours were pleasantly spent waiting on and conversing with my customers, the Cooper case was never far from my thoughts. I kept asking the cops who were in the place if they had heard anything new, but when I sensed they were getting tired of my constant questioning, I backed off. Twice I poked my head into my office to check on Cora, who was so into whatever she was doing she didn't hear me enter. I made sure she had food and plenty of Chardonnay to keep her going.

It was just before eleven when Duncan finally showed up, and I took him into my office where Cora was still at it on her laptop. As soon as the door was closed, I hit him up for any news.

"I don't have much to tell you," he said. "The public records for both Alberto and Juanita are squeaky clean. They are legal immigrants with no outstanding warrants, no crime histories, not even a parking ticket. And I can't get any bank information until the morning."

"I can," Cora said. "But I don't think it's going to be of any help. The Alvarezes' shared checking account shows the biweekly deposits from both of their paychecks and no unusual expenditures that I can see."

"How did you—?" Duncan started to ask; then he shook his head and said, "Never mind."

"The only other thing I turned up was a cosigner on Juanita's car loan four years ago, a woman named Margaret Heine. Apparently she was a practicing attorney at one time here in town, but she has since either retired, or quit, or moved on. At first I thought she might have died, but I wasn't able to find any evidence of that. She simply disappeared about three years ago. Then I got to thinking about how women change their names when they get married, and I went searching through the county records looking for the name Heine and hit pay dirt. It seems Margaret Heine used to have another name until she got married four years ago, not long before she cosigned on that loan for Juanita. So I did a little more digging and came up with the name she'd had before the marriage. It's one you'll recognize," she said to Duncan. "It was Peggy Smith, and Peggy is often used as a nickname by women named Margaret."

"Oh!" I said, excited, looking over at Duncan. "Peggy Smith is the name of the lawyer who you said posted bail for Jamie Cooper when he had his first DUI. It can't be a coincidence that this woman is connected to both Jamie Cooper and Juanita Alvarez."

"Probably not," Cora said, "but good luck figuring it out. Peggy Smith managed to pull a disappearing act, too. I can't find any work, death, or finance records with the name Peggy Smith and the corresponding date of birth, for the past three years either, so Margaret Heine didn't revert back to the older name. It's as if the woman just appeared out of nowhere and then vanished."

"Mack's right," Duncan said, looking deep in thought. "The key has to be with the Alvarez family. I need to take another run at Juanita."

"How does someone just vanish?" I asked. "Especially in this day and age when it seems Big Brother is watching every move we make. I mean, if this Peggy Smith/Margaret Heine woman was practicing law just a few years ago, there should be some record of her somewhere, shouldn't there?"

"I have Margaret Heine's last known address," Cora said, typing away. "But the tax records show someone else living there for a little over three years now." After a few seconds, she said, "Here you go." She spun her laptop around and showed us what she had found.

Duncan scribbled down the address in his little notebook and then tucked it away in his pocket. "I'll check it out first thing in the morning. Want to come along?" he said, looking at me.

"Sure."

Duncan made a phone call to someone, asking them to look into the name Margaret Heine to see what they could find. When he was done, he looked at me and said, "I'm going to try to get a few hours of sleep tonight. I need to be sharp tomorrow. And I don't know about you, but I could use a nightcap to help me sleep."

We headed back out to the main bar area and joined the remaining group at the Capone table, which had shrunk in size. The threatened snow had finally started and it was coming down steady outside. Carter told us the Signoriello brothers had finally gone home, to "rest on the laurels of their clever riddle," and most of the newcomers had called it a night, typical for a weekday. Tiny, Alicia, and Tad Amundsen were still hanging out, although Alicia looked tired and ready to leave. I suspected the only reason she was still there was because Billy was tending bar. Two police officers who had finished their shifts were still there, too, and Dr. T had come in for a late-night toddy after finishing her stint in the ER.

The rest of the place was relatively empty with only a handful of tables still occupied, and Billy was taking a break and had joined the group at the Capone table with a sandwich.

With the snow still falling outside, I knew we weren't likely to get much more business into the bar that night, and after about an hour of conversation that centered around the Cooper case, with Duncan providing some limited updates, everyone was ready to go home.

"Let's close early," I suggested, worried about my employees getting home in the snow. Everyone agreed and, by one o'clock, the place was shut down for the night. Only Duncan remained.

We were standing in the kitchen where I had just finished washing the last of the dishes from the night's cleanup. He came up behind me and wrapped his arms around my waist, pulling me back against his body. His voice was a chocolate-flavored whisper in my ear.

"Mind if I spend the night here?"

"I thought you said you wanted to sleep."

"I'm thinking that certain activities might help me in that regard."

I leaned back against him, enjoying the fireworks his touch triggered in my body, fireworks that lasted until after three a.m.

Duncan's cell phone rang at a little after seven the next morning. Both of us groaned in unison as he rolled over to answer it. "Albright," he said, his voice hoarse. He listened for a few seconds and then got up, grabbed his pants, and took his notebook out of his pocket. He then grabbed a pen on the bedside stand and started writing something down. Then he said, "Thanks, Jimmy, I'll get right on it."

After disconnecting the call, he reached over and gave me a playful slap on the butt. "Time to get out of bed, wench," he said, arching one eyebrow. "I think we've just blown the Cooper case wide open."

Chapter 30

I was eager to hear the news, but when Duncan dragged me out of bed and into the shower—which briefly resurrected the fireworks—I momentarily forgot about it. Once we were dressed, Duncan finally shared his information while I brewed up a quick pot of coffee.

"I have good news and bad news. Which one do you want first?"

I thought a second and said, "The bad news."

"We got the final DNA results back from the toothbrush, and your instincts about it were spot on. The hair was only good for mitochondrial DNA, but we got a full profile from the toothbrush. And either both came from the same person or the hair is from a sibling of the person who used the toothbrush."

"Why is that bad news?"

"Because neither sample could have come from Davey Cooper."

"Why not?"

"Because they don't match Belinda's DNA at all. In fact, they are from a child of Hispanic descent."

"Juanita Alvarez again," I grumbled.

"Maybe . . . probably," Duncan said. "Except the DNA is from a boy, and the only child we saw with the Alvarezes was a girl."

"Okay, so what's the good news?"

"Jimmy is good friends with a retired judge and he called him last night to see what he might know about this Margaret Heine/Peggy Smith woman. It turns out she no longer practices law because she snagged herself a very rich husband two and a half years ago after she flew to Guam and got a quickie divorce from Mr. Heine. And she now has a new name: Meg Monroe. She no longer works, everything she buys is in her new name using her husband's credit cards or money, and she apparently managed to get her birth date changed on her DMV record, which is why we couldn't connect the two. She's trying to pass herself off as ten years younger than she is."

"Do you know where to find her?"

"I do," Duncan said. "And we're going to pay her a visit."

The coffee was done brewing so I poured us each a to-go cup and we headed out, taking Duncan's car.

The city snowplows had worked their magic during the night, and while the streets were a slushy mess with the morning rush hour traffic, the rest of the city was a sparkling bed of snowy white. The sky was clear blue, the sun was bright, and the snow was blinding.

"You seem pretty confident that this woman will be the key to everything," I said, a little puzzled by Duncan's enthusiasm.

"Oh, she is," he said. "It turns out that this isn't her third marriage. It's her fourth. And her first husband's name was Charles Cooper."

"Cooper? As in Jamie and Belinda Cooper?"

"Yep. Jimmy did some digging around and found a marriage certificate for Charles and Margaret Cooper. They had one kid, a boy. Mr. Cooper died in a car accident when the boy was five and Margaret remarried a year later to a man named Arnold Smith. She and Arnold had a girl a few months later. Apparently, that daughter was killed in a car accident seven years ago. Guess who was driving the car?"

"Jamie Cooper?" I said, feeling my own excitement grow.

"You got it. Jamie didn't lie to us, though technically it was his stepsister who died. He wasn't drinking when he had the accident, but he was charged with negligent homicide because he did have marijuana in his system, and he ran a red light. The judge Jimmy talked to said he'd heard that Peggy Smith had used her connections with the court system to pull some strings and get the charge dropped."

"But Jamie told us his parents were both dead."

"Yes, he did. It's because that's what he believed. His real father died when he was little and Arnold Smith died of a heart attack less than a year after the accident that took Jamie's stepsister. Apparently, Jamie's mother blamed Jamie for both deaths, and after she bailed him out following that DUI five years ago, she basically disowned him. What's more, it turns out this judge knows Margaret's last husband, Carl Heine, and he put Jimmy in touch with him. Carl told him an interesting story. It seems that Jamie called Carl three years ago because he was trying to track down his mother."

"That would have been around the time Belinda was pregnant with Davey," I said.

"You're right," Duncan said. "In fact, Carl said that was Jamie's impetus to try to reestablish a relationship with Margaret. Anyway, Carl and Margaret were separated at the time, and Carl knew Margaret wasn't keen on her son. She had told him that Jamie was a gang member and into drugs and that she was afraid of him. So Carl told Jamie that he and Margaret were separated and that he didn't feel comfortable giving him any additional information. Then Carl called Margaret to let her know the kid was looking for her. Three months later Margaret called Carl back and asked him to contact Jamie, say he'd had a change of heart, and give him Margaret's address. Carl thought it was an odd request but figured Margaret might have had a change of heart, so he did what she asked. Jamie then went to that address, which is the same one Cora found, hoping to find his mother. When he discovered someone else living in the house, he went next door to talk to a neighbor, to see if she might know where his mother had gone. The neighbor told him that she had some bad news—his mother had gone to California on vacation three months ago and had been killed in a car accident."

"Why would the neighbor tell him that?"

"Because she thought it was the truth. According to Carl, Jamie's mother set the whole thing up to make it appear that way because she didn't want her son to be able to find her. The neighbor told Jamie that his mother never returned from her vacation, and after a few weeks, some storage company came by and started emptying the place out. When the neighbor went over to ask what was going on, the workers told her the car accident story, stating that the owner of the house had been killed and that they had been hired by the woman's estate lawyer to clear the place out. The house went up for sale a few days after that and it sold a week later. By the time Jamie showed up, there was already another family living in the place. Jamie called Carl back and told him what he'd found. Carl knew Margaret wasn't really dead, but he assumed she did what she did so Jamie would stop looking for her."

"If both Carl Heine and this judge knew this information, why didn't either one come forward when Belinda was killed and Davey went missing?"

"Because they didn't make the connection. Margaret was only married to Carl for a little over a year and for a good portion of that time they were separated. Carl never met or saw Jamie; he only spoke on the phone with him. And Margaret never mentioned Jamie's last name so Carl assumed it was Smith.

"As for the judge, he remembered that Margaret Heine, who was Peggy Smith at the time, had a son and recalled her bailing him out after the DUI, and making the charges disappear after the accident that killed his sister, but he didn't remember the son's name and never made the connection between Margaret Heine and Jamie Cooper because he never knew Peggy-slash-Margaret as a Cooper."

"So Margaret, or Peggy, or Meg, whatever she calls herself, wrote off her only surviving child?"

"So it would appear."

"But that left her with no one," I said, struggling to understand how someone could do such a thing. Then it hit me and my eyes grew wide. "Except now there's a grandchild."

"Yes!" Duncan said enthusiastically, slapping my leg in a kudos gesture and making me see a distant swarm of bees.

"Davey is the only legacy she has left," I said, thinking it through. "He's her redemption, her last chance to make things right."

"Exactly! If she didn't want Jamie to know she was alive, or want him to have anything to do with Davey, she'd have to figure out a way to get her hands on the kid without anyone knowing. I don't know about you, but that sounds like potential motive to me."

"Yes, it does."

I sat in silence for a while, contemplating this new scenario. Duncan drove us across town and headed north in the same direction we'd gone when we'd followed Juanita Alvarez to the country club. Only this time, we ended up in a ritzy neighborhood of gated mansions that were built along the coast of Lake Michigan. Eventually, Duncan pulled up to a gate with a buzzer and a speaker. He rolled his window down and pushed the button. A moment later a tinny female voice came from the box. "Who is it, please?"

"Detective Duncan Albright with the Milwaukee Police Department. I'm here to see Meg Monroe."

There was a long period of silence. I imagined what might be going on in the house, whose stone façade I could only see a glimpse of past the trees at the top of the long circular drive beyond the fence. Eventually, the gate opened and Duncan drove in, stopping in front of a sprawling house with three levels. We got out of the car and climbed crescent-shaped stone steps to a huge front porch where the roof was supported by massive stone columns. Just as Duncan was about to ring the bell, the door opened, revealing a young, somewhat homely, blond woman who looked to be in her late twenties or early thirties. If not for the overly large nose, undersize chin, and pockmarked skin, she might have been pretty.

"My name is Sharon," she said. "May I see some ID, please?"

Duncan flashed his badge and Sharon took longer than what I felt was necessary to study it, making me wonder if she was stalling for time. I looked around the expansive grounds, searching for any sign that a child might be here, like some stray toys or a sled. I glanced over at the garage and wondered if there was a car in there with a child seat strapped into the backseat. Finally Sharon shifted her gaze to me. "And you are . . . ?"

"She's my assistant," Duncan said.

Sharon seemed amused by this but said nothing more. She stepped aside and waved us into a huge foyer with a marbled floor and a wide, winding staircase. The ceiling above us was three stories high and a crystal chandelier that looked bigger than Duncan's car hung down from it, stopping nearly level with the second floor.

"Mrs. Monroe will see you in her office," Sharon said.

"Her office?" Duncan echoed. "Does she work?"

"She works very hard managing her and her husband's various charities."

Ah, yes, I thought. *The working life of the filthy rich. Must be nice.*

"Please follow me."

We passed through the foyer into a sitting room that looked like it was rarely used. It was furnished with antiques and there was a huge stone fireplace on the wall to our left. From there we went through another door and down a long hallway, past several closed doors. Near the end of the hall, there was an open doorway on our right and Sharon stopped here and gestured for us to go inside. I heard a faint sound as we approached the door, one that piqued my curiosity. I tucked it away for now and, as we entered the room, Sharon disappeared back the way we had come. I had a feeling she wouldn't go far.

Meg Monroe was a tiny woman with a fashionable bob in platinum blond carefully coifed into place, and makeup that was artfully applied. She was wearing buff-colored stretch pants that revealed slender, toned legs, a royal blue sweater with a cowl neck, and blue pumps. Her light blue eyes looked icy, but her demeanor was warm and welcoming. She got up from a leather chair behind an antique desk and came around to greet us.

"Detective Albright," she said with a smile that looked genuine even though I doubted she was happy to see us. She shifted those icy blues my way. "And you are . . . ?" She gave me a quick head-to-toe perusal that left me feeling underdressed and gauche.

"This is Mackenzie Dalton, my assistant," Duncan said.

"An assistant? How quaint. I guess the city coffers must be well-endowed these days if the police can afford assistants." She looked back at Duncan and her smile broadened. "How may *I* be of assistance to you, Detective?"

Duncan ignored the not-so-subtle jibe and said, "I'd like to ask you some questions regarding a recent murder in the city."

Meg Monroe clutched a hand to her chest. "A murder? How awful. I'm not sure how I can be of any help to you, but go ahead and ask your questions. Please, have a seat."

Duncan didn't budge, so neither did I.

"Suit yourself," Meg said with a shrug. She backed up a step or two and leaned against the front edge of her desk.

"Are you related to Jamie Cooper?" Duncan asked, getting right to it.

There was the barest hint of a flinch, a tiny muscle twitch in one of her lower eyelids. "Who?" she said, and the smile faltered ever so slightly.

"I know who you are," Duncan said. "And I know that you're Jamie Cooper's mother."

Meg let out a little chuckle of amusement and pushed herself away from the desk. She turned away from us and walked over to a side window, gazing out at a snow-covered expanse of lawn. "Detective, I'm sure you're very good at what you do, and I hope you can solve this murder you mentioned. But I don't know what you're talking about."

"Cut the crap, Meg," Duncan said, "Or should I say Margaret. Or Peggy?"

Meg's shoulders stiffened ever so slightly, but she kept her back to us. I took advantage of her distraction to look at the top of her desk. There was an open laptop computer but I couldn't see the screen without going behind the desk, something I doubted Meg would let me do. Aside from the various typical office implements—a stapler, a tape dispenser, a paper clip holder that looked like it was made from carved ivory, and a metal rack with two shelves that were filled with papers that appeared to be letters—the only other objects on top of the desk were a cell phone and a Rolodex.

"I've never liked being called Margaret," she said in her cultured tone, still staring out the window.

I leaned a little to one side and saw that the Rolodex was open to the *W* section, and the card I could see had *Winston Children's Home* written on it, along with an Illinois address and phone number.

Duncan saw what I was doing and he moved closer to Meg, putting himself between her and me should she turn around. As soon as he did so, I grabbed the *A* tab on the Rolodex and flipped it over. I quickly paged through several cards until I reached one that made my heart skip a beat. I flipped it over so it wouldn't be the first thing Meg saw when she next used the Rolodex, but the name on the following card made my heart skip again. So I grabbed the *W* tab and returned the roll to that section. It was a move made none too soon. Meg was on the move.

She turned and marched over to the door of her office and stood there looking at the two of us. "I'm sure I don't know what you're talking about, Detective," she said, her tone now haughty. "So I would appreciate it if you would leave. Unless you have a search warrant."

It was a gutsy move, and given her legal background, I suspected it was also a knowing one.

Duncan didn't move and I stood beside him, trying not to look guilty, and hoping Meg hadn't seen me pawing through her Rolodex.

"Do I need to call the mayor?" Meg said, clearly irritated now. "Because my husband is a good friend of his. I'm sure he'd be interested in hearing how the Milwaukee police now get to bring assistants along when they go out and harass innocent people."

"Fine, have it your way," Duncan said coldly. He turned and headed for the door, while I followed on his heels. I could feel the icy glare of Meg boring through my back as we stepped over the threshold and into the hallway. That's when I noticed that sound again.

I stopped and turned around abruptly, nearly causing Meg to bump into me as she trailed us into the hall.

"Mrs. Monroe, do you have a pool?"

She cocked her head to one side and gave me a curious look. "Why do you want to know that?"

"Well, do you?" I pressed.

"Yes. We have an indoor lap pool down on the ground level. Why?"

"Is it beneath this part of the house?" I turned back and saw Duncan eyeing me with curiosity.

Meg huffed her irritation. "I really don't have time

for these inane questions of yours," she said. "You need to leave. I'm a very busy woman."

I had been right in thinking that Sharon wouldn't go far once she delivered us to Meg. She was hovering partway down the hall.

"Sharon, please see the detective and his assistant out," Meg said, saying the word *assistant* with a mocking tone. She then turned around and went back into her office, slamming the door behind her.

Sharon showed us to the front door, closing it behind us with a little more decorum than Meg had shown. As we descended the stone steps, I looked over toward the end of the house where Meg's office was located. The land beneath that part of the house was a downward slope, allowing for a basement with an exit on ground level. Beneath the windows of Meg's office, where I was willing to bet she stood watching us, was a solarium-style room. I nodded toward the floor-to-ceiling windows and said, "Look over there. I'm betting that's where the pool is."

Duncan waited until we were seated inside the car and pulling away before he spoke. "Did you see anything interesting in that Rolodex on her desk?"

"I sure did. I took a peek at the *A* section and guess whose name I saw on one of the cards?"

"Alvarez."

"Bingo. She had both Juanita's and Alberto's names on it, along with their address and phone numbers. And that's not all. When I flipped that card down so it wouldn't be the first thing she saw, guess whose name was on the next one?"

I had him puzzled with this question and he frowned as he tried to think. He gave up after only a few seconds. "I have no idea. Whose?"

"It was someone we both know very well, one of my regular customers." I waited to give him another chance, but he clearly wasn't in the mood for the game.

"Just tell me," he said.

So I did. "It was Tad Amundsen, Milwaukee's financial advisor to the rich and famous."

Chapter 31

We drove back to the bar and fixed ourselves a late breakfast using the bar kitchen. While Duncan was cooking, I placed calls to both Cora and Tad, telling them what we needed. Tad was reluctant to help at first, stating that it would be a violation of his fiduciary responsibilities to delve into one of his client's finances and share the information with us. I handed the phone to Duncan, who assured him that we wouldn't expose him as a source in any way, and when we told him who it was we wanted him to look into, he finally agreed.

"That Monroe woman is a bitch, and she's good friends with my wife," he said. Tad's wife was not high on his list of favorite people. "It will be a pleasure to take her down."

Once we were settled in at a table to eat, Duncan said, "I know Meg Monroe is behind this. It figures that she would try to mess with the DNA evidence, given her legal background. She knows what the procedures are in a case like this."

"But surely she must have known that the DNA would be compared to Belinda's."

"Probably, but I'm guessing she either hoped we wouldn't do the comparison, or figured at the least it would complicate things and slow down our progress in the investigation."

"It's a good thing Tad hates his rich wife so much."

"It's also a good thing you snuck a peek at that Rolodex. I'd like to have another chat with Juanita Alvarez, but I doubt she'll cooperate. Still, I think I'm going to send someone to get her and invite her down to the station for a chat."

Duncan made the call and we finished our breakfast. After cleaning up after ourselves, I started my morning prep for opening. A little after ten, Duncan gave me a kiss and headed out, saying he'd check back in later.

The next hour crawled by as I waited for opening time. When Pete and Debra came in at ten-thirty, I artfully dodged their questions when they asked if I had any news about the Cooper case. At eleven, we unlocked the doors and within half an hour, Carter and the Signoriello brothers had arrived. It was Wednesday, which is Larceny Day, and that meant the discounted drink of the day was a Ginger Snap made with Larceny Bourbon. Carter announced that he had come up with a riddle for the day and we listened as he recited it.

"The wealthy owner of a castle is throwing a masquerade party. There is a man who wants to rob a very valuable painting from the castle, but the entrance is guarded and in order to get inside, he needs to know the password. So he dresses as a minstrel and gets himself an empty violin case he intends to use to stash the rolled-up canvas from the picture. In order to figure out what the password is, he hides in some nearby bushes and listens as other guests arrive.

"The first guest is a woman and the guard asks her, 'Do you know the password?'

"The woman says she does.

"So the guard says *twelve*, to which the woman responds *six*. The guard lets the woman in.

"The robber now thinks that the proper response is half of whatever number the guard says, but he decides to wait for one more guest to see if his theory holds out. The second guest is a man and when the guard says *six*, the man responds with *three* and is allowed to go inside.

"Convinced his theory is right, the robber finally approaches the door and when the guard says *ten*, the robber confidently responds with *five*. The guard tells him he is wrong and he is then immediately taken prisoner. What should his answer have been?"

Joe Signoriello jumped in with, "I know, it's the numbers on a clock. The correct answer is whatever number is opposite the one stated."

"That can't be right," Frank said, rolling his eyes at his brother. "If it was, the answer to six would be twelve, not three."

"Oh, right," Joe said, looking dejected.

Before anyone else could offer up an answer, Cora came into the bar carrying her laptop. "I have something," she said, and despite protests from the others who wanted to know what it was she had, I ushered her into my office.

"What did you find?" I asked, as anxious as the others had been. "Any suspicious money transfers?"

Cora shook her head. "Tad was able to give me Douglas and Meg Monroe's bank account information, but I haven't been able to access them. Tad is still working on it. However, I did a little digging around online and found something interesting on Facebook."

Cora set down her laptop on my desk and settled into my chair while I wondered how on earth a social networking site was going to be of any help. She opened the computer and, as she typed something into it, said, "I don't want to say too much because I want your take on it."

I walked around behind the desk and peered over her shoulder. "Here we go," she said. "It turns out that Juanita Alvarez has her Facebook security options set at the highest level, but her password was painfully easy to guess." Cora shook her head and gave me a pitiful expression. "She uses her last name with the number one after it. I really thought she'd be smarter than that."

I looked at the page, which had Juanita's picture at the top and some innocuous posts featuring recipes, cartoons, and pithy sayings. There were also pictures of Alberto and their daughter.

"I was looking at some of Juanita's friends," Cora said, "and saw something interesting."

She clicked on one of the friend links and brought up another picture. Then she let me study it.

"Wow," I said after only a few seconds. "They taste almost exactly the same."

Cora gave me a quizzical smile.

"Visuals sometimes manifest as tastes for me, particularly pictures, TV, and movies, where the image isn't real life. Every image has its own unique taste, but Juanita's and this girl's picture both taste like freshly picked raspberries. There is a very, very slight difference, but it's barely noticeable."

"Good," Cora said. "Now look at this friend."

She clicked on another picture and within seconds of viewing it, I got another raspberry taste, though this one was also slightly different, a tiny bit tarter.

"They all taste like fresh raspberries. One is a little sweeter than Juanita's, and the other has a hint of tartness to it."

"What does that tell you?" Cora asked.

"That they look very much alike," I said. "They have the same shaped noses, the same dark hair, the same dark brown eyes, and even the shapes of their faces are the same. The teeth are a little different, and the haircuts aren't alike, but other than that . . ."

"What are the odds of that?"

"Well, from a visual perspective, I've seen people who look a lot alike, but other than identical twins, the only time two pictures taste so similar is when they are siblings who strongly resemble one another."

"I saw the similarities the instant I clicked on the pictures," Cora said. "And there's something else. Most of Juanita's posts are the typical social chatter, happy birthday wishes, congratulatory comments, responses to cute kid and animal pictures, that sort of thing. But with these two friends, she shares some private messages. Nearly all of them are like this one." She clicked back to Juanita's page and then to a private message sent from one of the look-alike girls. The look-alike had written: Hey, do you remember Mateo Gutierrez? He married Mia Hernandez even though he is ten years older than she is. She's only eighteen. And she's pregnant already!

Juanita's response, which was posted two days later, was: Of course I do. I will send them a gift right away. Beneath that she had typed two rows of numbers: 01241986-2145067210 on the first line, and 10141975-3127423450 on the second line. Then Juanita had written, Tell them Consuela Garcia and Anthony Perez say hi.

I frowned and looked at Cora. "What am I missing here?"

"Not much . . . yet. Check the date of the post. This exchange occurred nearly a year ago. Now look at this one." She then clicked on the next message in the exchange, from the look-alike girl: Mia and Mateo got your gift and are very grateful!

"Sorry, Cora, but I'm still not seeing it. What is the significance of the numbers?"

"I wondered about that, too, at first, but when I found three more messages with an exchange like this, also with a string of numbers, I started to wonder. All three say something like: *ran into so-and-so today and his thirtieth birthday is next week*. And then Juanita says she will send a gift and lists a string of numbers. Then she includes a closing line of some sort that mentions another name. The digits appear to be two separate numbers separated by a dash. In both messages, the first string of numbers is eight digits long. The second string of numbers is ten digits long and at first I thought they might be phone numbers. But when I tried calling the first one, I got a recording telling me that the number I dialed wasn't in service. The second one was for a restaurant in Canton, Georgia, and the third one was for a construction company in Dayton, Ohio.

"Then I noticed that all of those second string numbers ended in a zero, and I started to wonder if perhaps the zero was superfluous. If you take away the zero, you have nine digits left, and what common number contains nine digits?"

"Social Security numbers?"

"Right. And the first string of numbers could easily be dates—birth dates in fact."

"In fact? You verified this?"

"I did," Cora said, looking very pleased with herself. "Those Social Security numbers and birth dates happen to belong to people who are dead, and not just any dead people, but babies and children who died at Milwaukee Memorial Hospital back in the sixties, seventies, and eighties. Except they've recently been resurrected."

"She's creating false IDs?" I said, finally making the connection.

"That's what I think, yes. I think she's using them to bring people into the country from Mexico, because these two friends of hers on Facebook, the ones who look so much like her? Their names and birthdays—at least the day and month, which is all they have listed on Facebook—also belong to people who died at Milwaukee Memorial years ago. I bet twenty bucks those two girls are her sisters and they established fake identities so they could get into the country."

"Juanita used her access to old medical records at the hospital to help them."

"It sure looks that way, and since the death records are public, Duncan should be able to obtain them. There are enough coincidences here to get a search warrant, I would think. Maybe even an arrest warrant."

"Have you told him yet?"

Cora shook her head. "I wanted to test you with those pictures first, to make sure I wasn't seeing a resemblance because I wanted to, but because there really was one. I'll call him now."

I stood and listened as she relayed her information to Duncan over the phone. It took her awhile to explain it all and without the visual of the Facebook pages, I imagine Duncan had a hard time understanding at first. When she was done, she listened for a minute and then said, "Okay, I will," and hung up. "Duncan was on his way here when I called him. He said he'll be here in a few minutes and to tell you he has more good news and bad news."

"Great, that again," I said.

Cora gave me a curious smile, and though I'm sure she would have liked me to explain further, I kept mum.

While we waited, Cora showed me the other posts on

Facebook. As promised, Duncan showed up about three minutes later.

"So which one do you want first this time, the good news or the bad news?" he said as I shut my office door.

"Let's go with the good news first this time," I decided.

"Tad has found something that might help us."

"That's great! What's the bad news?"

"Juanita Alvarez has flown the coop."

Chapter 32

"Oh, no," I said to the news about Juanita. "Where did she go?"

Duncan shrugged. "I'm not sure. Her husband is still here. We found him at the house, but he told us that Juanita took their daughter and split after they had a big fight at the country club last night, right after we left. She didn't come home, and she didn't show up for work this morning, either, or call in. So I can only assume she's in the wind. Alberto says he has no idea where she might have gone and, oddly enough, when I asked him if Juanita had any family she might have gone to stay with, he said her family were all back in Mexico."

"Did you believe him?" I asked.

"I did. He seemed genuinely shaken up by it all. I talked with him at length and I don't think he knows what Juanita has been up to. But he did confirm, once I promised I wouldn't turn him over to the IRS, that he not only takes care of the country club pool, he has a number of private accounts he does pool care for, all of them for cash under the table. And included in those accounts are the Monroes. He said Juanita often helps him out with these private cash jobs and that she was the one who typically did the Monroe pool."

"Hence the chlorine smell," I said, feeling redeemed. "What did Tad turn up?"

"Several things. First, he gave me bank account information for the Monroes and I had a look at their recent transactions. It seems that Douglas is the only name on the accounts—keeping with Meg's desire to fly under the radar, I imagine—but she is an authorized signer for his checks. And even more interesting was the discovery that she got herself a new Social Security number for the bank's records to go along with her new date of birth and name. I traced that Social Security number and discovered that it really does belong to a woman named Meg Monroe who is the same age our Meg is claiming to be. But that Meg Monroe lives in San Francisco. Coincidentally, she was born here in Milwaukee at the same hospital where Juanita works. That leads me to assume that Meg got the number from Juanita and the two of them are in cahoots together."

"Cahoots?" Cora said, smiling flirtatiously. "How cute."

Duncan frowned at her and then continued with his story. "Anyway, we found two ten-thousand-dollar checks written to the same charity within the past two weeks from one of Douglas Monroe's accounts, and Meg was the one who wrote them."

"So?" I said.

"The charity they were made out to only exists on paper. It's called CALM, supposedly an acronym for Cleanup All of Lake Michigan. And after tracking down the ownership of the organization, all I came up with was a dummy corporation called M&M Enterprises."

"M&M? As in Meg Monroe?" Cora said.

"That's my guess," Duncan said. "I don't know if Meg's husband has a clue about what she's doing. But I'm betting that money went to Juanita Alvarez. We had a look at the Alvarezes' bank accounts, too, and there aren't any unusual deposits, so I'm guessing Juanita kept the money as cash. And that means we're likely to have trouble finding her."

"You think Meg Monroe hired Juanita to kidnap her grandson?" I said to Duncan.

"I do."

"Do you think she wanted Juanita to kill Belinda, or was that solely Juanita's doing?"

"I don't know," Duncan said. "But clearly Juanita knows how to create a false identity, and I'm betting that Meg either knew what Juanita was doing and was helping her with the illegals she was bringing over, or Meg found out what Juanita was doing and asked her to do the same thing for her and Davey."

"Which means she probably has a new identity established for both herself and Davey," Cora said.

"Yes, and that's good news and bad news for us, too," Duncan said. "It certainly bodes well for the boy's safety and future, but it also means it will be painfully easy for them to disappear. Given Meg's resources, I'm sure she has everything planned down to the last detail."

"Then why hasn't she disappeared already?" I asked. "I mean, if she used the money she took from her husband for this fake charity to pay Juanita to kidnap Davey, then why is she still hanging around? He's been missing for several days and I would imagine she had everything ready to go the instant she got her hands on the boy. Why would she wait?"

"That's an excellent question," Duncan said. "And I think I know the answer because of what Tad found. While going over Douglas Monroe's retirement portfolio this morning, he noticed that one of the funds was missing a substantial chunk of money—fifty grand to be exact. And Douglas doesn't know anything about it."

"Oh, that sneaky bitch, Juanita," Cora said. "She's holding the kid for ransom, to get more money out of Monroe."

"That's my guess," Duncan agreed.

"If that's the case, isn't it likely that Juanita is still somewhere in the area?" I asked. "If she still has Davey, he must be somewhere close by."

"Maybe," Duncan said doubtfully. "If Juanita was really smart, she'd be as far from here as possible and get some locals to do her dirty work. But I'm thinking she wants to get her hands on that money personally, with no go-betweens to mess things up. Even if she has distanced herself, I'm betting Davey is somewhere close by."

"I think those look-alike Facebook friends, who I'm betting are Juanita's sisters, would be a good place to start," Cora said. "I looked them up and they both live in the area." She handed him a piece of paper with the addresses written on it.

Duncan took the info and gave Cora a quick kiss on the cheek. "You rock, m'lady."

For the first time since I've known her, Cora blushed.

Duncan turned to me next but I didn't get a kiss, just an invitation. "Mack, will you come with me? If I need to question these women, I wouldn't mind having you there to help me interpret their responses."

Once again I had mixed feelings on the matter, but my desire to see little Davey brought home outweighed any reservations I had. And I sensed that we were closer now than ever before. So I said, "Sure, I'd be happy to."

Cora promised to keep us posted if she found anything else and, after checking in with my staff to let them know what I was doing, Duncan and I headed out.

When we were settled in his car, he started the engine to warm both it and us up, and then stared at the two addresses. "One of these addresses is in the same neighborhood that Juanita lives in. The other is across town near Brewer's Hill. I'm not sure which one to go to first."

"Go to the one closest to Juanita's house first," I said. "She knows that area better and I think she'd be more comfortable there."

"Fair enough. That's as good a logic as anything I can come up with."

We arrived at the first location, which was about six blocks from Juanita's house, a short while later. The home resembled Juanita's in that it was a bungalow dating back to the early half of the twentieth century with a tidy, well-manicured lawn. The curtains were all drawn, which I took to be both an encouraging sign and an ominous one.

Duncan parked in the street a few houses down, and called in his location with his cell phone. Then he turned off the engine and pocketed the keys. I started to open my door but he grabbed my arm to stop me. "Hold on a second," he said. "Let me think this through."

I sat patiently as Duncan stared out the windshield at the house. The windows began to fog up as the cold seeped into the car. Cold always tastes tart when I feel it, like a sour orange or lemon, which I've always thought was odd given that both the fruits and their respective colors tend to be associated with warmth.

"Tell you what. If you don't mind waiting here, I'm going to go up and knock on the door. I can't tell if anyone is home or not, but if they are and they let me in, I'll motion for you to join me once I've determined it's safe."

I nodded my agreement, resigned to sitting in the chilly air a little longer. I watched, hugging myself for warmth, as Duncan got out of the car and approached the house. He opened a small, knee-high gate in the white picket fence surrounding the front yard and climbed the steps to the front porch. My breath was making tiny clouds in the air as I exhaled, and I held it as Duncan knocked on the door. No one answered.

By the time I was forced to let my breath out, Duncan had walked over and tried to peer in through a front window. When he stepped off the front porch and headed around to the back of the house, my body relaxed, making me aware of just how tensed up I had been. He disappeared from my view and I took advantage of the moment to look around at the other houses.

My cell phone rang then and when I answered, I heard Kevin Baldwin on the line.

"Hey, Mack, I just wanted to let you know that I went through that trash from the Alvarez home like you asked."

"Did you find anything?"

"There were food items that would typically be for kids."

"That's not much help. The Alvarezes have a young daughter."

"Ah, that would explain the empty package for a doll. There was some junk mail addressed to Alberto Alvarez, and the usual items you'd find in any other house trash. The only thing I found that might be of help was a used box of hair dye in a black color. What color hair does the missus have?"

"She's dark haired, but not jet black. Was it a true black?"

"It was."

"Kevin, you rock! The next time you come into the bar, your meal is on me."

"Thanks, Mack. Let me know if there is anything else I can do for you or Duncan."

"I will." I disconnected the call and slipped the phone back into my coat pocket. Then I went back to staring out the windshield.

The minutes ticked by with no sign of Duncan's return, and the windows were now so fogged up I could barely see out of them. When I couldn't stand it any longer, I got out of the car and began walking toward the house.

From the sidewalk, my view of the side and backyards was limited until I had almost reached the far corner of the neighboring lot. That's when I finally saw Duncan.

He was lying on the ground alongside the house, blood seeping into the snow around him.

Chapter 33

I ran up to Duncan as fast as I could and knelt down beside him. There was an ugly gash on the side of his head that was still bleeding. Judging from the amount of blood on the snow around him, it must have bled fiercely initially, but the cold had slowed it down to a constant ooze. At least, I hoped it was because of the cold, and not because Duncan had no blood pressure.

He was breathing, but his eyes were closed and he wasn't moving. Panicked, I tried to roll him over, but he was too heavy and the snow kept bunching up behind him, thwarting my efforts. So I reached into my coat pocket for my cell phone, took it out, and dialed 9-1-1. That's when I heard the slam of a door.

I froze and looked in the direction of the noise, which had come from the back of the house, just around the corner. I couldn't see the back door from where I was, but I heard a female voice say, "Come on now, you two. We're going on an adventure."

Three figures emerged in the backyard. Two of them were tiny figures wearing snow pants and winter coats. Between them, holding their hands and directing them toward the rear portion of the yard and the house beyond, was Juanita.

I heard a faint, distant ringing followed by a voice coming from my phone and I slid it back into my coat pocket. Then I yelled, "Juanita Alvarez!"

Juanita froze in her tracks, her back to me, still facing the way she'd been headed. The two smaller figures turned to look at me, and I saw that one of them was Juanita's daughter, Sofia. The other was a little boy, smaller than the girl, with black eyebrows and jet black hair sticking out from beneath a woolen hat. He was carrying a dingy blue blanket, its tattered edges dragging in the snow. He was the right size for Davey Cooper, but his hair was the wrong color. Fortunately, I knew from my conversation with Kevin the reason for that and, even though I could only see a profile of his face, I knew it was him.

"Give me Davey Cooper!" I yelled at Juanita.

She turned to face me then and stood there a moment, chewing on her lip. "This is my friend's boy, Carlos. I'm taking him and Sofia to another friend's house to play."

"And for that you had to whack Detective Albright here on the head? He needs an ambulance," I said loudly, hoping the emergency operator was listening in. I got to my feet, wanting to be ready for a quick escape if I needed it or to make a quick pursuit.

"This is none of your business, lady," Juanita said.

"Detective Albright," I said loudly again, "is very much my business."

Davey wriggled loose from Juanita's grip and dropped to the ground, sitting in the snow. He began to cry.

"Carlos, it's okay," Juanita said, keeping up her façade and reaching down to grab his hand again. She pulled him back up to his feet.

Duncan moved then, pulling a splayed-out arm in toward his body, and I heard him moan.

Juanita saw and heard it, too, and the distraction was enough for the little boy to get away from her. He started to run across the snow toward me, but his feet got tangled in the blanket he was dragging with him, and he fell. Juanita let go of her daughter's hand and dashed after the boy, yanking him back against her while kicking the blanket away. Then she lifted him up and held him in one arm, causing him to go into a minitantrum, kicking his feet and screaming. "Mommy, Mommy!" he yelled, and at the sound of it, that strange, nasty taste I'd experienced at the Cooper house that first night came back to me. I knew then that it had been the residue from Davey's screams that had triggered it.

"Want my bumpy . . . my bumpy," Davey cried, reaching for and looking at the blanket on the ground.

"You and that damned bumpy," Juanita muttered.

I took a few steps forward and picked up the tattered blanket. Then I heard something, a sound I had only heard once before—when I'd been standing beside Davey's bunk bed. I realized now that it was the smell of this blanket, Davey's "bumpy" as he called it, that had triggered that sound. In essence, it was the smell of Davey himself.

As I looked at that little boy's terror-stricken face and thought about those photos of him and his mother back at the house, I knew there was no way I was going to let Juanita Alvarez leave with the child. Angry and desperate, I dropped the blanket and tried to make a lunge for Juanita, hoping to wrest the boy away from her. But my feet slipped in the snow and I fell to my knees. Juanita backed away several steps and glared at me, her face suffused with anger. Then she went suddenly pale. I realized she wasn't looking at me any longer; she was looking over and behind me.

I glanced over my shoulder, thinking that Duncan must have recovered, or that the cops had arrived, managing a miraculously speedy response. But it wasn't Duncan or the cops. It was Meg Monroe, holding a large canvas bag in one hand and a gun in the other. The gun was pointed straight at Juanita.

I shuddered and tasted something metallic. For a second, I thought I'd bitten the inside of my mouth and it was my own blood I tasted. But then I recognized it as a synesthetic taste, one I'd experienced many times before. It was the distant sound of a voice coming from the phone in my pocket. It boosted my spirits a little, but I wasn't sure it had come in time, or that the person on the other end had been able to hear what was going on.

Meg Monroe glanced down at Duncan's inert form with a faint smile and huffed her amusement. Then she turned her steely gaze back to Juanita. "Give me my grandson," she said, her voice as cold as the surrounding snow.

Juanita pulled the boy close to her chest with both arms and backed up a few steps. "Shoot at me and you run the risk of hitting him," she said, her voice low. So far, everyone but me was speaking in low tones, probably to avoid attracting attention from anyone in the neighboring houses. Carefully, slowly, Juanita backed up until she reached her daughter. "Get behind me, Sofia," she instructed, and the little girl hid behind her mother's legs. Davey stopped squirming and hung helpless in Juanita's arms, sobbing. "Do you have my money?" Juanita asked Meg.

"We had an agreement, you greedy bitch," Meg seethed through clenched teeth. "Twenty grand, all of which you have already. Plus all the money I fronted you for the other stuff." I sensed she would have loved to scream at Juanita and go all shrieking harridan on the woman.

"I don't think you are in a position to argue," Juanita said. "The price went up when I had to kill the boy's mother. Fifty grand or you will never see him again. I have a car parked in front of the house behind me and once I'm in it, we're gone."

Now it was Meg's turn to look indecisive, but she kept the gun aimed at Juanita, who was slowly backing up into the yard of the house behind her.

I tasted metal again and decided it was time for a desperate move. "That was very clever of you, hiding here at your sister's house," I said in a loud voice. I recalled how Duncan had phoned in his position and hoped that this would be enough information.

"How do you know who my sister is?" Juanita asked, looking mildly surprised but still taking one small step at a time back toward the house behind her.

"It was easy once we figured out that you were using death records from the hospital to create new identities for people. How many did you help across the border?"

"You know about that?"

"You didn't hide your tracks as well as you thought."

"Oh, cut the crap," Meg said from behind me. "You win, Juanita. I have your money right here in this bag. Just give me my grandson and it's all yours."

This was enough to make Juanita halt her retreat. She thought for a minute and then said, "Open the bag and let me see it."

Still holding the gun, Meg knelt down and set the bag on the ground. With one hand she unzipped it, keeping an eye on Juanita the entire time. When she had it open, she tipped it up, revealing a bunch of banded bills inside.

"Okay, close it back up and toss it over here," Juanita said.

"First let my grandson go."

"No way," Juanita said with a mirthless laugh. "You're the one holding the gun."

Meg zipped the bag closed and picked it up from the ground, but then she just stood there holding it.

"Throw her the money, Mrs. Monroe," I yelled. "It's your only grandson, your only remaining chance at a legacy. You've already paid her twenty grand, what's another fifty? I'm sure Douglas won't miss it given all the money he has."

"Shut up!" Meg snapped at me. "And quit yelling. There's nothing wrong with my hearing."

I watched as Meg weighed the options and saw it in her face when she made her decision.

"We'll use her as an intermediary," Meg said, gesturing at me. "I'll give her the money and you give her Davey."

"No way," Juanita said again. "Do you think I'm that stupid? There's no way she's going to give me the money. Now toss it over here or I swear you'll never see your grandson again."

Davey had quit sobbing and he hung limp in Juanita's arms. She pulled him close to her, preventing Meg from taking a shot without hitting the boy.

Resigned to her fate, Meg Monroe swung her arm and tossed the bag over my head. It landed in the snow with a soft *whump!* about five feet in front of Juanita, who then told her daughter, "Sofia, go run to the car and wait for me there. You know where it is, yes?"

Sofia nodded.

"Go! Now!"

Sofia turned and ran down between the two houses bordering the backyard. As soon as she was gone,

Juanita slowly walked toward the bag and picked it up, taking care to hold Davey in front of her as a shield the entire time.

"Put the boy down," Meg said.

"So you can shoot me? I don't think so. I'll leave him somewhere you can pick him up." With that, she started backing up again, much faster than before, still using Davey as a shield.

"We had a deal, Juanita. Give me the boy." Meg was clearly growing impatient.

Juanita just shook her head and kept back-stepping, so Meg upped her efforts.

"Okay, look," Meg said, "I'm putting the gun down on the ground." She bent over and did just that. Then she held her empty hands up in the air. "Please, Juanita, give him to me."

Juanita halted, eyeing the weapon. "Kick the gun away," she said, "and I'll let him go."

Meg kicked the gun and it slid across the snow. It ended up near Duncan's feet.

"Okay," Juanita said, and she set Davey down on the ground. He sat down on the snow, looking stunned, staring off at nothing, not moving a muscle. Juanita turned and started to run, but then a shot rang out and she dropped into the snow, writhing in pain.

"Are you crazy, Sharon?" Meg screeched, no longer caring who heard, after the sound of the gunshot had echoed between the houses. "You could have hit Davey."

I turned and looked to my left, where I saw Sharon, Meg's blond assistant, step into the backyard from the other side of the house. Meg was behind me and couldn't see her from where she was, so I assumed she had known Sharon was there all along. That must have been why she was willing to put the gun down and kick it away.

"I aimed high," Sharon said. "He was in no danger."

Davey was still a huddled heap in the snow, but he was no longer staring off at nothing. His eyes were focused on me—frightened, sad, appealing. I've never felt so desperately helpless.

"We need to get out of here," Meg said, hurrying over toward Duncan to fetch her gun. Just as she reached down for it, Duncan sprang up and grabbed her arm, yanking her down to the ground.

"Mack, run!" he yelled.

After that, everything seemed to happen in slow motion, though I know looking back that it had to have been mere seconds. I watched as Duncan and Meg wrestled with one another, and my gut told me to do what Duncan said. But when I looked back at Davey, I knew I couldn't leave him behind. Then I saw Sharon come charging across the back of the house. At first I thought she was going to make a grab for Davey. I started to get to my feet, determined to stop her from taking him—gun or no gun—but she headed for the corner of the house instead, and I knew then that she was running to help Meg.

I glanced over my shoulder again and saw that Duncan had managed to get to his feet. He had Meg wrapped in his arms in a bear hug, her back to him, but Meg wasn't giving up easily. She kicked and wriggled and tried to bite him on the arm through his coat sleeve, anything to get free. At least she didn't have a gun; it was still on the ground.

But Sharon did have one and she was almost by the struggling pair.

I screamed, "Duncan, watch out!" And as Sharon dashed past me, I lunged forward and grabbed her legs.

Sharon went sprawling in the snow face first, but she was quick to recover and get back on her feet. She whirled on me with a furious expression and I saw the gun she still held in her hand swing around and aim at my head.

"You bitch!" she yelled.

It was then that I realized my greatest fear about working for Duncan was about to come true: it was going to cost me my life.

The sound of the shot when it came seemed oddly distant to me, and I wondered if that was because I was dead already, or because that's what it sounded like when a synesthete died.

Chapter 34

It was Thursday afternoon and the bar was full. There was an air of excitement in the place, in part because of the resolution to the Cooper case, and in part because the last of the items I needed for the new section had arrived. I planned to open it to the public tomorrow but I was giving tours to certain select customers ahead of time.

The Capone Club was gathered in their usual corner of my bar, celebrating the successful end to the Cooper case. Everyone was there: Sam, Alicia, Holly, Kevin, Tad, Cora, Carter, Frank, Joe, Tiny, and Dr. T. Also present were Billy, Missy, and Debra, who were working, and a couple of new employees I'd hired: a bartender named Mike and a waitress named Linda, who were training. Several cops were there, too, including Tyrese and Nick. The only person missing was Duncan, but I was expecting him any time.

Yes, I was there, too, and no, I wasn't dead. But my encounter with Juanita, Meg, and Sharon was the closest I've ever come to being dead and I can say without hesitation that I hope to never come that close again.

My narrow escape was the current topic under discussion.

"It was a stroke of genius for you to leave your cell phone open after calling nine-one-one," Frank said to me. "It not only saved your life, it gave the police recorded evidence of both Juanita's and Meg's involvement. If Tyrese here hadn't arrived when he did and shot Sharon, you would have been mincemeat."

"I thought I was," I told the group. "I heard the shot and I remember thinking that it sounded like it was too far away. I figured it was just another one of my weird synesthetic experiences . . . my last, in fact. I had no idea Tyrese and Nick had responded as a result of my nine-one-one call."

"It was lucky the nine-one-one dispatcher was able to hear what was going on," Tyrese said. "But, to be honest, you should have stayed in the car."

"If I had, Davey might have never been found. And who knows what would have happened to Duncan."

"Duncan would have been okay, most likely," Nick said. "Juanita only knocked him out so she could get away with the kid. She said she had no intention of killing him. And I doubt Meg and Sharon would have done anything to him as long as he was out cold."

"There's something I don't understand," Tad said. "I saw this Juanita Alvarez woman on the news and she's not a big woman. How did she get the jump on Duncan in the first place?"

Nick fielded this one. "Juanita's sister and nephew had gone to the store and when Juanita saw Duncan come up and knock on the front door she knew she couldn't answer it. She figured he would eventually go around to the back, so she grabbed the fireplace poker, went out the back door of the house, and waited just around the corner for him. When he was walking down the side of the house, she jumped out and whacked him before he even knew she was there. Once she knew he was down, she ran back inside, grabbed the kids, and got their coats on so she could make a run for it. Just in case Duncan had somebody out front, she left out the back. She had already parked her car over on the next block in anticipation of just such an event."

"I'm glad Duncan is going to be okay," Holly said.

"He'll be fine," I told her. "He has a bunch of stitches in his head and a whopper of a headache, but his CT scan came back normal."

"He'll probably have a headache for a while," Tyrese said. "If not from that concussion he got, then from all the paperwork he has to do."

I had gotten a glimpse of some of that paperwork, along with some of the interrogations that had followed the arrests. I'd spent nearly the entire day at the police station yesterday after Duncan and I were released from the hospital. Other than a few minor scrapes, I was fine. It was Duncan who had borne the brunt of Meg's and Juanita's wrath. Juanita was going to be fine, too, eventually, but it would be awhile and a surgery or two before she was brought to justice.

Cora said, "Juanita was smart in a lot of ways, but taking on Meg Monroe wasn't one of them. Whose idea was it to put the hair in the brush and use the toothbrush from another child?"

"That was Meg," Nick said. "She told Juanita to brush her nephew's hair and leave the hair in the brush, which was new. Juanita took the old hairbrush with her. The toothbrush was new, too, and Meg told Juanita to rub it over the gums of the same kid. I guess she hoped that we either wouldn't compare the DNA from those items to Belinda, or if we did, it would take long enough to get the results that she would have time to disappear with the boy."

"And what will happen to the little boy now?" Joe asked.

"He's going to stay with Belinda's family in Ohio," I said.

Tad jumped in next. "So, Mack, that taste you experienced at the Cooper house—what was that?"

"I'm pretty sure it was from little Davey's cries. Juanita said the kid had put up quite a fuss, screaming and carrying on about his bumpy. She didn't know what that meant and in an effort to calm him down, she kept going about the house, trying different things she thought might be what he wanted. She collected some toys, some videos, even a box of juice from the fridge, but none of those seemed to work. When she went out to the garage to get the car seat, she set Davey down and he ran back to his bedroom and got a blanket from his bed. Once he had that, he calmed down and he kept calling it his bumpy. That's when Juanita figured it out. But then, after she loaded all the stuff she had into the car and went back for Davey, she found him standing in the hallway looking into his mother's bedroom. She grabbed him and headed for the front door, and that got him started again. He screamed at the top of his lungs as she took him out of the house and that's what the neighbor heard. I think the residue from those screams is what I picked up on."

"I'm surprised Juanita bothered to take all that stuff with her," Cora said. "It seems like a hassle and it delayed things. Plus, the neighbors might have seen her."

"It was dark and she used her sister's car," Tyrese said. "She was wearing all black clothing—black coat, black gloves, black boots, and a black wool cap. And she temporarily switched out the license plates on her sister's car with ones she took off another car. So even if someone had looked out and seen her or the car, they wouldn't have had any useful information. She knew they were calling for snow to come in the next few days, so she figured Saturday night was going to be her best chance for getting in and out as invisibly as possible."

"As for Juanita grabbing all the stuff she did," Nick said, taking over, "that was per Meg's instructions. She didn't want any receipts, or incidental camera recordings, of her buying any kid stuff anywhere because she was afraid it would provide a trail that would lead to her. So she told Juanita to grab the basics . . . some clothing, some toys the kid was familiar with, that sort of thing. She figured it would also help him adapt more easily if he had some familiar items around him."

"Was it part of the plan to kill Belinda all along?" Cora asked.

Nick shrugged. "Meg swears she told Juanita to snatch the kid, but not to kill anyone. Juanita says Meg told her to do whatever was necessary to get the kid, but from what we overheard on the phone call recorded by the nine-one-one center from Mack's phone, it sounds like it was Juanita's doing. We don't think she planned it that way, though."

"How did she get into Belinda's house?" Joe asked.

Tyrese resumed the explanations. "She knocked on the door, told Belinda she had just moved into the neighborhood two streets up and was looking for a day care for her daughter, and that someone had mentioned that Belinda worked for one. At some point, Belinda turned to get something to write down the address of the day care center and that's when Juanita stepped inside and closed the door. This got Belinda suspicious, so she asked her to leave. When Juanita stalled, Belinda threatened to call the police. Unfortunately, her cell phone was in her bedroom on the charger and when she went to get it, Juanita followed her. When she realized Belinda was going for her phone, Juanita used a Taser her sister had loaned her, some cheap thing the sister had brought along with her from Mexico. But the Taser wouldn't fire, so Juanita then grabbed a pair of panty hose from the bedroom trash and threw them around Belinda's neck, pulling her back. Juanita swears that all she wanted to do was disable Belinda long enough to grab Davey, but Belinda put up quite a fight. Eventually, their scuffle ended up in the master bath off the bedroom. Afraid she was losing the battle, Juanita grabbed a pair of scissors that were sitting by the sink and stabbed Belinda. Belinda then staggered out into the bedroom and collapsed."

"That poor woman," I said, feeling an ache in my heart when I recalled those photos at the Cooper house. "She loved that boy so much she was willing to die for him."

"Was Meg's husband aware of what she was doing?" Frank asked.

Nick shook his head. "It doesn't appear so. We have questioned him at length and his story has stayed pretty consistent. He had no idea what Meg was up to, which is amazing when you consider that the woman had to have been planning this for a long time. All of her efforts to reinvent herself, to hide her identity and such, make it clear that she was planning to take Davey and then disappear. She knew what a drunkard Jamie was and that he'd make a lousy father, and she was afraid that Belinda would be so horrified by the way Meg treated Jamie that she would never let her near the child. Since her original family was destroyed and she was too old to have more kids of her own, Meg thought

Jamie's child would give her a second chance at it. So she started scheming, beginning with the faked death and the identity change. I wouldn't be surprised to learn that her marriage to Monroe was also part of the plan. She was well off enough financially before the marriage, but his money gave her much more in the way of resources."

Tyrese jumped in with more. "Juanita was the final piece of the puzzle. Meg is a longtime member of the country club where Juanita's husband worked. She liked and respected Alberto as a hardworking man who put in long hours, and met Juanita when she used to come to the club to pick up Alberto. When Juanita got pregnant, Meg overheard them talking about how hard it was going to be to coordinate things once the baby came along because they only had one car. So Meg offered to cosign on a loan so Juanita could buy a second car. Meg moved in with Douglas Monroe several months before they got married and she talked him into hiring Alberto to take care of the pool. Juanita quickly took it over and one day, Meg happened to overhear a phone conversation Juanita was having with one of her sisters about establishing a new identity for someone who wanted to come over from Mexico. It was in Spanish, but it turns out Meg is fairly fluent.

"Knowing she had something on Juanita, and seeing how Juanita's little talent with false identities might help her own cause, Meg basically blackmailed Juanita into helping her. Juanita saw a chance to make a little side money, and she didn't want to jeopardize the family members she'd brought over the border, so the two women worked out a deal. They spent over two years talking and planning it all out. That camper that Juanita was using was bought using cash that Meg gave her, though it was one of Juanita's sisters who made the actual purchase. Then Juanita stole some plates to put on it and went about wooing Jamie at night, thinking that she could figure out a way to snatch Davey by learning more about his and Belinda's habits and routines."

"If Juanita hadn't gotten greedy at the end, they might have all gotten away with it," I said. "But apparently Juanita wanted to relocate with her sisters and she needed more money to do that. She knew Meg had the resources, and she also knew how badly Meg wanted the kid."

"Juanita's husband wasn't in on it, either?" Cora asked.

"It doesn't appear so," Nick said. "He was clueless and pretty devastated by it all."

"Well, at least Sofia will still have a parent," I said, thinking that at least one child would come out of this half okay.

Billy, who had been tending bar and eavesdropping when he could, answered the bar cell phone and, after listening for a few seconds, walked over and handed it to me. "It's Duncan," he said.

I got up and walked away from the group, heading for my office so I could talk to Duncan in private. "Hello there, stranger," I said once I was inside behind closed doors. "Everyone here is wondering when you're going to put in an appearance."

"Something has come up, Mack," he said, and I didn't like the tone in his voice. "I can't drop by right now."

"Why not?"

"My superiors aren't too happy that I dragged you along with me to Juanita's sister's house. In fact, they aren't too happy that I involved you in any of this. They've said it sheds a bad light on the department, that it looks like we're using voodoo to help solve cases, that I put a citizen in unnecessary danger, yada, yada,

yada. I've been suspended for two weeks and they're doing an investigation to determine if I can keep my job."

"Oh, no, Duncan," I said, feeling my heart ache.

"We'll just have to hope for the best until the verdict comes down."

"And what about after the verdict comes down? If they let you come back to work, does that mean I can't help you anymore?"

"I suppose. I don't know. The fact that we did solve the case weighs in our favor, and I've been pretty upfront with my immediate boss as to how big a part you played in that. But he's afraid of the publicity and how it might impact our reputation, our funding . . . that sort of stuff. He said your involvement makes the police force look like a bunch of bumbling idiots. And he doesn't even know about Cora, Tad, or Kevin and the roles they all played in this."

"I'm so sorry, Duncan. I never meant to get you into trouble."

"It's not your fault, Mack. I brought you into this knowing that it was a bit dicey. But there's something else."

I braced myself, wondering how things could possibly get any worse.

"I just learned that the press knows about your involvement. I'm not sure how, but they do. And you need to prepare yourself, because you're going to be on the evening news."

"Oh, no."

"I know. I'm sorry. They're probably going to show up there any moment. Your best bet is to just not say anything to them."

"Okay."

"And given everything that's going on, I think it would be best if I stayed away from you and the bar for a while, at least until all the hubbub dies down."

"Okay, if you think that's best."

"I do. I'll keep in touch by phone, but for now, a little distance will help us both out."

I wasn't sure I agreed with him on this point, but I said nothing.

"Take care of yourself, Mack. I'll talk to you soon."

"Okay." He disconnected the call and I held the phone out and stared at it for a moment, still trying to comprehend everything he'd said. I took a few minutes to gather myself together and then headed out to the main bar area.

The reporters were there already and as soon as I came out of my office, a woman reporter saw me and said, "There she is!" She and a cameraman rushed over to me and the reporter started badgering me with questions.

"You're Mackenzie Dalton, right? Is it true that you helped the police solve the Cooper murder and kidnapping by using ESP? Are you the Milwaukee Police Department's secret weapon? How did it feel when you were involved in the shoot-out?"

"I have nothing to say to you," I grumbled. The man she was with shoved his camera at my face. "I have nothing to say," I repeated more vehemently. "And I would appreciate it if you would leave."

"Come on, Mack," the reporter cajoled. "Give us something. Is it true that you and Detective Duncan Albright are a couple? Is that how he discovered this disease you have?"

"I don't have a disease," I snapped, immediately wishing I could take the words back. I realized the reporter was trying to goad me into a response and I'd played right into her hands. To avoid any further inquiries, I turned and stormed back into my office, slamming the door behind me.

I fell onto my couch and closed my eyes. After several minutes of sitting there trying not to cry, the door to the office opened. I surged upward, thinking it was going to be the pushy reporter. But it was just Cora, Frank, and Joe.

Joe and Frank settled in on either side of me and Frank draped an arm over my shoulders. Cora grabbed a nearby chair and set it down in front of me. Then she sat in it and put her hands on my knees.

"Are you okay?" Cora asked.

"No, I'm not okay," I hiccupped, the tears I'd been fighting coming on full force. "Everything is all screwed up. Duncan got into trouble for using me. He's been suspended and might lose his job. And with the press knowing all about it, I'm now the laughingstock of the city."

"It's not that bad," Cora said, and I shot her a look that told her what I thought of her comment.

"Duncan can't even come by the bar now," I told them. "He said he needs to keep his distance until they decide what to do with him."

"I'm sorry, Mack," Cora said.

Frank massaged my shoulders, and Joe said, "It will be okay. Just give it some time until all the interest dies down. You know how the news is. Something else will be the top story in a day or two."

"I don't know," I said. Cora reached over to my desk and grabbed a box of tissues, handing them to me. I took one out and swiped at my face. Then I blew my nose. "How did they even find out about all this?"

"It was Tiny," Cora said, looking guilty. "I'm sorry. If I'd known . . ."

"Tiny? Why?"

"He didn't know that Duncan was trying to keep your—and our—involvement under the radar. And when we told him that we might be able to help him solve his sister's murder, he went to the press and told them about you, Duncan, the Capone Club . . . all of it. He didn't mean any harm by it. He just wanted to generate some renewed interest in his sister's case."

"Well, I can't blame him for that," I said, knowing what it was like to feel as if your loved one's murder had been forgotten. "I might have done the same thing before my dad's murder was solved if given the chance."

"This will pass," Cora said. "You'll see. And, in the meantime, we'll do our best to keep the reporters at bay."

I nodded and sniffed, my eyes nearly dry now.

"Come on back out and join us," Joe said. "The reporter is gone. And if she or any others come back, we'll chase them away."

"Yeah, our cousin Guido has a way of being very convincing," Frank added.

I smiled at that. "You don't really have a cousin Guido, do you?"

Joe shrugged. "Who knows? Maybe we do and maybe we don't. It doesn't matter. What matters is whether or not anyone believes we do."

I turned and gave Joe a big hug, then I did the same for Frank. "Thanks, guys."

"Anything for our Mack," Joe said.

I looked at Cora then and said, "And you, too. Lord knows this case might never have been solved if it wasn't for you."

"Hey, I do what I can," Cora said with a dismissive shrug.

I slapped my hands on my knees and said, "You know, there's something that's been bothering me and I keep forgetting to ask."

"What's that?" Cora asked.

"That puzzle yesterday, the one about the guard and the castle and the secret password?"

Cora nodded.

"I never heard the answer to it."

"Oh, it was easy," Joe said. "The answer to the guard's question was the number of letters in the number he stated."

"The letters, of course!" I said, shaking my head. "The correct response to twelve was six because twelve has six letters, and the answer to six was three for the same reason. So the correct response to ten should have been three, not five."

"You got it," Frank said.

"And for that, I'm going to buy you a drink," Joe said with a wink. "Let's see, it's Assault and Battery Thursday, right? So that means you need a Sledgehammer."

"How appropriate," I said. "Because I feel as if I've been hit with one."

"Come on, then," Cora said, getting to her feet and returning her chair to its original position. "We'll all have a Sledgehammer and then you can hear the case I cooked up for everyone today. Trust me, it's a doozy!"

With my Italian uncles at my side and Cora leading the way, I headed out to the bar, back to my customers, back to my business, back to my old life, wondering what the future held in store for me.

Drink Recipes

SIMPLE SYRUP

Simple syrup is a sugar-based mixer that is used in a lot of drinks to add sweetness, volume, or both. It's sold premade in most stores that sell liquors, but it's easy to make at home. Simply put 3 cups of sugar and 2 cups of water in a saucepan and bring it to a boil. Turn the heat to low and simmer the mixture for 4 to 5 minutes, stirring occasionally. (Spices, juice, or fruit can be added during this stage if you want to make a flavored version—strain as needed.) Remove from the heat and let the syrup cool. The syrup can be kept in the refrigerator in an airtight container for several weeks. If you prefer it a little less sweet, use 2½ cups of water.

SNEAKY PETE

(I've seen several different drinks that were called a Sneaky Pete, but this is by far my favorite.)

1 shot coffee-based liqueur (such as Kahlua)
1 shot whisky or bourbon
4 ounces milk or cream

Stir ingredients together and pour over ice.

For a nonalcoholic version, use one shot of chilled espresso, one shot of simple syrup, a teaspoon of vanilla flavoring, a few drops of maple flavoring, and 4 ounces of milk or cream. Stir and serve over ice.

BAD ATTITUDE

1 shot coconut rum
1 shot spiced rum
2 ounces pineapple juice

In a cocktail shaker, combine rums and juice, shake, and strain into a glass over ice.

For the virgin version, use one ounce of coconut-flavored coffee syrup, one ounce of chilled black tea, 3 ounces of pineapple juice, 1/2 teaspoon of rum flavoring, and a pinch each of ground ginger and cloves. Shake very well and serve as above.

GINGER SNAP

2 ounces apple juice
2 ounces ginger ale
2 ounces bourbon

Pour everything over ice, stir, and serve with a slice of apple for a garnish.

For a nonalcoholic version, use an ounce of chilled black tea with a teaspoon of vanilla extract in place of the bourbon.

THE SLEDGEHAMMER

2 ounces vodka
2 ounces rum
3 ounces Galliano
1 ounce apricot brandy
2 ounces pineapple juice

Stir ingredients together and serve over ice.

For a nonalcoholic version, use ½ teaspoon of rum flavoring, 1 teaspoon of vanilla flavoring, and ½ teaspoon of anise flavoring mixed well into 2 ounces of simple syrup. Add 2½ ounces of pineapple juice and one ounce of heavy or light syrup from canned peaches (or apricot nectar, if you can find it). Top off with a splash of club soda. Stir and serve over ice. If you prefer, you can substitute 2 to 3 ounces of Italian anise soda in place of the flavored simple syrup.

THE ALIBI

1 ounce ginger simple syrup (*see below*)
2 ounces vodka
1 tablespoon of fresh squeezed or bottled lime juice
Splash of club soda

Shake the first three ingredients with ice, pour into a highball glass, and top off with a splash of club soda.

For a virgin Alibi, eliminate the vodka and add three ounces of club soda.

The ginger simple syrup can easily be made by peeling two inches of fresh ginger (or one teaspoon of ground ginger) and adding it to ¾ cup of sugar and ½ cup of water. Simmer over a low flame for five minutes, remove the ginger, and chill.

DUNCAN'S GRANNY'S HOT BUTTERED RUM

HOT BUTTERED RUM BATTER:

1 cup butter
1 cup brown sugar
1 cup white sugar
¾ teaspoon cinnamon
1 teaspoon nutmeg
2 cups softened vanilla ice cream

Melt butter in a saucepan, add sugars and spices, and stir over low heat until well blended. Remove from heat and stir in the ice cream. Mix at medium speed with an electric mixer until well blended. Pour into container. The batter will keep for three weeks in the refrigerator or for two months in the freezer; the batter can be used straight from the freezer.

To make the drink, place three heaping tablespoons of batter into a mug and add 6 ounces of hot water. Add one shot of the rum of your choice (dark or light). For a nonalcoholic version, add one teaspoon of rum flavoring. Stir well and serve with a cinnamon stick.

This recipe is so good I make it in huge batches during the holidays and give it away as gifts in containers that are decorated with mini bottles of rum and some cinnamon sticks tied together with holiday ribbon. Guaranteed to warm you on a cold winter's night!

GREAT BOOKS,
GREAT SAVINGS!

When You Visit Our Website:
www.kensingtonbooks.com
You Can Save Money Off The Retail Price
Of Any Book You Purchase!

- **All Your Favorite Kensington Authors**
- **New Releases & Timeless Classics**
- **Overnight Shipping Available**
- **eBooks Available For Many Titles**
- **All Major Credit Cards Accepted**

Visit Us Today To Start Saving!
www.kensingtonbooks.com

Grab These Cozy Mysteries
from
Kensington Books